THE ghost of
ANNA

THE ghost of ANNA

S.J. GROVES

authorHOUSE®

AuthorHouse™
1663 Liberty Drive
Bloomington, IN 47403
www.authorhouse.com
Phone: 1-800-839-8640

Published by AuthorHouse   09/17/2012

ISBN: 978-1-4772-2259-1 (sc)
ISBN: 978-1-4772-2260-7 (hc)
ISBN: 978-1-4772-2258-4 (e)

INTRODUCTION

This is a story of a little girl Sarah Jones and her family living in an old house in the Town of Bristol in the southwest of England set in around mid 1974 to the end of 1984. Sarah's inescapable haunting memories growing up in this house but this was no ordinary house it had a dark past; Seeing these haunting memories through Sarah's eyes growing up as a little girl of 6 years in 1980, when it became more apparent. Sarah and her family will learn of dark secrets this house holds, through Sarah's experiences as a child. The story is based on true events that accrued in an actual house; its one of the first of three books, a trilogy. Second a prequel and the third a sequel to the first book.

CHAPTER 1

Sarah Ann Jones was just an ordinary little baby girl with pale blonde hair like her dad and brown eyed girl like her mum; growing up in their family home in Bristol in the southwest of England with her mum Susan and dad Michael. Who were in fact her grandparents! They were young grandparents too Susan was 33 years old and Michael 34 years old when Sarah came along.

They had adopted her when she was only 3 years old, in the beginning of August. Her mum Ashley was a very young mum at 13 years, a month before her 14th birthday, just a kid herself still at school. Ashley could not cope at that point with being a mother but she could not bring herself to abort this life growing inside of her, so Ashley's grandparents took drastic action, so that Sarah would not be adopted outside the family, Sarah would always know her real family and where she came from.

Sarah never met her real dad as he was only 16 himself, Sarah was told when she got old enough to understand that she was adopted and that her dad's name was Jack Haskins he had wanted to be a father, even though it was not planned and even said he would marry Ashley but being just under 14 year old girl, she was scared of being a young mum and pushed him away, so he left before Sarah was born. Growing up Sarah never blamed her real mum for pushing her real dad away, she understood.

Sarah understood a lot of things from a very young, even though she had a good childhood with her Grandparents as her parents and the rest of the family playing different roles through the adoption. An Auntie becoming a Sister, a Uncle becoming a brother and her real mum in a way becoming her sister, she grew up quick in other ways and understood things about life far quicker than most children growing up due to her family circumstances and the haunted house that she was growing up in also the bullying in and out of school, this gave her different aspect on life with a different take on things.

Sarah was shy, sensitive and down to earth, also stubborn at times but knowledge of things beyond her years, made her feel different from the rest of the kids and also because of this she became a bit of a loner, did not make friends that easy, growing up.

Susan and Michael felt it was important to be completely honest about the fact that she was adopted by her grandparents and Sarah knew her real mum from the very beginning of her childhood.

Michael and Susan had three other older children, Sarah's mum Ashley was the eldest, Antony was 12 years and Diane was 10 years, when Sarah came along. Susan had always wanted a big family, she loved children more than anything in the world but this was unattainable twisted hand of fate, Susan had a lot of love to give and wanted to give that love to all her children.

Susan was going to have another baby boy before Sarah came along but he died. The baby was born he was alive for few minutes! Just enough time to take a few last breathes of air! Then he slipped away into eternally sleep peaceful without pain and died in Susan arms.

This was upsetting but worse news of all was to come because with all her pregnancies there were complications, Susan always had high blood pressure and other issues when she was pregnant, which meant she was very ill, through out her pregnancies, each one more and more dangerous to herself and the unborn baby, so by this time of her forth infant, she was advised not to have anymore children, as her body would be able to cope with any other pregnancy! Which for Susan was devastating and for Michael but mainly for Susan.

Susan found this hard to take being that she always wanted a large family but Michael thought his wife's health was more important than having other children. After all they had three lovely, healthy children already.

At that time Susan was just 32 years old, so this was extremely frustrating to be told by the doctors and midwifes, she could not have anymore children and if she were to fall pregnant, the consequences of this would be probably losing it before it was born or it would be at risk to her health and Susan could die herself.

If she was healthy it would not be too late to have one more. This news was not taken well by Susan and for a while she was very down and depressed about this. As her need to be a mum and have other children was still there.

When they adopted Sarah, Susan was 36 years old and Michael was 37 years old. In a way adopting Sarah was nice for Susan, it was her chance and only chance to be a mother once again. She could be Sarah's mum and her grandmother all at the same time, this was to become a strong bond for Sarah, in time she was to become her mum, grandmother and best friend all rolled into one.

Susan also became like a mum to her kid's friends when her kids were growing up, as she was kind and understanding to all that knew her, always there to help others if they had a problem and needed to talk.

When Sarah was adopted Michael had mellowed from his younger years, he had a bit more of a temper before and very little patience before Sarah came along he became more of a soft touch but still proud and logical with everything.

Ashley was a bubbly brown eyed brunette strong opinionated girl a little bit impulsive at times when growing up, but she was a good listener to her friends and was good in a crisis. About two years after Sarah's dad Jack, Ashley had met a young man about two years older than her called Tom Hall, Ashley was 16 by this time, he was a very obsessive and abusive man, so this relationship did not last at all, Ashley was not the sort of girl to put up with this but Ashley had one more child to come from this failed relationship, it was a little baby boy Jason which meant Sarah had a half brother, which was nice for Sarah. This gave Ashley a second chance to be a mum. Ashley and her dad was not that close, she was a dad's girl but he was never a brilliant dad or husband at that time when she was little and she could remember his temper towards her mother. Antony and Diane was too young to remember.

Ashley was a bit older by that time and was able to look after her son Jason but was not easy at time as she was still a young single mum at 17. By this time Sarah was about 3 years old and had just been adopted by her grandparents when Jason came along.

Antony was the 2nd eldest, the middle child a rebel and stubborn but caring and funny too, black hair with blue eyes, when he grew up he would be very tall.

Diane was shy mummies girl, patient and sensitive with a big heart, brunette and hazel eyes, when she grew up she was also going to be very tall like a model.

Sarah family was very complicated through her adoption by her grandparents, her uncle Antony was now her brother and her auntie Diane became her sister. As growing up she called her real mum by her name Ashley, as having two mums was confusing enough! It was not easy trying to explain her family.

Sarah never knew her real father, she never really missed him but Sarah often wondered what he was like growing up and imagined what it would be like to meet him from time to time but she was told about him as she grew up, mostly by her mum and Auntie Emily who thought her dad was such a lovely man, so at the time that was good enough, as she had all her other family around her. Sarah got on quite well with her Auntie Emily! It was nice hearing stories about her real dad from her.

Sarah's dad had a kind heart a really genuine person and loved the sea. Jack would help her auntie do the soup runs for the homeless sometimes, that's the sort of person he was.

When Emily was a child she was not a prefect child sometimes a little selfish and bit of a bully like having her own way, as she got older, she had changed and like helping out people that were less fortunate. Still showed off at times the material things she had but treated her sister better than when, she was young. Emily was a charity worker for the homeless as well as working in a supermarket and worked her way up to in the end being the manager. Emily got to know Sarah's father quiet well, as most people did. Emily was a strong follower of the church and its faith. She went to the church every Sunday.

Something else her mum mentioned when Sarah was about 6 years, which at the time when she was told this, Sarah was not to sure what her mum actually meant by this but she said that 'her father was a sensitive man, sensed things about people and places and seemed to be able to see things before they happened'. As Sarah got older, she realised what her mum had meant and realised that this was probably where she got her insight from.

By this time, her mother Ashley was 20 years old, bringing up Jason and had moved out of the family home when she was 17 years and got a job in a corner shop after she had Jason part time. Where Ashley lived in a council terrace house, it was a bit run down but cheap and liveable, with their personal bank, dad's financial services.

Antony was just under 18 when he moved out and had got a job in a shoe shop part time, making and fixing shoes. Antony was going to save up for a car; he was starting his driving lessons when he turned 18. Antony could not wait to have a set of wheels.

Diane was 15 years old when her brother moved and 13 years old when her sister moved out the family home but when she was 17, after her exams, she had planned to move in with her older brother and sister.

At home it was just going to be Sarah growing up in the family home after Diane was going to move out when she was 17, which was good in one way as it was a bit of a squeeze before when her older brother and sister were at home.

Michael and Susan had moved into this home when they got married, Susan was only 18 years and Michael was only 19 years, a year later Susan was pregnant with their first child Ashley, Michael grew up in the same street as Susan with his foster parents. Michael's mum had given him up and his brother, who lived with a different foster parents; Michael was separated from his brother when he was only about 3 years old.

Michael's brother moved away with his foster parents when David was on only 1 years old, Michael never really knew his brother all through his childhood and did not get in touch with him not till he was in his 50's as he never was given any information were his brother had moved to. Their mum was a single young mother bringing up two children in war time Britain, it was a hard life.

This was not an uncommon thing to happen in war time England with a single mother she thought she was doing the best things for her children at the time. She could not provide for them. Michael's foster parents were called Mrs Katie Beecham and Mr Ben Beecham.

Susan's family was her mum Hilary and dad Henry, Susan's older brother harry, younger sister Emily and younger brother Mark. Susan's family surname was Walsh. Emily had married Peter Keane they had a Daughter Jessica, who was a year older than Sarah and Mark meet

Vivian Muller, got married and they had two daughter's Natasha and Nicole.

Michael and Susan's house was a 1960's property in style, a red brick, 3 bedroom, detached medium sized house, with a medium size front and back garden. It was along street, off a main busy street.

The long street had lots of houses; that had two turnings that went round the back of the main houses, which also had a few houses. The back gardens on these houses would face each other, which was handy if you wanted to speak to a neighbour from the other street. Didn't even have to go to their house, just pop your head over the back fence and have a chat with cup of tea or coffee.

The houses on both streets were red brick detached or semi detached three to four bedroom houses. Susan and Michael had two very good friends, their garden faced on to their friend's garden; their names were Maggie and Keith Barns. They often came over for coffee or just chatted over the fence as the Barns and Jones like being out in the garden when the weather was good, sometimes they would have their son Danny and his young daughter round who was about the same age as Sarah her name was Karen. Danny was about 3 years older than Ashley. Karen's mum and dad were no longer together.

Sometimes they were go to each other houses with lovely homemade cakes that they had made that morning to have with a cup of tea or coffee. Susan and Maggie were very good cooks, especially their baking.

In the Jones house as you came in, their was a hallway, with a downstairs bathroom straight a head with a separate toilet to the right, at the end of the hallway and living room/ dinning room and kitchen to the left of the hallway via sliding door and stairs to the right as you came in. The house decorated in the 1960 style floral dated carpets and magnolia walls and thick old wooden white doors.

Upstairs was a small landing with one small bedroom to the right, which was Sarah's bedroom before Sarah it was Antony's bedroom, to the left there was a medium bedroom which was Michael and Susan's bedroom and straight on from the landing another medium room which was Diane and Ashley's bedroom. They also had an attic that no one went in as they didn't likes the cobwebs, especially Antony he seemed to be scared of the attic growing up. Antony thought that the cyber men from Dr Who were watching him from the attic. Although it did feel at times that something was hiding up there, until it was that time to come out from the darkness of the attic to haunt once again.

The Jones were well liked and had lots of friends in the street, the house was always busy in the day friends, popping round for coffee and a gossip when Sarah was growing up, it was a little community all of its own, which was nice. Most of the time in the day, if Susan was home and was a nice day, she would have the back door open all day, to let some air in the 1980's, you could do that then, leave doors open or unlocked.

The paranormal activity seemed to start happening for Sarah when she moved into her mum and dad's old room at 6 years old, for some reason the entity's were drawn to her. Which also she would find out as she got older, that sort of thing, seemed to be drawn to her.

Diane was going to be moving out very soon so she moved into the small bedroom, Michael and Susan had Diane's old room and let Sarah have their room as it was bigger room, than her old room plus she was always drawn to that room from a very young age.

Sarah for some strange reason even before, she moved into that bedroom, she was drawn to it, like she had been their before. Even as a baby, her eyes would open wide if her mum or dad took her in their room, Sarah eyes would slowly look around as if she was watching something move around her, or she would stare into space and smile at something but there was nothing there to smile at, only her mum or who ever was holding her. Suddenly Sarah would cry for no reason then give a really frightened look. Which Susan noticed this fascination and moods from the very beginning, Susan was always puzzled by this, as none of her other children reacted in this way to the room, Michael thought nothing of it.

As a toddler she was just as intrigued, Sarah was always running into her mum and dad's room and wanted to play in that room. Sarah would look up and smile or laugh or point to something that was not there, an unseen presence but Sarah was also afraid of the built in cupboard in her parent's bedroom, even as a toddler, she would not venture near it at all. Sarah never really understood why at the time being so young, she would never open it or try too and for some reason neither would anyone else. It was bad!

As Sarah was growing up, Sarah would always stop by the bottom of the stairs! Sarah always felt strange and uneasy as far back as she could remember. She was drawn to the top of them, Sarah felt as if someone was staring at her from the top of the stairs, so much so it would make her look up the stairs, this made her feel really unnerved. Sarah could always feel things about places or people that no one else could see or feel. What she didn't know that she had the gift of forth sight from her father.

It was the day that Sarah had moved all her stuff into her new bedroom, her mum and dad's old bedroom. Michael and Susan had put their old bedroom furniture into the back middle bedroom and moved Sarah's wardrobe in to her new room. They had brought a lovely dressing table with a mirror, painted white to match her wardrobe and shelves. They had placed the dressing table under the window to give the best natural light for styling her hair. Sarah loved it, she felt like a little princess with her new dressing table and mirror; it had a pretty pink Barbie lamp too.

It was light and airy too with a lovely long window to the far wall, which when the sun shone let lots of light and warmth as it was south facing window. She always felt a strange sense of being in a filmier place in that room, even though it was her mum and dad's old room, which would explain why! Bizarrely this felt more deep routed than that. Now this was her room the feeling became stronger as she grew up.

For Jason and Ashley when they came up on the weekends and if they wanted to stay, they stayed in the small room, it was not a huge room but good enough for a spare room or Antony if they wanted to stay over, Diane would sleep in with her Nephew and sister. Sometimes Jason would sleep in the same room as his half sister.

It had a bed to the left side by the door and storage unit in a shape of a car to put Jason toys in, to the right that was next to a pine wardrobe, next to that a desk and a long window at the far wall, facing onto the back garden, with blue curtains and a night light, it looked a great bedroom, there was also a spare mattress under the bed.

Jason had come with his mum that day, he could not wait to see what the spare room looked like, although for now he did have to share it with his Auntie Diane but only till she moved out, Jason came round so he could put a few toys in the room, so he would have something to play with when he came over his Nan and Granddad's house. This was the prefect time for a clear out with three of their children all grown up. With three children plus two grandchildren and nearly 30 years of marriage a lot of clutter had built up over time.

They would clear away the old to make way for the new, as it would not be much longer before Diane would move out then it would just be Sarah there. Diane still was at home at that time and shared the room if her sister and nephew stayed over. There was a mattress that Ashley would use that was placed under the spare bed when not in use, they had to sleep on the floor of the room, they didn't mind; it was just about big enough.

Susan and Michael also decided it would be nice to have a couple of cats, they had cats in the past but one died of old age and another had unfortunately got run over. They had got two kittens from one of their friends that lived in the street that had a cat that just had a litter of kittens, so Michael and Susan had two of the kittens from this litter a brother and sister.

They called the male kitten Felix and female kitten tabby; they were both tabby cats, both full of character. They also picked up that there were things of the spooky nature there too; tabby and Felix would stare at things that were not there, even chase things that no one could see.

Sarah's new bedroom somehow felt suspiciously familiar to her, even though it was the family house! Which she would feel as if it was familiar but this Always felt deeper routed at the time; she thought nothing more of it. In the corner of the left hand side there was an old built—in cupboard, something was telling her never to open this cupboard, like a gut feeling, instinctively that it would very bad, if she was to do so.

Sarah put her box of personal persuasions down on the bed, then suddenly she her a voice, a child's soft voice say "Sara" Sarah did not take much notice as the voice was very faint almost like a whisper in a gentle breeze! Sarah carried on unpacking her box of things; she just thought to herself 'it must be my imagination or just the wind' as a window was slightly open; there was a light cool breeze blowing through the room.

Felix came wobbling along as he was only about 6 weeks old and started to purr at first, Sarah thought this purr of affection was intended for her but Felix was clearly purring strangely enough at something else as he was in the middle of the room and seemed to be purring rubbing himself up against something that was not there. "You silly thing Felix, What are you purring at? there is nothing there!" Sarah said as she picked Felix up and took him downstairs, Sarah did feel the same as her kitten. Sarah also felt as if there was something in her room "I will get you something to eat" Sarah added getting Felix some go cat.

For the next few weeks she heard nothing. So she didn't really think much about it. It was to be a busy few weeks in any case. Sarah had to get to know their new furry additions to the family! Maybe that voice or what she thought she heard was just the wind, blowing through the house. In her mind something was telling her this was not the wind, a gut feeling that would not go away and her mum had always said to her kids to trust their instincts.

Michael and Susan had always been ok in their house while the kids were growing up. Michael was never the prefect man, growing up he did not have much guidance, which a child relies on to show them right from wrong and how to be a good person as you grow.

Now three of the kids had grown up and Michael had changed into much softer temperament and tolerant man and was doing well at work. This was a good time to redecorate the downstairs as it was dated and style was very much 1960's décor. It needed to be brought into the 1980's.

Susan always felt something was in the house, like invisible presence in the house but as none of her children said anything about the house, she was not really bothered by it. It didn't seem to bother anyone at least that's what she thought!

It was the summer holidays so no school for Sarah. They had the whole of the summer holidays to sort their things out, it was a busy time. Give this 1960's property a lick of paint to give the house a fresh feel to it. Ashley with Jason and Antony came over in the summer holidays a lot to see their mum, dad and sisters, when they were not working to lend a hand, to help with the house.

They too had memories of their home growing up some good and some not so good but they also all had some strange memories too, Sarah had no idea about the rest of the families experiences, for one thing she was only little girl when her real mum and brother left to live their lives. Even other family members and friends of the family that had stayed in this house, had all experienced something over the years but it was never talked about, as that sort of thing was not.

People would think you were mad talking about ghosts in the 1980, although little did Susan's kids know that Susan and a few friends, Maggie Barns, Sally Milton and Rebecca Williams, one night did a Ouija board, it seemed a good idea at the time, which was a dangerous and foolish thing to do but being only 18 years at the time Susan was naïve and impulsive, as were her friends.

Susan and her friend's had freaked themselves out as what was meant to be a laugh at the time that became serious, as they got a response, which was not what they had excepted; The four friends put their index finger on the tablet and as you do, Susan asked timidly "Is there, anyone there!" the tablets moved by itself and the kitchen door slammed shut suddenly, which made the four friends jump out of their skins.

This made her friends really frightened and the four friends stopped, stupidly quickly took their fingers off the board, this scared the living daylights out of them and they didn't know where to run, Susan and Maggie getting stuck in the kitchen doorway, as they open the kitchen door then tried to get through the door at the same time, which their other two friends did find amusing.

Michael was not very happy when he found out they did this but he did see the funny side to his wife and friend getting stuck in the doorway. Michael did say at the time that it silly thing to do and you should not mess around with things like that.

Susan's friends went home, this made them feel uncomfortable staying in their friend's house after that, they promised each other never to do or speak of this again to anyone; they all had a very bad feeling. Which under the circumstances they did not know that then but they were wise to stop and the entity that was trying to communicate was not very nice.

By this time though it was already too late, this unseen presence had been there for a hundred years, lying dormant for a hundred years, what they had done unwittingly was very bad they had awoken this evil Spirit from it entail sleep and allow it to come through! This family would just be another family he would have to see to and this was not the sort of entity to poke fun at. There was another entity there though and this was something angelic and good.

This family was different though, it would be a strong family and close family in the end, that already had been through tough times and had giving them each strength in their own ways, that they would not scare or be moved easily. This entity would be faced with a face from it's past and would subconsciously know it's dark past; that in the end would challenge this entity, as memories never get truly forgotten, just stored away in the subconscious, until a trigger, a catalyst to bring those memories forward.

CHAPTER 2

The first night in Sarah's new bedroom, this is when the paranormal activity really started for Sarah, just small little things to begin with. It was their first night, all in their new bedrooms an early night as they all were very busy moving furniture upstairs and getting rid of old furniture that they didn't want anymore, so they were all tired.

Jason had come up with his mum, Ashley was just stayed for tea and to help out then go home, Jason was going to stay the night, being the younger only three! Jason just ran around or played with his toys, even he was tired with excitement of his first day in his bedroom, even though really it was his auntie's room. That night they had a take away, fish and chips all round with lots of bread to make chip butties. Jason wanted to stay with his grandparents, half sister and Auntie that night. Jason fell fast asleep within minutes of going to bed that night. For that night Diane slept on the spare mattress on the floor so Jason could have her bed as he was so tired.

Sarah could not help feeling as she was not alone in her room that day but as Sarah was so tired from the moving things around, she tried to ignore her feeling and drifted of to a deep sleep but Sarah had a tormented and restless night, something was not right in that room.

Michael and Susan talked about their day, as they normally did before they went to sleep in their new bedroom. They had all these plans for their home. After their tabulate past together as a young married couple! They wanted it to be a fresh start, they seemed to be getting on a lot better since Sarah and Jason had come along and their three children had all grown up.

Michael had a small bottle of Asti on ice by the bed to toast to the fresh start; at that point they were so happy. Nothing could spoil their new future!

"I love you so very much Susan, I'm sorry for the things in the past. I've not been the best husband or dad. This is to us to look to the future" Michael said raising his glass towards Susan's glass and gave her a passionate kiss as they lay in bed sat up a little.

"I love you too so much, well let's put that behind us now" Susan replied taking a sip of Asti; She felt a fresh new start for the Jones family.

That night they had more than one way of celebrating fresh start a glass of bubbly then had a loving and passionate celebration between the sheets while the children slept.

They were totally unawares that Sarah was having an irritable night, Sarah kept tossing and turning all through the night, the feeling of not being alone would not leave her, something that was not nice, something that had personal interest in Sarah.

This was not the only haunted house in their family, Susan and Michael's kids growing up, did not like their Nan and Granddad's house. There was something there too, another troubled soul, none of kids like going to the bathroom up the stairs. It would feel like from the landing something was watching them! Going up to the bathroom to go a toilet and coming down from the bathroom. It would feel like you were being followed.

If at any time the kids went to visit and really had to go they would run up the stairs then after run down them as fast as their legs could carry them. Ashley, Antony and Diane all felt this way about that house; Including Sarah. Jason was very young at the time.

Sarah sometimes would see a dark figure dart across the landing as she went to the bathroom or when she was leaving the bathroom. No one ever mentioned their experiences in their Nan and Granddad's house, so no one ever knew. Again this entity did not feel nice, not as bad as the entity in their house but apparently their Nan and Granddad's house was around in the 2nd war and was that part of Bristol that had been affected by the bombs.

So this was another house that had history running through its very walls, but it was unclear who this entity actually was! Just like the Jones house. Sarah was good at picking up vibes in houses good or bad, she could feel the history in a house, like pictures in her head of what once was; or if something was there a haunting again good or bad, even as a baby, she always had this insight, as she got older, this insight grew stronger.

After Sarah first night in her new room, the next morning after Sarah restless night! The Jones all woke up feeling fresh with the morning summer sun upon their faces as they arose from their sleep it was the Jones first day, with the move around with the bedrooms, this year felt different. They had changed things around and got rid of the past. Sarah on the other hand was still feeling tired from her lack of sleep. Sarah did not feel as the rest of family and felt nervous about the year, she unclear why she felt this but never the less she did!

Susan did the family a lovely cooked breakfast, the full works sausage, bacon, mushrooms, eggs and beans with loads of toast. The smell was lovely of the sizzling bacon, the smell filled the house. Michael, Diane, Jason and Sarah came down for breakfast. Diane had got her sister and nephew up and dressed for her mum.

Susan thought it would be nice idea to have a family get together, they had not had one in a while; but as it normally ending up in Susan getting hurt from her family, as there was always some disagreement, Susan did not have them as often as she would of liked. Susan's family didn't always like Michael not at first as he was not the best husband to Susan or a brilliant dad in the early years but they were not prefect to Susan either, Michael was not that struck on his wife's family either.

But since Sarah and Jason had come along a lot had changed for all the family. They all had realised that they had not been perfect in the past and wanted to start and move on from it, leave the past in the past, try to move forward.

Michael went to work, while Susan set about making a few phone calls to her family to organise a family get together, a party. Sarah and Jason went upstairs to play, Diane just watched some telly. Later on Ashley came up to pick up Jason and to see her sister also her daughter Sarah. She missed her daughter when she went but she knew her daughter was settled and she knew that giving her daughter up for adoption to her mum and dad, Ashley had done the right thing at the time for her daughter's welfare.

Meanwhile Susan had managed to round their family up plus their three older kids, son and two daughter's Ashley, Antony and

Diane. There was going to be Susan's mum Hilary and dad Henry. Susan's younger sister Emily her husband Peter and their daughter Jessica, Susan's younger brother Mark and his wife Vivian and their daughters Nicole and Natasha and Susan's other older brother Harry. Michael had no family his foster parents had moved away and he did have a brother but he had no idea where is brother was living. Michael foster parents moved away when he moved into the house with Susan.

It was going to be a nice night although, Susan was not that close to her family as she would of liked to be, they were a little mean to her growing up and she was not her mum's favourite child but maybe now as they were older and maybe with this gathering they could finally put the past behind them. Her younger sister Emily was always the favourite with her mother and Susan felt it at times.

Ashley, Antony and Diane got on ok with Susan's side of the family but knew that their mum had not always been treated that good by their Nan, when their mum was growing up. In years gone by they had tried to put the past behind them, but sometimes that it is not that easy.

Susan had arranged it to be on a Saturday in a fortnight time, just a buffet and drinks nothing fancy, with the new furniture and decorating the house they did not have a lot of cash to spare. This gathering was not about the food and drink, it was hopefully to close a chapter in the past of Susan's family and move forward, to look to the future and leave the past firmly where it belongs!

CHAPTER 3

Those two weeks had flown round, within that week Sarah sometimes would hear a little girl's voice quietly almost like a whisper or a little giggle. Sarah was curious who this little girl was? She knew now that it was not the wind but something else! Sarah could feel the little girls presence around her. The attic always had a unsettling feel to it too as it was above the landing and directly in between the small spare bedroom and Sarah's bedroom, somewhere for a unwanted spirit to hide!

It was time for the family gathering Ashley, little Jason and Antony came over to help with the preparations with getting the house ready with their dad's help none of them had work that day. The night of the party was upon them!! That day Susan was nervous, she wanted her family to give praise.

Susan wanted her family to be proud of her rather than, not having anything good to say in the past but she knew what they were like! They had never thought Susan would not amount to anything, as she never wanted a career and became a mother when she was just 19 years old, her brothers and sister had all been very successful with their careers. Susan was never as career minded as her brothers and sister! Just wanted to do well at school and always wanted to be a mother from a young age.

Susan had decided that she would be a mum first and be there for her children, rather than a stranger bringing up her children. Michael grew up with Susan as their families lived on the same street to each other. Michael saw how they would treat her and in a way empathised with her.

Michael came into the kitchen where Susan was cooking some mini sausages and making a homemade quiche. Michael could see that she was stressed and worried. Even though she blamed the odd tear on the onions she was chopping.

"Don't worry it will be ok, I'm here. If they don't approve that is their loss, you have nothing to prove to them, your wonderful mother, loving wife and an extra special person if they cant see that stuff them" Michael said holding her hand and giving her a much needed comforting cuddle and kiss.

"Thank you, I needed that! How are the kids getting on with the living room" Susan replied. She felt happier with her husband by her side and gave the strength that she knew, she would need.

"Yep their doing great" the table all set out and the décor looks stunning, Cream and gold tableware on their dinning table with vases of fresh flowers put around the room to give the living room a lovely fresh smell, like summer fields of flowers in bloom and gold candles along the mantel place; .

"I know you too well! STOP worrying" Michael said as he went into the living room to help his children finish up. Susan finished preparing the buffet with the help of Ashley and Diane. Antony helped with the dinning/living room.

Ashley said to her mum also giving her support, she also picked up the fact that their mum was worried too "It will be ok, mum. You got us too!" Ashley and Diane gave their mum a hug and smiled.

"It will be fine, mum" Antony said over hearing his sister, all three of them loved their mum very much and wanted to show that they were behind her a hundred per cent too.

It was an hour till all the guests were due to arrive, all the family was coming. It took time but now the food was all ready. The wine, champers and beers were cooling in a huge bucket of ice. It looked great, a joint effort from her husband and her kids with a little help from Jason at only just 3 years also wanted to help.

Susan got on ok with Michael's foster parents although she had noticed he was not shown a lot of love or guidance by them. Mr and Mrs Beecham were down to earth and always thought that Susan was a lovely person and that was enough for them. They knew that Michael was really happy, when he was with her.

Ashley and Antony were already, they got ready before they came up to their mum and dad's house. Ashley and Diane had summer floral party dresses on. Antony was in navy chinos and a shirt. So they sat down and watched some telly while their mum and dad finished getting ready. Antony arranged the music for the party. He picked out the best records and tapes. The party was ready!

Susan went upstairs to get ready, while Sarah got ready. Sarah had a new dress white with pink flowers. She had it for her birthday, which Sarah was going to wear. Sarah helped Jason to get ready he looked cute a stone chinos with a white shirt so her mum had more chance to get ready herself.

Michael went upstairs to get ready too but being a man he could be ready in ten minutes. Michael went into their bedroom "WOW, you look stunning and rather sexy if I do say so" Michael smiled grabbing his wife close and give a seductive kiss on her neck. Susan was wearing a tailored cerise chiffon knee length, sleeveless dress scooped neck, her lovely light brunette shoulder wavy hair and make up to match her hazel eyes, all to match her glamorous and chic look.

"Are you sure I look ok?" Susan had always doubted herself. Even though she grew up to be a beautiful swan, she always saw herself as the ugly duckling. She was never made to feel anything else. Not necessarily by her family but she was also badly bullied at school, which this did affect her self esteem growing up.

"Yes, you look lovely, stop putting yourself down" Michael said with a bit of a stern tone. Susan just gave a little unconvincing smile. Michael gave his wife another reassuring hug and kiss.

It was time for the party and her family was due to arrive. Susan was feeling very nervous as if she was a child all over again. She did every time her family got together. Every time there was a get together there was always some row or harsh words spoken about the past.

Michael got ready he was going for the smart casual look beige chinos, with cream shirt to match his dark hair and blue eyes. He still looked rather handsome. They all made an effort to look nice. The family knew how important it was to Susan.

"Let's get this show on the road!" Michael said giving his wife a much needed hug of support, once again. The Jones all went downstairs to wait for the guests to arrive. Michael lit the candles and dimmed the lights. Then put some music on just for in the background.

"Mum, dad you both look amazing" Diane said smiling, as she went into the kitchen to get some wine glasses out from the fridge, that were chilling.

All the guests started to arrive; first it was Susan's mum Hilary, dad Henry and younger sister Emily with her husband Peter Keane and their daughter Jessica. Then her older brother Harry came with his girlfriend. Susan's younger brother Mark came next with his family. Then finally their friends came in Maggie and Keith Barns they were invited too as they were Michael and Susan's friends; It was a full house!

The kids went upstairs to play while the adults mingled down stairs. Ashley sorted out the drinks for everyone so her mum could talk to her family, a glass of wine for the ladies and a beer for the men in the family, soft drinks for the kids and the older kids.

Ashley, Antony and Diane hoped that it would go well for their mum. This was the first time they had all been together in long time the memories of the past always got in the way of them all moving forward.

Maggie was not to keen on Susan's family, they sometimes came across a bit two faced at times, also Maggie remembered that Susan had told Maggie how she was never treated that fairly by her family. Susan never acted like the rest of her family. She was down to earth person, kind and caring always thinking of others. Although Susan's family had changed as she got older, she felt she had to prove herself to them.

Mark, Emily and Harry did try to make it up to their sister and seemed more caring and loving towards her. They still thought she could done better than just being a mum, have more ambition and drive.

Although Susan did work in a factory for a little bit after school, she didn't get much chance to do anything else as she fell pregnant but to her that was wonderful, she had always wanted to be a mother. Harry and his girlfriend Jane did not stay that long, mainly through that his sister could not get past how she was treated and Harry through guilt.

As normal for most of the evening, nothing was not quite good enough for Susan's family they picked at everything she had done nothing was not up to their standards. They could not help it talking about the latest gadget.

Upstairs things were not much better Jessica, Nicole and Natasha, Sarah and Jason's cousins were doing the same sort of thing. They wanted everything for themselves and talked about the new gadgets they had. Spoilt was an understatement! But the table were about to be turned as this was not an ordinary house!!!

Meanwhile downstairs Michael, Maggie and Keith had enough of Susan's ungrateful and spiteful family, Michael could see Susan's face, even though she tried to hide it. She always would feel the pain that her family was causing; the consequences of their actions were plain to see!

Michael had to say something but he had to be careful, he didn't want his wife to feel any more pain than what she was feeling already. He could tell his older kids were not happy either, they could see that their mum was upset by the put downs and every little things their Auntie and Uncles picked at.

"TRY and be a bit more supportive to Susan, I don't care what you think of me? But she is your family and I wont have Susan treated in such a spiteful way! This is our home" Ashley, Antony and Diane thought well done dad. Maggie smiled Michael had said what Maggie and Michael's kids were thinking. After that Susan's brothers and sister were a little better behaved.

Through the rest of the evening things were better as Susan's family did apologise in person to Susan, they realised how they acted and wanted to put things right; This was the start of the family finally coming together. Slowly start to put the past behind them, with of course a bit of time and patience!

The rest of the family met the two latest members of the family Felix and Tabby, Felix loving the attention, as thought he was top cat. Tabby just wanted to be left alone to sleep curled up by the fire. The rest evening was an enjoyable one!

Upstairs things were getting interesting in Sarah's room. Sarah and Jason's cousins were still being spoilt, when the bedroom door opened and one of Jason's cars that he had collected went racing into Sarah's room! But there was no one out on the landing to make this car move and it was in Diane's room stroke spare room, no one was in Diane's bedroom!

All the adults were downstairs as this happened. Then Jessica, Natasha and Nicole, Sarah and Jason heard a child's laughter. They all looked at each other, Sarah for some reason was not afraid or Jason but Jessica and Nicole that thought they were so cool were scared stiff, then Nicole, Natasha and Jessica heard something in their ear, a gentle whisper "BOO"

This frightened them too death "It's a ghost" all three shouted in chorus and ran down the stairs as fast as their legs could carry them to be with their parents. Sarah and Jason looked at each other it was kind of strange, what had just happened! They did find it funny in one way and in a way their cousins did deserve it. Sarah and Jason went downstairs too, trying not to laugh at their cousin's reactions.

"Have you been trying to frighten my poor little girl Jessica, Sarah" Auntie Emily said grabbing Sarah by the arm with anger. Emily had noticed that Sarah was grinning when she came into the living room so she assumed by her face that Sarah had done something to her precious little angel.

"NO of course not, why would I do that!" Sarah replied in a cheeky tone, Sarah was annoyed with her Auntie thinking that she could be that cruel and a little hurt by her accusations.

"Get your hand off my daughter" Michael said and continued "IF Sarah says she didn't do anything, well she didn't!" Michael was not happy at all.

"Sarah is not the sort of girl to do that, she not spiteful or wicked!" Susan said trying to be the diplomat "You know Sarah!" Susan added she was annoyed that her sister could think that of Sarah too.

"I know my little sister and she would not do that" Antony said shaking his head with annoyance, Diane and Ashley nodding with agreement with their brother.

"OK we are leaving, something happened and I see no one is going to tell me what! Then I'm not staying her any longer" Emily said in a real mood patronising tone then Emily moodily grabbed her coat.

Emily had only been there for a couple of hours, but was adamant that she was right and they were wrong. Sarah had played a trick on her daughter, she was determined to leave. Emily left without even saying goodbye, along with her husband Peter and her poor daughter Jessica and Emily along with her older brother Harry and his girlfriend, who gave his sister Susan an evil look as he left.

Susan was upset it was all falling apart again, Susan thought everything was just started to get better, Susan had tried so hard to bury the past "I AM sorry, but I had to say something love! That was the last straw for me" Michael said putting his arm around his wife.

"That's ok I know" Susan said as she started to tidy up a little, trying to be strong and not to cry, Susan looked really crushed.

Then Mark put his penny in "I Know kids will be kids, but still I think its time to say sorry to each other kids. It probably just a kids prank, you know what kids are like!"

"I DONT know what happened, but I swear I did not do anything" Sarah said still trying to work it out in her own head, Sarah ran upstairs. It did not feel nice being accused of something she did not do and that her Auntie did not believe her.

"My sister didn't do it" Jason added sticking up for his big sister, at only three.

"Ok will leave it at that, its just one of those life little mysteries. I've got to go soon sis and I am sorry for the digs at you and the way you done things, I didn't mean anything by it but it was wrong of me, I do love you sis and I really never meant to upset you. Nicole got her piano class in the morning, so I have to say goodbye now. This was an interesting night to say the least!" Mark stayed for another half an hour but then they had to leave. "I will give you a call" he said he gave his sis a hug as they left, he could tell that she was a little upset.

"I got to go now, sis" Mark said smiling getting his wife and his two daughter's coats. Susan said goodnight to her brother and his family. Then it was just Maggie and Keith, they sat downstairs with Susan, Michael and Susan's kids. Ashley went upstairs to check on Sarah.

"Are you ok, Sarah?" Ashley asked as she sat on Sarah's bed giving her daughter a hug and kiss on the forehead.

Sarah was playing with her dolls, with her head down. She did not look very happy at all "I be ok, it's just Auntie Emily should of believe me, I swear I did not do anything. I know it sounds strange but Jason's car really did move by itself when it came into my room! And I did not say anything either, it was little girls voice that spoke but not mine!" Sarah explained frustrated and upset at the same time

"Ok I do believe you and so does mum, dad, Antony, Diane and Jason. SO before you go a bed say goodnight to everyone" Ashley said and gave Sarah a big cuddle again. Ashley went downstairs.

"Are you ok? Michael has only said what we all were feeling tonight!" Maggie and Keith said to Susan, they could tell that Susan was not happy and stayed on a bit to make sure Susan was ok as they only lived up the next street.

"I will be ok, just hope Sarah is ok!" Susan replied, she wanted her family to be there that night, as despite it all she still loved them, but she did like it when it was just Michael, Maggie and Keith were more down to earth, had always treated her with kindness.

Sarah went to bed not long after, before she went to bed she came downstairs to give her mum Susan a cuddle, she knew that her mum would be upset and worried about her, then said goodnight to everyone else, she was very tired she went to bed. So it was just the adults up, for the rest of that evening Michael and Susan had a good night, they had a laugh.

Sarah felt that night that she was not alone once more but this time it was a nice feeling like, something good and kind was watching over her, something that could feel that she was upset and could indentify with Sarah.

Ashley left a little after as Jason was getting tired it had been a long evening, Antony paid for a taxi for his sister and Nephew to go home Antony was going to stay with his younger sister Diane and his parents. He didn't have any work the next day, so he could have a few drinks, so Antony was going to share a taxi with his sister Diane as she was staying over with Ashley and Antony that night.

Maggie and Keith stayed till midnight then they left and took a slow walk back to their house as they were a little drunk. Antony and Diane taxi pulled up just after Maggie and Keith left. Diane and Antony gave their mum a huge hug before they left to show their support "I will give you a call mum and arrange something" Antony said as he left. It was a good night. Michael and Susan went upstairs to bed hand in hand and a little bit tippy.

Ashley brought Jason up most weekends so he could see his sister and Ashley could see her daughter. For Sarah she was not so close to her real mum Ashley always felt like a big sister, rather than a mum to Sarah but as time went on, they did become closer. This was something that would take time, probably years even to develop. Sarah was closer to her Grandparents at the time they had brought her up.

Sarah still enjoyed Ashley and Jason coming up it was nice when the family was together Ashley, Jason and Diane, when he could get away from work Antony.

The next morning after the party Susan and Michael got up with a bit of a sore head from drinking the night before. It was the big clean up dishes to do and general tidying, rubbish to clear up paper plates, beer cans and wine bottles.

Sarah was already up. Susan made a start on the cleaning with Sarah help and Michael. It took time but they got their in the end. Later that day in the afternoon, Michael was going to do some decorating, while Susan did the general housework, Sarah tidy her room up and put the duster round.

Michael had got some paint to refresh the walls in cream and had order some beige carpets for the house to be delivered for the living room hallway and landing. The rest of house would have to wait, till he had saved up more money.

Sarah had that morning done breakfast for herself, a Banana with glass of apple juice, which was nice for mum not to have to worry about for once. Michael put the kettle on for coffee. Then there was a phone call, Susan picked the phone up it was her sister Emily. She wanted to say sorry for how she was at the party and how she behaved to her sister.

"I am sorry about how I treated you at the party? and I'm sorry about how I treated Sarah I know she is a good girl!" Emily knew that she had been in the wrong and was really sorry she loved her sister. Even though sometimes she didn't always say it or show it.

"OK, I accept your apology, let's just forget about it and move on!" Susan replied she knew that for her sister to ever say sorry, she would mean it and that this was not a word that came easily to Emily at times.

Susan got of the phone then went into the kitchen, to get her and her husband a coffee. "Who was that?" Michael asked out of curiosity.

"Oh it was Emily she said sorry about how she was last night? and said to say sorry to Sarah too" Susan said pleased that things were back on track, with her and her sister's relationship.

"That's ok mum. I can see in a way why, she thought it was me playing a trick, it was kind of strange!" Sarah said as Sarah went upstairs to her room, to play some music.

"I should think so too! Well let's forget about it, for now" Michael responded.

Sarah got herself dressed to help her mum and dad. she knew they had a bit of a hang over.

Maggie also gave Susan a call just to make sure she was ok. Susan said that she was fine and that her sister had called to say sorry. Maggie was a lot happier knowing her friend was ok, Maggie could hear in her friend's voice that seemed happier now.

Michael had to work that day, it was meant to be a day off but someone called in sick and they needed cover plus this would be extra money in the kitty to make home improvements like decorating. While Susan sorted more stuff out and painted the landing and hallway. Mid afternoon the Carpets were due to come and be laid.

Sarah watched her mum paint the hallway in a medium green, she sat on the stairs. Tabby and Felix were sat either side of her on the stairs like two book ends! They too were watching the paint brush going up and down the walls as Susan painted.

Sarah had a strange feeling in her mind, she felt as if there should be old fashioned bells lined up along the hallway! The sort they use to have in manor houses or country house or a large farm house like in the old times! That would ring to let someone like staff, that someone from the main part of the house wanted something! Also the colour of the paint that her mum had picked was the colour of the walls a long time ago, Sarah felt.

Sarah could not understand this feeling, why would she know that or even feel that, this made her feel confused growing up as this would not be the only feeling that she would have about the house. She would get this feeling a few times, a feeling that never really went away. How could she know this? She was only 6 years old! So she ignored this feeling Felix or Tabby their kittens also sometimes acted strange too. They too could sense something in the house. Sometimes they would purr or run away for some bizarre reason! Sarah knew that animals were sensitive to things, could pick up on things that people could not.

CHAPTER 4

Not much happened through the summer holidays, Emily and Mark would sometimes visit on an evening or pop round lunchtime or Susan would go up to them by bus. Harry and Susan were still not that close, he never really said sorry about how he treated his sister but he was proud and really it was more out of guilt why he never said sorry He bullied her a lot as kids and was cruel to her, rather than being the big brother that he should have been. Susan would visit her parents too once a week, in the morning or afternoon when Sarah was at school.

It was Antony's birthday in august but as he was older now. Too old now to go out with his parents or birthday party's, the normal thing was to just go out for something to eat with his friends and his mum and dad would give him money rather than a birthday present, he was 18 years. Antony was going to start his driving lessons and was already saving for a car. Not new one, just second hand car. He did not take that long to have his driving lessons and pass his test, first time. By that time he had saved enough money for a car.

By this time Sarah started to hear footsteps in the middle of night! Not every night though, it would happen between about half one and half two in the morning when everyone was asleep, Sarah had always been a light sleeper but she was not the only one to hear them, little did she know at the time so did her sister Diane. The days were not so strange, as the nights.

Sarah at first didn't think much of these footsteps for one thing she was only 6 years old, the age of innocence and didn't know anything about ghosts. At first she would think it was her dad going to bed, it sounded heavy like a man's footstep. Sarah would be half asleep when she would hear them so she was not sure if it was just her imagination or the heating going through the pipes. Sarah was aware and was told that old houses do creak and make strange noises.

As the Jones family did not have a huge amount of money. The summer holidays would be Just a day out to the park or to the seaside, so the summer holidays went slow. Having one wage coming in meant that they never had loads of money but they were for the most part, a happy family. Sarah didn't mind as long as the family was together, cant miss what you never had! That was the way Sarah thought and family was more important than material things, even though it was a complicated family.

When the family had a day in, Sarah would amuse her self by playing with her dolls most of the time outside, on an old blanket in the warm summers sun or play on the old swing they had in the garden. Sometimes the neighbour's kids would come round, Lucy and Tom. Unless it rained it which case they would play in Sarah's room or watch telly downstairs, Tom and Lucy did prefer playing in the garden, they always felt unsure in the house.

Sarah did not mind playing inside or out as in the day, things were not as spooky as the night, although the feeling of being watched was always there day or night and there were other noises, sounds in the day. But nothing that bad, voices, like an impression from the past echoing through the walls. Voices of the past bleeding into the present, a child's giggle or voice whispering in the Sarah's room!

It was the end of summer holidays Sarah had to go back to school. Her school was ok, she did find it difficult. It was the other children that were the problem. Sarah was shy and reserved child, not confident. In a years time she would be starting her first year in junior school. Sarah was not looking forward to the change. She knew school would get harder and harder dealing with more and more name calling.

The kids teased her, as she was shy and quiet, never really said a lot. Sarah didn't really like school and for the coming weeks, Sarah started to feel different from the other kids, she didn't fit in and never made friends very easily. Also made to feel different by the harsh words of other children 'you smell' they would say 'and you are strange, you don't talk! What's wrong with you?' so that would make her feel more alone in everyway.

Her mum had always said not to take any notice of other children, their just cruel and mean it is the people that love you that count. But it was hard, not to listen, this was constant. Her older brother and sister were brilliant too, they tried to support her but as they were a lot older they had their own lives to lead, so they were not there all the time.

Sarah seen her real mum, older and younger brother mostly on weekend or they would go round on an evening, Diane was still living at home but as she was 16 years old she was out a lot with her friends. Sarah still felt lonely a lot of the time. The family always tried to spend as much time together as they could. Even though Antony and Ashley were grown up, even Diane was leaving home soon. They always stuck together and did things as a family.

Sarah made friends with the next door neighbour's kids, tom and Lucy Chapel but they were never close friends, it was someone to play with outside when the weather was nice.

The rest of the children in the neighbourhood would not really play with her either. Again they would tease her, they too would think she was strange as Sarah did not say much, keep herself to herself. Growing up she always felt different from anyone even though her parents would never make her feel this way. The feeling came from within but she never knew why or understood the feeling.

Her mum was brilliant, understanding and caring always there for her. Sarah's mum was the glue of the family. But Sarah didn't want to say too much about anything to her mum. She did not want to worry her mum, but sometimes she could not help it, her mum always had a knack for knowing when something was wrong with her kids even if she was not sure what it was that was bothering her kids she knew!

Sarah's mum never had a brilliant childhood. Susan was mistreated by her older brother and did a lot of things for her younger brother and sister. Which she never got thanks for, she felt she was made to grow up to quick and she was bullied too, quiet badly at school, even by one of her teachers. The teacher if she not paying attention to the teacher, she put to the back of the class with own desk, which children would call this Susan's island, the teacher never stood up for her. This affected Susan's confidence and self esteem growing up, this made her feel isolated. She suffered at times with depression from teens upwards. This in turn affected her ability to work.

Susan felt as if she was not good enough by her mum at times, she was the older daughter she had to do a lot of things to help more than maybe she should of, at her age. Susan's dad was away a lot as he served in the navy. For her mum Hilary it was not very easy in a way, left with four children to bring up. Sometimes felt like she was on her own, with her husband away sometimes for months at a time sometimes longer with the impending knowledge, that he might not return through loss of life or injury, it was hard. Susan's sister and her two brothers had always put her down.

Susan made up for that with her own children, who she tried to be supportive and kind but also firm but fair. Her children would always come to her as she was a mum that listened to her children, her children were her everything, her world.

Susan's dad Henry made up for it when he was home, he would spend his time with his family and bring back something for them all, just a little something. When he went away he would write letters to his family, from the battleship that he was on where he was based. Henry was loved and well respected man with a big heart, he would make people laugh with his funny faces. His most well known face was Popeye the sailor man. Henry did like his spinach!

Susan and Michael were childhood sweethearts, grew up together and married when they were young. Michael had fallen in love with Susan when he was a young man. They were each others first loves and only love. They were happy in the very beginning but like all couples did have their heated talks, it was a very much up and down marriage, by the time Sarah came along Susan and Michael marriage had settled down, lot more calmer.

Michael to Sarah was a great dad the best. A proud and loving husband, worked hard as a Welder in a small factory to support his family. He had this job since the time he left school at 16 years old. Michael was logical and stubborn, believed in the facts only of life but a little of a soft touch to Sarah, she was a daddy's girl and could whined him round her little finger.

Michael had only Susan's family and their kids as his family, Susan's family would visit Susan and Sarah, the grown up kids would visit too, mostly on weekends. With Susan's side there was a lot of ground work to make up. The family had to get over the past to move on admit their mistakes, which was not easy for Susan's family.

Ashley, Antony and Diane were not as close to their dad as their mum. Michael was not a perfect dad or husband but they could see that when Sarah and Jason came along he had changed. Michael's kids did understand why he was like he was when they were kids as he was brought up in a home with fosters parents, not that all foster parents were bad. Just that these foster parents, more firm than loving and did not show their dad as a kid the guidance he needed.

Sarah loved her brother Jason but being a younger brother, he could be annoying too at times. Her brother was opposite to her, he was confident little boy, he was always on about something. Dark strawberry blonde hair and brown eyed little boy; 'Jason will be a hit with the ladies, when he gets older' his granddad would say. Where as Sarah was more shy and reserved. One minute they loved each other the next they hated each other. But they loved each other really. It was just the usual sibling rivalry, although they sometimes did have really big fights but Sarah being the eldest, she would be the one to get told off, as begin the eldest, she should know better, her parents would say. This use to whined Sarah up even more and Jason knew it.

Sarah was close to her older brother and sister's but it was a big age difference, ten years between her and Diane and twelve years between her and Antony. So they were into different things plus they were old enough that they were dating too, also going out with friends on nights out. Ashley and Antony did find time though to visit their mum, dad, Sarah and Diane as she was still living at home at this time. Jason did stay a lot at his Nan's in the day before he started school as Ashley had a little part time job in the mornings for a couple of hours a few days a week.

To Sarah in other ways it was nice having a big brother and sister, also a real mum that was kind of a sister too! It was someone else she could talk to rather than her mum, who was really her Nan. Sarah looked up to Diane a lot and as she was still at home they talked a lot to each other. Sarah never mentioned her feeling about the house, she did tell her sister a bit more about the kids teasing her at school to Diane rather than her mum. Sarah just didn't want to worry her mum, with what was going on.

CHAPTER 5

One day after a hard day at school, when the kids yet again calling her names. Sarah came in and went straight to her room, trying to hide her bruised heart. Sarah was not happy, she felt sad, Sarah was glad to be home. Her mum had noticed that Sarah went straight upstairs. Susan sensed that her daughter was upset about something but thought that she would give Sarah a bit of space. So she could come to her mum when she was ready to.

Sarah unpacked her school bag and got changed. Her mum was getting the tea on the go. Sarah all of a sudden heard a little girl voice again! The girl voice just said "Hello". Then Sarah heard a faint giggle, as if this little girl could sense Sarah needed a friend.

"Who's there"; Sarah demanded, but there was no reply. Sarah had heard this little girl voice before. She was not in the mood for little games! Although she sensed that this little girl was trying to communicate with her!

"Tea is ready" Susan called to Sarah from the bottom of the stairs. Five minutes later Diane came from seeing her friend. She had finished school now she had not done to bad with her grades too.

Sarah went downstairs to have her tea, as her dad walked in from work, Sarah gave her sister and her dad a cuddle, then went over to her mum and gave her a hug. They all sat round for their tea. They had an open plan living stroke dinning room.

Mum and dad talking about their day and what other plans they had for the house, with Diane giving her input how she like the house decorated too. They wanted decorate the whole house but a bit at a time, each room to be up lifted with light shades of colour and more up to date carpets.

Susan asked her daughter how her day was at school. Susan was little concerned with Sarah as she knew something was up. Diane knew her sister well too and could tell that something was on her mind. Sarah didn't say much, just made out she was tried! One of the lessons was not that easy. But she was ok, nothing she could not handle? That was Sarah's excuse. After that Sarah's mum didn't push it and just gave her daughter a hug.

"Well, if you ever need to talk about anything, you know you can talk to us!" Susan said to reassure her.

"Whenever you need us" Michael added giving his support but was not really worried about Sarah, he just though it probably just did not like her school that much.

"I know but I'm fine really" Sarah replied with a smile. They carry on eating.

Sarah however could not get this little girl's voice off her mind, what had happened that day. It was nice for her parents to ask about her day. But she could not tell them what had happened? Sarah was too frightened to say what she heard, as they would think she was telling tales and would not believe her plus, her dad did not believe in that sort of thing.

For the next few weeks, Sarah would hear a child voice, laughter or something would move in her room, when she was not looking almost, as if the little girl was trying to make contact with her or make her presence known. This never made Sarah afraid at first. The footsteps she still did not take any notice at that time, it was just now and again, in the middle of night, that could be anything.

They just did their normal routines. Susan would take Sarah to school. Michael would go a work in the week. Susan just did the odd trip to the park to be in her own peaceful thoughts or shops, or see her family or have a coffee with her friend Maggie. On the weekend Michael and Susan would do something to the house like the odd bit of painting and decorating. Or take the kids out or Susan and Michael's older kids would visit.

The paranormal activity would start with little things to being with, in the house. Just the feeling of being watched, if Sarah came down the stairs or the odd word from this little girl or sound of laughter, Sarah would hear in her bedroom, while playing on her own or when her brother would play. Her brother would never say anything about it, what Sarah would hear from this little girl so Sarah did not mention about it, or sometimes her dolls would move when she was not looking, not much, just a little.

'Why would this little girl not speak to Sarah properly? Maybe she was shy like her!' Sarah would ponder over this, she really wanted to able to speak to this little girl 'Maybe they could be best friends' Sarah thought to herself.

It was a Friday, Sarah was glad there was no school on the weekend. After school Sarah was always in a rush to get home with her mum. The weekend had started. Diane had come home from going out with her friends, as Friday night was their family night and Diane had a sat job so she had to work lunchtime for a few hours. It was going to be a nice relaxing evening. Michael was home from work early as normal on a Friday. So mum, dad, Sarah and Diane had their tea together and sat down to watch the soaps. Friday night always seemed to pass quickly. Sometimes they would have a take away night on the Friday, like fish and chips or pizza or a Chinese. It was always a nice evening for the four of them.

After tea and a bit of telly Sarah went upstairs to play to give her mum and dad a bit of space for an hour before she had to go a bed. Sarah was always good at amusing herself, if she needed to. Diane just went upstairs to play some music and did some writing in her diary that she had, about her week.

Sarah just watched a bit of telly, on her black and white telly to play with her dolls. She felt as if she was not alone, but she did not feel afraid, she felt that it was the little girl that she had heard before. Sarah felt that this spirit could tell that Sarah always felt lonely. Even though this presence at the time would not speak, it gave her comfort that she was not alone. 'Maybe this little girl was just hiding from her! This little girl did not know her. Maybe she was just shy like herself' Sarah thought at first.

An hour pasted very quickly and now it was time for Sarah to go a bed. Sarah got ready for bed, then said goodnight to her mum, dad and big sister. She drifted off to sleep, fell in a deep sleep. Sarah's mum and dad went to bed too an hour later, her sister Diane went a bed half an hour after her mum and dad.

The house was all calm and quite, just the sound of the old floor boards creaking as the hot water went through the pipes, only the landing light on. The rest of the house in darkness and silence!

Sarah was awoken from her sleep about half one in the morning. She heard what sounded like an old bell tinning and creak of a door, it sounded like it came from downstairs in the hallway, where she had imaged bells would be. She thought it was an odd sound! there was nothing in the house that would make that noise in the dead of night!

This woke her up out of her sleep. She was curious 'what was that?' Sarah thought to herself. Then she heard the little girl's voice once again. This time it came from the cupboard that she would not dare to open. It was the little girl soft voice; "Its Anna, help me please Sara". The little girl voice said in scared tone. The little girl seemed nervous and upset!

Sarah jumped up an in a timid voice said "Who are you? My name not Sara, its Sarah, please come out of the cupboard, I know it would be really bad to open it".

"I CAN'T, he won't let me. I've been a bad girl" this scared voice whispered.

"What do you mean?" Sarah asked. The little girl did not speak back to her. That night Sarah found it hard to go back to sleep and the next day it was still on her mind. Sarah heard this bell noise a few times at random, sometimes in the day and sometimes at night. But she never really took much notice of it, even though it was an odd sound to hear with a house that had no bells or anything that could make that sound.

The next day was a Saturday. Ashley was going to come round with Jason as she did most weekends. Sarah loved seeing her brother and her real mum Ashley.

This family was a closer family now, the past mostly laid to rest, and it felt special to be part of this family. It was nice that Sarah was able to see her real mum too. That the family had always been honest with her, also that they had kept her in the family. For Sarah her life could have been much different but fate seemed to play a hand and she was still part of the family. Ashley and Jason stayed for the day; it gave Ashley also chance to catch up with her sister Diane. Diane came back from work mid afternoon with some cakes for after tea for them all.

Jason and Sarah played together in her room, Jason liked the spare room but he liked his big sister's room too, it felt nice. Sarah felt the little girl presence with them watching her and her brother play but Sarah did not feel afraid of this, she smiled to herself. Jason stayed for tea with his mum, Ashley and Jason stayed, until about half 8 in the evening went home on the bus.

Then the next night the little girl started to talk to Sarah from that night, on most nights. It was Sarah's own friend, someone she could talk to, even though in her heart, she knew that this was the voice of a ghost! But Anna had a kind, soft voice and somehow felt filmier to her! So Sarah never felt afraid of her. She knew that this little girl meant her no harm.

Anna never mentioned why, she called Sarah Sara? Also what she meant when Anna said she was not allowed out of the cupboard for being a bad girl, Sarah never pushed for an answer.

She told Sarah 'her name was Anna and her mother was Helena. They lived in that house a long, long time ago' Anna never mentioned about her father. Only that his name was 'Edward Carter' but that was it, which Sarah thought was a bit strange. Sarah always talked about her dad. The tone of her voice would change if Anna mentioned her dad. Anna did not like talking about him, almost as if she feared him. Sarah never brought Anna's father up in conversation.

Sarah never said anything to her mum and dad or the rest of her family about her new friend Anna. It was her secret, it felt special to have a secret friend that no else knew about and that Anna would only speak to her, no one else. No one would believe Sarah anyway . . . .

The next day at school it was the same old thing the children would make fun of her and call names. Sarah tried to think of what her mum said to her 'sticks and stones will break my bones but names will never hurt me' as much as she tried to think of this, the names did hurt though and they did bruise but the sort of bruises that did not show, it was felt inside her heart.

But at least she had a friend and now had something to look forward to at night, beside her family. Sarah needed someone to turn to after school; Anna came to her when she needed someone the most.

The teachers at Sarah's school were good to her and did try to help her fit in. They could see that she felt lonely, out of place to the other pupils and did want to learn. Sarah tried her hardest in lessons. It did show in her school reports. After school was better Sarah thought at least she had her own special friend . . . .

Sarah came home, went upstairs, as usual to sort her school stuff out and change as normal. Sarah had a feeling that something was not right in her room, the ore of the room had changed drastically and it was bad, this was not Anna.

Sarah was horrified when she went into her room. She noticed in the corner of her eye the built in cupboard door in her room, was wide open. Her brother Jason foolishly had opened it, not knowing he was doing anything wrong. Even though Sarah had told him never to open it, as it was bad.

Jason was over that day to see his nanny as Ashley had to work, Susan babysat for her daughter most of the time when she was at work. This time Jason had been in Sarah's room. Sarah felt as something bad would happen if anyone opened it, Sarah called Jason into her room, Jason came running in from Diane's room. "What have you done Jason? Come here it was you!" she shouted at him.

Jason said unexpectedly "Yes, the man wanted to come out" Jason said "but he was stuck I heard him" Jason added, being only just under three years old he was too young to understand what he had done wrong.

Then her mum came up stairs, then Sarah's dad who had come home early, came up stairs. Susan asked in annoyance "What on earth is gone on?" Susan said firmly, she noticed the cupboard was open.

"It's just a cupboard but just keep it closed as it will let in a draft" Michael just said being his logical self.

Sarah's mum said something that surprised Sarah "Best not to open this door! Some things should be left alone" Susan closed it and just smiled. Jason did not take any notice of what his Nan had just said, as he was too young to think anything strange.

Sarah was confused, not by her dad as he pretty much said what Sarah thought he would say. But why would her mother say that, only if she felt the same way as her daughter! Also what her brother had said! If it was Anna stuck Jason would of said it's a she not a he, who was it that spoke to her brother! Her brother went into Diane's room to play with his toys in his toy box after and said no more about the voice in fact later that day, when Sarah asked about this voice he said "What voice?" as if Jason had completely forgotten all about it, like it never happened.

Sarah knew that it was not the case of him just forgetting or just saying it never happened. He really had no recollection of what had happened! It was as if his memories were wiped from his mind. So much so that he looked confused, as he had no idea what on earth his sister was talking about with vague expression on his face.

Sarah closed her door to after that incident, her mum and dad had gone down stairs. Sarah walked over to her wardrobe, to put her school bag away. Her bedroom door opened by it self, about halfway, which she seen from the corner of her eye. Sarah felt a cold breeze go pass her back almost, like someone had walked past. It made her shiver, like someone had just walked over grave. This did not feel like Anna, it made her feel uneasy and wary but Sarah tried to dismiss it.

Then Sarah plucked up the courage and opened the very cupboard, she said she would never open, even though something inside was telling her not to. 'It is just a cupboard like Jason said! How can it be bad?' Sarah tried to convince herself. Sarah slowly open it, she did feel edgy about it.

The cupboard was empty just a dark and creepy storage cupboard. But she noticed it was very cold up to the rest of the house, like ice. It felt filmier in some strange way. There was something eerie, amnions feel about it. As she peered into the cupboard to take a closer look, it felt like a dark and intimidating place. Her mum shouted from the bottom of the stairs "Tea is ready;" She had done Jacket potatoes for tea.

As she turned around to close the cupboard door, she felt two cold icy hands on the back of her neck; in her mind she felt green piercing eyes on her back, Sarah was petrified; she always knew there was a dark force in the house, a demonic presence. Sarah had never felt like that before and did not like it one bit, as she turned a dark figure appeared from the darkness, it went to reach for her but she quickly closed the door and ran downstairs.

She knew that bad things were going to happen. Sarah knew this entity meant business and was nothing like her friend Anna, who she had always felt safe, this made her feel terrified to her bones, she was not wrong! Maybe this was the ghost of Anna's father Edward? This was his cupboard of secrets.

For the next few days, she would chat to her friend Anna some evenings, when she was in bed. Sarah did ask Anna about the cupboard and what she had felt but Anna would not talk about it or maybe, she didn't want to! Sarah thought.

Anna would never talk about herself much just sometimes! She would talk about her mother or what she could remember. Anna's mother Helena had died when Anna was about seven years old. She missed her mother Helena so very much. Anna mentioned her mother was a teacher in a local school, what she could remember of her mother, she was kind, loving person and beautiful. Her mother was always helping others and she was well loved by the people that lived in her village.

Anna only said that her father Edward was a doctor that had moved there from the big city, before he had met her mother that was all she said about him. Back then the house was a bigger house, then it was now.

Sarah instinct felt like Anna was holding back something about him, something bad, that she was too afraid to speak of. So Sarah never push it, she just mainly talked about things that was going on with her like school, or just things that two little girls would talk about. For Sarah it was nice to talk to someone that could understand. Sarah did not feel so alone anymore. Even if her best friend was a ghost she did not care. It was nice, to finally have a friend, a best friend. Someone that understood! Anna felt the same.

The next few weeks Sarah was aware of the feeling of being watched by a presence that was not her dear friend Anna, she had always felt this but only now and again but now she had stronger feeling of this, Sarah was being monitored; closely.

CHAPTER 6

Meanwhile in those weeks Susan went up to see her sister Emily in her house for coffee and another day would see her brother Mark in his house for coffee, she was getting on much better with Emily and Mark but she could not get along with her older brother Harry and Harry never wanted to bother much with his sister.

Susan was always busy in the day in the week, coffee morning with her friends or family or doing things in the home like housework and washing or just odd jobs.

The following fortnight Ashley, Antony with Jason was coming over for a visit to see their mum, dad and two sisters, they were coming over around about six after tea. It would be nice to catch up, it was on a Friday. It was going to be a take away night. Fish and chips all round with mushy peas, also bread and butter, to make the perfect chip butties for Susan, Michael, Sarah and Diane.

They all arrived at the same time "Hi mum and dad" they all said together as their mum and dad got the door. They came in as Sarah came running out from the living room to give them a hug, along with Diane she had just got in from seeing her friends.

"Come on, lets all have a sit down in the living room and I will stick the kettle on" Michael said as they all went into the living room and all sat down.

"SO how's everyone been?" Ashley asked with curiosity.

"Yes were all been fine, Sarah is doing well at school, how is things with you lot?" Susan replied trying to change the subject on to her older children and their lives. "How is Jason getting on" Susan added.

"Yes he is doing fine; I'm ok too, getting on well with Terry" Ashley replied. Ashley had been seeing terry for about a year now.

"GOOD, he seems a nice young man" Susan replied back with an approving tone. Jason went upstairs to play.

Diane who was the more sensitive out of the three could tell something was not quiet right, that Sarah was quieter than normal. She had noticed this for sometime now. Diane was curious what was on Sarah's mind!

"Is everything ok Sarah? You seem a bit quiet today!" Diane asked her young sister. Hoping that all was ok

"Yes I'm ok but the cupboard door in mum and dad's old room was opened, I don't like that cupboard! It's creepy, Jason opened it" Sarah said just to see the reaction! Sarah wanted to know if her real mum, older brother and sister would say anything about it.

"Oh right, it is a creepy cupboard but cupboards are like that, as it is old, don't worry. I'm sure there is nothing to worry about!" Diane replied looking over to Ashley and Antony they were all scared of that cupboard growing up and always dared each other to open it but never did. They would always chicken out at last minute and make some random excuse not to open it! They too felt something bad would happen if it were to be opened;

"Well keep it closed if you are that scared of it but it is just a cupboard nothing to be afraid of!" Susan added although she felt the same as everyone else, she did not want to scare her children, plus she thought if they left it alone nothing would happen! 'It's just a plain old cupboard' Susan convinced herself 'nothing more, nothing less'

Michael came in with tea and coffees for everyone with squash for Sarah and Jason "So what is everyone talking about?" Michael said in a curious manor, Jason at that time came down for a drink, with a few toys in his hands.

"Not much dad, just about how things are going for us" Ashley replied smiling at him. She did not tell the truth, she knew her dad would just think their all being silly about this cupboard, begin the logical person he was seeing was believing; in his eyes.

That night they all had a lovely catch up Ashley was dating Terry for a while but no plans to marry. Ashley was getting on well in her job and was also doing Agony Auntie in a local magazine. Felix and Tabby came over to say hello to the family too. Tabby sat on Ashley's lap purring, Felix popped himself in front of fireplace and curled up on the floor to sleep.

Antony was doing well in his job. He had been going steady with a girl for about a year Susie Gibbs, they had just got engaged. So a wedding was on the cards sometime soon. Antony and Susie did not want to wait that long, they were young and totally in love.

Diane was doing well in the restaurant it was just a Saturday and a few hours on a lunch time but it was nice to have a bit of money. Diane was single but she was only 16 she had plenty of time to find her true love.

Michael popped out to get some drinks in the news agents down the road after their cups of coffees and teas! The take away was only 5 minutes away. It was a nice evening, catching up. The take away was naughty but very nice as a treat.

Ashley left around half 8 with Jason as he was getting tired. She had got a bus up but she had decided to get a taxi home. Antony stayed till about half ten and went home.

By this time Sarah was tired, so she said goodnight to her parents and went to bed, her parents went to bed about eleven, the same time as Diane. The house was still and silent once more, just the sounds that an old house makes.

It was about half two in the morning, something stirred Sarah, she opened her eyes, she heard footsteps. She had heard them before, they never were that loud but this time she did take notice as they seemed louder and more defined. Sarah felt unnerved by this. She had a bad feeling that this was just the start, a taster of things to come. It only lasted for a few minutes but it was long enough to stick in her mind and stopped her from having a good nights sleep.

The next day was a Saturday, so just a chilled day! It was beginning to get cold now on the evening as it was mid September but still not too bad in the day, warm sun with sometimes the odd shower so still nice enough to play a little in the garden.

Susan and Emily and the rest of Susan's family were getting on a lot better by now, they had well and truly put the past behind them and mended bridges. Mark was getting on better with his sister, apart from Harry. Emily offered to babysit for her sister Susan and Michael, as this was her way of making it up to her sister, plus it was coming up for Susan and Michael anniversary.

They had been married for 27 years but they had been together for around 29 years. Susan was now 47 years old and Michael was 48. Michael wanted it to do something special! he had booked a table at nice restaurant in the country. It was about half an hour from where they lived, it had an inn.

Michael had also booked a room for a night, so they could spend a bit of time together without any children. Even though they loved their children they needed some time on their own as a couple, up till now they had always done something with the kids on their anniversary.

Their friend from over the fence Keith Barns had offered to take them and pick them up as Michael did not drive, just walked or got buses everywhere, with work it was only a 15 minute walk away, he did not miss having a car. He really was not that bothered about learning to drive; he never felt the need to learn!

That night Emily came over to her sister's house to babysit. She was stopping the night. She would go back in the morning to see her daughter and husband. Emily would go home when Susan and Michael came back home from their night away.

Susan and Michael left half an hour later from Emily arriving, as Keith had pulled up to pick them up and beeped the car horn. They both looked very smart, Susan had a fitted red sleeveless dress with red silky shawl and Michael was wearing his black chinos and black silk shirt.

They said goodbye to Sarah as they left. Sarah was not happy for her mum and dad leaving after all that was going in the house. Susan being a mum felt guilty for leaving their child but this was first time they been out together in a few years! They always did things with their children as both were family orientated. But they needed time together as a couple, a loving married couple.

Sarah really didn't want her mum and dad to go out, she was a little upset, when they left but Auntie Emily gave her a big hug. She was close to her auntie, they seemed to gel well and for the most part Sarah got on well with her cousin Jessica too. Sarah didn't want them to go out to but she even at that age, she knew that her mum and dad needed time alone together as husband and wife.

Susan and Michael left for their lift, while Emily brought out a big bar of lovely chocolate as a bribe, Sarah was fine then!

Emily had already done tea before coming over she had cooked a chicken casserole, then had put it in a container and brought it over for their tea. It was still piping hot as Emily had a car, so it only took her about ten minutes to come over. It was rather yummy. Sarah polished off her plate, she even had seconds.

After tea Sarah did some homework, while Auntie Emily did the dishes and tided up in the kitchen. Then Emily sat down to watch the telly, Emily brought round the chocolate for herself and Sarah, she had broken it into two large chunks for the two of them.

"How is school going?" Auntie Emily asked to how her niece was getting on.

"Yeah, ok" Sarah sighed, Sarah did not want to tell her the truth about school, it might get back to her mum and dad! They would only worry.

"I bet your looking forward to Christmas? Only a few months away" Emily said trying to get a little more out of Sarah, she did not seem that happy with something.

"Yes, I like Christmases with the family and the snow" Sarah replied it was the one time of the year Sarah always liked, it had a special feel to it, not like any other day and it was not about the presents for Sarah.

Emily did not push it about what was wrong, Sarah was not ready to talk about it. So they both watched telly as by this time Sarah had finished her homework. The house was peaceful and silent. Just the sound of the telly, it was time to watch the soaps. Susan called up to see how her daughter was, knowing that she was upset before they had left, Susan was still feeling guilty for leaving Sarah.

"Hi just called up mostly to see how Sarah is?" Susan asked hoping that her daughter was ok.

"YES Sarah's fine we have had tea, Sarah finished homework and now she just eating chocolate. Are you both having a nice time?" Emily replied.

"Yes its lovely here. Missing Sarah, give her a big kiss and cuddle from us. We will see you all in the morning" Susan said "Bye"

"OK, bye." Emily said putting the phone down.

The thought that her daughter was ok now, Susan felt that she could enjoy herself more and not have to worry, that all was well. Susan and Michael were having a lovely time, they missed Sarah like mad but they needed this time, they both looked very smart. Michael grabbed his wife hand and kissed it, he looked lovingly into her hazel blue eyes.

Susan and Michael had a drink and chat at the bar first then the meal. The meal was outstanding a bottle of Champagne to drink, for food scallops with cream and white wine sauce to start followed by sea bass as a main and a really thick chocolate tart with proper clotted cream for desert, they were stuffed after.

It was naughty but very nice, a treat for themselves. Then upstairs to watch some telly and snuggle in bed, followed by a second desert between the sheets before bed!!

Meanwhile at home Emily took Sarah upstairs to get her ready for bed after watching telly for a bit and play for an hour, later Sarah went to bed.

Emily got her bed ready too; she decided to sleep on the sofa. Emily set her bed up on the sofa with a sleeping bag, a blanket and a couple of pillows but she was not that tired, so to tire herself a bit, she settled down on the sofa and read some of her book . . . .

Emily had the night light on. The house was still and quiet, just the odd sound of the house settling, with hot water running through, the creak of the floor boards. The normal sounds of a house as Emily read her book.

Then she heard what sounded like the bathroom door creak open, she wasn't sure, she knew that the doors to the bathroom and toilet were closed, it was one of the doors downstairs at least that's what it sounded like, which would have to be the bathroom door or the toilet door, as the living door was close to the bathroom and the toilet door, it was hard to figure out which door it was for sure.

Emily didn't think much of it. It was a cold, blustery windy night! Maybe it was just a draft coming from somewhere or maybe Sarah going to the toilet, even though she did not hear her coming down the stairs! So Emily put her book down and turned off the night light then settled down to sleep for the night. The house was dark and cold; Just the landing light on upstairs.

As Emily drifted of to sleep something woke her, she thought she saw a figure. A dark figure standing over her, she was half a sleep, so she didn't really take it in, as in a blink of an eye this dark figure was gone.

She sat up a little but what she thought she saw had vanished, so Emily just laid back down and went to go asleep again, when this time she heard footsteps that sounded like they were going up the stairs.

Emily was still sleepy so she got up thinking maybe it was Sarah but why would she be up at this time. It was about half one in the night, if it was Sarah she would of asked what was she was doing up this late!

So Emily went out to the landing to investigate, the footsteps had stopped by the time, when she got there! Emily for some reason felt uneasy, she felt something not right. Emily looked down the hallway to the stairs, the hallway was dark just the light shinning down from the landing light that was on upstairs. She did not feel comfortable at all. Emily could not see anything but she still felt as if something was there looking right at her, through the darkness of the hallway. It was she felt an evil presence . . . .

Emily went back to bed, she felt too uncomfortable to stay in the hallway. She wrapped her covers around her, hoping that whatever it was, it would go away and leave her alone. Emily did not hear the footsteps again that night but she still could not rest. This feeling she felt was not a good feeling. As if she was not welcome!

In the morning Sarah got up it was a Saturday, no school for her. So Sarah watched morning telly as she normally did on a Saturday morning. Sarah did think that her Auntie was acting strange, like she was on edge about something.

Emily got up and made Sarah some breakfast, bacon butties all round. Emily said nothing about the footsteps! She did not want to scare Sarah. Even though unbeknown to her, Sarah already knew about the footsteps.

Later that morning Susan and Michael returned from their big night out. They had a lovely time but were really pleased to see Sarah they had missed their little girl a great deal. Sarah ran over to give her mum and dad a cuddle. Emily did not say anything to them, as she thought they might think she was going mad!

"Thanks for having Sarah for us, maybe you, Peter and Jessica can come over for a meal one night? Just to say thank you" Susan said noticing that her sister seemed odd and quieter than usual.

"Yes that would be really nice, well got to now. I've got to get back for Peter and Jessica" Emily said she didn't want to say no to her sister's offer, as it would be rude but she felt very uncomfortable in the house after her experience.

"Is everything ok you seem a little odd" Susan asked her sister as Emily said goodbye to Sarah.

"Yes I'm ok just got to go, get back home for Jessica" Emily replied giving her sister a kiss on the cheek and said goodbye to Michael.

"Speak to you soon sis" Susan said as Emily went out the door, Susan thought how strange but really did not think much of it and she sat down with Michael. Susan and Michael told Sarah about their night out, leaving certain bits out!!

Later that day Susan phoned up her sister to ask if anything was ok! She was still puzzled by Emily peculiar behaviour and that she seemed in a rush to get out of the house! "Hi Ems, are you ok? You were acting very strange when I got home and you seemed to be in a hurry to get out of our house!" Susan asked in a concerned manor for her sister.

"YES, I am fine just missing Peter and Jessica" Emily replied she felt she could not tell her sister the truth, maybe this could make things worse for her sister and her sister's family.

"Well ok, As long as you are sure! Maybe you could pop round next week for tea with Jessica and Peter? A way of us to say thank you for babysitting and it would be nice to catch up too" Susan added not convinced by her sister story but didn't take it any further.

"Ok that would be lovely" Emily said she could not say no to her sister, even though the thought of being in that house again made her uneasy. She never wanted to step one foot in that house again. The thought of being there terrified her.

Emily like most people had always felt uneasy in that house and she had heard what sounded like footsteps before but it was in the middle of the night when Emily was half asleep. This time the footsteps were louder. There was no mistaking that was footsteps. She never heard the bathroom door open in the middle of the night for no reason. Emily had not felt that threatened before either, so much so that she needed to get out of the house, made to feel that unwelcome. She was concerned now for her sister.

The following week Susan had arranged for her sister Emily, Peter and Jessica to come up for tea on the Friday. That day had arrived, to Emily's dread.

Susan was doing roast beef with all the trimmings and a lovely homemade apple crumble with custard for afters, it was October and it was getting wet, windy and cold! Susan also wanted to discuss Christmas too. Susan was looking forward to her sister coming round this time with her family as Emily had made up for the past. Susan could not forget her part in making her childhood not brilliant but she could forgive, it was a long time ago and she had moved on.

Meanwhile at the Keane household Emily was getting ready, she was very nervous and tried to hide it to the best of her ability but it proofing very difficult to do so. She was looking forward to seeing her sister and catching up but she just wished it was not in that house.

"Are you alright, Love?" Peter asked his wife as he noticed she seemed a little quieter than normal and quite agitated.

"Yes I'm fine" Emily replied holding back her thoughts.

They all left their house and got into the car to drive to Emily's sister house. It was not a long drive; the traffic was not bad it took approximately 15 minutes.

Susan had finished cooking tea and was ready to dish up, while Sarah helped to lay the table and Michael sorted out the wine. Susan was looking forward to the evening. Diane had not planned to see her friends that evening so she helped her mum in the kitchen and was going to help her mum dish up.

Emily knocked on the door with Peter and Jessica behind her. They had brought a bottle of wine with them and a bottle of coke for Sarah, Jessica and Diane, Michael opened the door.

"Hi come in, I see you have not come empty handed!" Michael said jokingly as Peter handed him the bottles. Peter and Jessica came in first with Emily following behind. She could not help it she felt tensed. Emily was drawn to the top of the stairs! She felt something looking at them from the top of the stairs. The same evil presence she had felt the week before, this was a horrible feeling.

"Come on Emily don't just stand there, in the doorway" Peter said noticing that his wife was staring up the stairs. Jessica just gave her mother a strange as if to say 'what are you looking at mum!'

They all went into the living room where Susan was dishing up the roast with the help of Diane. Susan went up to her sister and she gave her a hug then she gave her niece a hug and a big kiss on her cheek.

"Every time I see Jessica she has grown" Susan said and continued "I hope you are all hungry" she said as she went out to the kitchen to get the plates. "If you all sit at the table I will be in now with tea" Susan added while they took their seats around the table.

The smells that were coming from the kitchen were mouth watering. Susan brought out everyone plates on a little trolley. It looked as good as it smelt. Michael poured the wine for the adults and then poured out a glass of coke each for Sarah, Jessica and Diane.

"This looks and smells amazing Susan! Thank you" Peter said licking his lips and taking a bite of the tender roast beef.

"No worries, dig in and enjoy guys" Susan said she was pleased that they were all sat down together and that there was no tension between them all, like the other time they all were together. This would be a good night Susan felt.

Emily was having a lovely time with her sister but her mind was always conscious of the presence, she had felt the week before and when she came in.

There were clean plates all round. After tea they all felt stuffed, it was lovely roast and pudding. The adults settle down on the sofa with a bottle of wine. Diane stayed downstairs with the adults, while Sarah and Jessica went upstairs to play. Jessica did feel slightly nervous, the last time she played upstairs one of Jason's cars came hurtling in from Diane's room, when there was no one there to make this happen!

Jessica behaved herself this time and did not show off at all. Jessica hoped that if she played nice nothing would happen. So Jessica just nicely built things with Lego with her cousin and talk about normal things like about school, toys and music as her mother told her not to show off and act spoilt or she would be in trouble. Emily was not happy about Jessica going upstairs to play but 'she was with her cousin' Emily thought.

It was an interesting and enjoyable night. Emily did not mention about what had happened to her the week before. She was not sure how to approach the situation! She knew her husband and Michael would probably laugh at her. That was not the sort things they believed in, so she said nothing about it.

Susan mentioned that for this Christmas they were having their kids and partner's up for Christmas dinner, it would be a full house. Which Emily was happy about 'at least she did not have to come to this house' she thought to herself. Peter offered to pop the presents over to their house and to collect any presents on the Christmas day, late morning, which Emily agreed to.

The night flew by and it was time for Susan sister to go home with Peter and Jessica. Jessica had enjoyed herself too, nothing had happened that night to her while she was upstairs.

"Thank you for having me, the food and evening was nice. Take care. Love you, I'm always here for you" Emily said to Susan and gave a cuddle, a tender cuddle. Susan knew by her sister's actions that there was defiantly something wrong.

"Ok! I love you too. I give you a call" Susan replied as her sister and her family left. "Maybe we can meet for coffee" Susan added determined to get to the bottom of what was up with her sister!

"Yeah ok, speak to you soon" Emily said as they left, Emily giving her sister half a false smile.

"Is your sister ok? She not normally an emotional type! Maybe it's the wine talking?" Michael said non serious expression, not really thinking anything by Emily and how she acted.

"Maybe your right, It is probably the wine talking" Susan said grinning but she knew her sister that was not like her at all, there was defiantly something going on.

"You put your feet up love. I will tidy up in the kitchen, then I get us a cup of tea and coffee" Michael insisted as Susan when upstairs to get Sarah ready for bed.

"Ok I will put my feet up, just sort Sarah out and put her to bed" Susan said.

Diane went upstairs to her room, till she went to bed to give her mum and dad a bit of space. Susan sorted out the Sarah, Sarah said goodnight to her dad and sister then went to bed; she was tired, so Sarah hit the pillow that night.

Michael had tidy up the kitchen and put the kettle on, when Susan came down stairs. Susan and Michael embraced and Michael gave his wife a kiss on her forehead.

"You have a sit down love and bring our drinks in" Michael said as the kettle clicked off.

Michael brought their hot drinks in. Susan and Michael cuddled up on the sofa as they normally did on the end of an evening, when

Sarah had gone a bed and before they would go to bed themselves. They had their coffee and went to bed too.

Sarah was awoken again by footsteps in the night, by now Sarah was a use to them, she did not like them but it was nothing more at this point, so she was that tired that she drifted off into a heavy sleep.

The next day Susan did call her sister Emily and asked if she was ok. Emily did not give anything away. Emily just said that it was nice to feel close to her sister. She had realised what she had missed growing up! She knew she was not the best sister to Susan. Susan just left it at that. She believed her sister's cover story. Emily could not tell her sister the truth, she afraid that she would make things a lot worse in doing so.

That day Susan had another call from her younger brother Mark. He said that Harry had said that he was moving away to New Zealand. Harry and his girlfriend Jane were getting on very well. They had been going out for nearly a year. She happened to come from New Zealand and had family over there, so Harry was going to move away with her.

Susan was a bit shocked that her older brother had not told her that himself but although it was her brother, she was not really upset to see him go maybe it would be good for Harry anyway Susan thought to herself, there was no love lost between them sadly.

Harry had planned to marry Jane over there too in a year time. This move was his way of getting to know his future in laws. He had also a chance of working over there with Jane's father selling show homes. He was moving over there just before Christmas, end of November. Harry had decided to have a little gathering at his house just before he was due to leave in mid November.

CHAPTER 7

Sarah always felt unsettled about the house, now that the cupboard in her room had been opened. She did not like the attic either! It also had a strange vibe too! She felt almost as if her brother had unknowingly let something or someone out and whatever it was, it was bad and evil. Sarah would always feel as if someone was watching her down the stairs or something behind her with an icy stare, right through her very soul.

Whatever was there was always there but by opening the cupboard. It had some how made things more intensive, there was some sort of secret to that cupboard. The secrets had been let out! This cupboard was the bad entity domain and was not to be entered.

Sarah's real mum Ashley, older brother and older sister, never really had much happen to them as they grow up in that house. Just they felt the same as Sarah and didn't like the cupboard or the attic, the feeling of uneasiness like being watched. Now and again hearing the footsteps in the middle of the night, or the odd giggle or a little girl's voice whispering. But nothing like what was happening to Sarah. Not that Sarah had any idea that her family had experienced anything. It was never talked about in any case.

The ghost of Anna and her father Edward seemed to just contact her for some reason. Her only excuse for that is that maybe as she could sense things about the house for example; that the layout of the house was different in the house years ago when Anna and Edward were living there, when they were alive to what the house was like now.

Sarah could also sense a negative and positive charge going through the house, like waves of emotions that had imprinted it self to the walls of this house. A link to the past, that no one else seemed to pick up on. Maybe with Anna the fact that Sarah felt lonely, sad at time, like she never fitted in and felt different to everyone else. Maybe that's why Anna came to her and no one else. Maybe Anna felt the same sort of feeling, therefore they understood one another.

In the house there was an electric meter, which you top up the electric in the paper shop via a key. Sarah dreaded every time it would run out especially, now that the cupboard in Sarah's room had been opened, which it would not very often as her dad was quite good remembering to top it up, but from time to time he would forget. It was bad enough in the day, but at night! It was worse the house would be in total darkness. Just shadows cased from the light coming in from the street lights, or lights and shadows of cars driving by.

Sarah would never go upstairs! When this happened, or if she was in bed she would run into her mum and dad's or sister's bedroom or would run downstairs, if her mum and dad were downstairs. Sarah felt too unsafe to be upstairs but she could not be in a room on her own, she would be too scared.

Sarah knew something was just waiting for her to come out into the landing or hallway, almost that this sincere presence was laying in wait for her. She could feel those piercing green eyes, as if he would be staring though the very walls from the hallway, to the living room were she would sit with her mum.

The house would be in pitch black nothing but silence and darkness! Her dad would never take that long to get the electric. The shop was just a few minutes down the street but it felt like an eternity. It also sometimes would happen in the middle of the night when the local shop was closed. When that happened they would be in darkness all night long, which she would be scared stiff. She knew she was never alone. It would not be her friend Anna, when this happened she always felt a dark figure over her, haunting her.

Sarah would sometimes feel other times that, someone was waiting for her on the other side of the door, if she was in the bathroom or toilet. Some days she would see the bathroom door slightly open by it self or the door handle would move or shake slightly like someone was trying to get in, trying to torment her.

Whenever she was having a bath, she would think it was her friend Anna but knowing in her gut it was something else was with her. Something was very wrong with this house! Sarah seemed to draw this demonic entity's attention.

On one of the days Sarah was having a bath, which she did every other day. Sarah's mum had washed her hair and given her soak down, then left her to have 5 minutes play before she had to come out. Sarah just laid in the baths warm water to relax and let her mind completely unwind to the worries of the day, as sometimes she did, it was nice to relax. She closed her eyes just for a moment, when she opened them, Sarah seen a dark menacing figure standing over the bath and looking straight at her, she was frozen with fear, she could not move.

This was a tall dark figure and those green eyes that would pierce right through her, which she felt many times. Sarah always felt that this figure for some reason wanted not to harm her but to frighten her, as this presence wanted to feed on her fear. She closed her eyes again for a second, when she opened them the dark horrible haunting figure had vanished without a trace.

Then her mum came in to get her out of the bath, Sarah said nothing of what had happened! She hid what had happened to herself well. Sarah didn't know how to explain it! 'How could she explain? OH by the way our lovely house is haunted?'

Sarah knew that this dark figure and this cupboard in her bedroom were connected in some way. What was the dark secret to this cupboard all about? After all it was just a cupboard! But yet it was the coldest part of the house and Sarah felt as if this was the key to another story. What tales did this old house have to tell? The truth in the end would be shown and all the evils that had gone before it. This old house would be revealed, this cupboard was somewhere to hide or something to hide, dead or alive!

CHAPTER 8

Jason birthday was coming up he would be 3 years old. Susan and Michael wanted to give their grandson a nice birthday; his birthday was in mid October. It was about a week away. Then they would have to think about Christmas. Jason was looking forward to it. All kids looked forward to their birthdays! It was going to be a family do just Jason's mum, nanny, granddad and his half sister. They did not have much money, so this was the cheapest option and Jason was only 3 he did not have any friends like that. It was a week away by this time.

The week went past fairly quickly as the normal routine of the week made it feel like it was a short week and with things to do for the party. It was Friday at last and Jason's third birthday was upon them. Susan was going to do just a small party but as Jason did not have any friends like that, Susan decided to invite all the family. This time the family gathering should better, up to the last time her family was there. Susan was getting on far better with her sister and brother. They were also bothering with their sister more as well! Even Susan's mum had changed through the years and now was a supportive and loving mum to her daughter. Also her kids were there to defend their mum in any case and would stick up for her, if need be.

All the family more or less had turned up at the same time. Susan had done a buffet with a homemade double chocolate cake. 'It looks scummy' Jessica thought as she came in. She loved chocolate cake, so did the rest of the kids.

Jason did well with presents more little cars and a car that he could sit in and move around with his legs, sweets and chocolates. Nicole and Natasha stayed downstairs with the adults as they were far too old to play kiddies game at the age of nearly 9 and 12 years old. Jessica, Sarah and Jason went upstairs to play with Jason's new things after stuffing their faces. The adults just chatted not about old times but the future.

Antony wedding was going to be in one or two years. They had to save up and they only known each other a year. So they felt it was a bit too soon. Antony knew that he did not have the money to afford to pay for the wedding. Antony had said it would in two years and it would be in mid July. It was good to have a few celebrations on the horizons; this family had its fair share of bad luck in the past. This would be something positive to happen with the family.

It was time to cut the cake, Michael called the kids down. They knew what it was time for 'Cake time' the kids came running down the stairs like a herd of elephants, of course kids begin kids. Susan sorted out the cake and put a candle on it that was in the shape of the number 3 which she then lit. They all sang happy birthday to Jason as Susan brought the cake into the living room. Jason blew out the candle and made a wish as they all cheered.

The family sat round the table while Susan cut the cake and served them all a nice big slice. It was delicious, after the kids had their slice of yummy cake! They all went back upstairs to play. The cake did not last long at all.

All the kids were having a whale of a time, by this time it was about six after they had stuffed their faces. They played well together for quite a few hours. It was getting on for about just after 8. Poor Jason was getting tired, so Sarah said if they just played for ten minutes more, then it would be time to go downstairs.

Sarah was enjoying herself and Even though Jason was tired, he had enjoyed his birthday too, Sarah was missing Anna though, she understood her more than her cousins, it was not the same, but she could feel Anna's presence with her smiling at them, while they played. But then she felt another presence, Sarah felt that something had frightened Anna off, as Sarah no longer felt her spirit there.

The bedroom became very, very cold, she felt that Anna was too afraid to stay, this was warning. Sarah knew when Anna had that feeling and would disappear like that; she knew that Anna's father Edward was there.

This presence did not like the laughter and happiness of her cousin or any children! Anna's father liked people feeling fear and negative feelings which he feed on, to give himself power and control over his environment.

Sarah's bedroom door that was open! It suddenly slammed shut by itself. This was just a warning to Sarah. Sarah's cousin and Jason were freaked out by this and opened the door, quickly ran down the stairs. Sarah was about to follow when the door closed on her. Sarah tried the door handle but she could not open the door, whatever it was! It would not let her escape "Please let me go. I wont say anything" Sarah pleaded she was scared near to tears.

The door opened but she knew that this was just a warning. Sarah could feel this spirit was pleased with himself this spirit was still in control, not Sarah. As long as Sarah was afraid, she would not question herself and start asking questions.

Sarah went downstairs. Her cousin had said nothing they just all said, that they wanted to come downstairs. Jessica did want to tell the truth but she was too afraid. The family thought it was strange but didn't really question it.

Emily knew that there was more to the story. She had first hand experience of things that were in the house. She looked across at Sarah. Emily could tell that she was really scared about something along with her daughter!! Even though Sarah tired her hardest to hide it and Sarah's mum could see it too.

No one said anything more about it. No one wanted to spoil Jason's birthday. Plus him being only 3 years old, they didn't want to scare him or worry him. They had an enjoyable rest of the night nothing else happened. It was time for the family to leave. Ashley with Jason, Antony and Diane stayed for an extra hour before going home. Antony was going to take them home in a taxi he had booked and already paid for.

They all said their goodbyes and left to go home. For Sarah it was time for bed, as by this time it was getting on for quarter to ten. An hour later Susan and Michael went up to bed.

The house was silent once again, dark and still with the sound of the old floor boards and the wind blowing through the house. Sarah found it hard to settle with her ghostly and nasty presence of Edward.

That night she was not alone and it was not Anna. It was him again, she felt almost as if he was mocking and laughing at her. Sarah had been his amusement for the evening. Sarah felt sad and upset, 'why was this happening? why did he taunt her like this?' she thought to herself as she felt her eyes watering with tears that felt cold running down her face as the temperature dropped.

Sarah just hid under the covers hoping that he would in time leave her alone, just fade away, but he didn't. Sarah in the end was so tired and exhausted, Sarah couldn't help it! She fell into a deep sleep. This was just the beginning for Sarah, a battle of wills.

CHAPTER 9

It was coming up for the big move for Harry and his future wife to be Jane. They were living together at the time, they had managed to sale the house and moving in two weeks, it was time for Harry to say farewell to the family.

Hilary and Henry, Emily, Peter and Jessica were invited along with Mark, Vivian, Nicole and Natasha and Susan, Michael, Ashley, Antony, Diane, Sarah and Jason.

Hilary and Henry were going to miss their son. Emily and Mark were going to miss their big brother and in a way Susan would too. Jane was nice down to earth girl and had been good for him. The evening went well! Harry had laid on plenty of food and drink for the party.

Hilary, Henry, Emily, Mark and Harry talked about the past about funny and fond memories but for Susan there was not many fond memories she remembered, he treated her unfairly and cruel at times for them, too much water under the bridge, although Susan did wish her brother well as for all his faults he was still Susan's older brother and could see that he had changed a lot since then.

The night ended about midnight and had started about 6 in the evening so it was a long night. Poor Jason had fallen asleep on one of the sofas; Harry had arranged a few taxi's to get people home. Ashley, Antony and Jason went home first followed by Susan, Michael, Diane and Sarah. The other taxi was for Emily, her mum and dad with Peter and Jessica and another for Mark, Vivian and the girls being the last to leave.

They all said their goodbye and it was very emotional but Susan was not upset like that. Susan could not forgive her brother's harsh words and the way he made her feel as a child, instead of being able to look up to her older brother and feel protected.

Ashley, Antony and Diane knew how their mum was treated and that their Uncle Harry was responsible for a big part of their mum's unhappy childhood. They did like him for whom he was now but did not like for what he did to their mum when they were kids.

A few weeks later Harry went off to his new life in New Zealand with Jane, he was happy but he wished that he could make things better with his sister Susan before he had left. He knew that the past was his fault, that he was not the sort of brother he should have been. When Harry got to his new home, he called his brother and sister's, now that he had arrived at his new home and things were going well.

The weeks went by and it was coming up for Christmas, the paranormal activity carry on still with no one really saying anything about it, hoping the less they talked about it all of a sudden it would go away! Even though, there had always been something in the house for a long time.

For Christmas all Michael and Susan's kids would be there and their partners, Terry and Susie in the house for their Christmas Dinner. Nine people to cook Christmas dinner for, Susan would have her work cut out for herself. She wanted to make it really special, by this time it was end November. Susan thought she would trim up a week early, with the help of Sarah, Diane and Michael. This was the time of the year they could all get creative, as each year they would make a Christmas trimming for the tree or for around the house, the trimmings that the children had made would be used every year. It was a family tradition in the Jones household, a special tradition.

Ashley, Antony Diane all did it as kids, every year and still did but now Sarah and Jason would have their chance to make a decoration. This was a special time for the family. So that Friday, the fourth week in November.

Susan decided to trim up on that Friday, it was the start of the weekend and Michael came home early from work on a Friday, so Michael to could get involved with his wife and kids. Susan had done a little pre-Christmas buffet for the family, lots of family favourites like cheese and pineapple on sticks, mini sausages on sticks, crisps, different cheeses and cold meats also of course chocolate fingers, it was yummy.

Michael got the Christmas tree down from the attic. Jason didn't like the attic he thought that cyber man was hiding up in the attic, at night watching him. As he liked Dr who! Which the family found quite amusing and funny enough Antony had thought that too, when he was growing up in the house, poor Antony was teased over it, even though he was grown up now.

Then they all helped to trim up. Michael put the Christmas tree up while Susan and Diane got the decorations for the tree and house out of the trimming boxes. As they got the boxes down, Sarah happened to look out the window. It had started to snow. Little white crisp cold snowflakes had started to full and settle on the ground as if Mother Nature knew it was that time of the year once more!

"It's snowing" Sarah said with excitement, now it felt like Christmas, there was something magical about snow. Even though it was cold it was a warm happy feeling inside, with the trees, the ground and rooftops glistened with white soft snow. It became an enchanted winter wonderland as the blanket of white covered everything within minutes.

Susan put some Christmas music on, while they were trimming up. It was really festive, the whole family was happy, even Sarah was excited too. They all made something each for the tree. Ashley little Jason and Antony came round too, to help as it was a family tradition to put the trimmings up together. As Christmases gone by it was really nice and gave everyone a warm festival glow with warmth in their hearts.

Susan gave them all a glass of mulled wine to warm the cockles, on what was a cold winter's evening apart from Sarah and Jason. Who had warm berry juice that was homemade, that tasted scummy and sweet with warm homemade chocolate chip cookies!

When they were done the house looked lovely warm and welcoming with the dazzling multi coloured fairy lights all around the living room on and the Christmas tree and fireplace pretty bobbles that would catch all the aluminous colours from the fairy lights and sparkling gold, silver and red tinsel with the candle lights flickering away living/dinning room looked stunning; Felix liked the Christmas tree too! He would try his best to get away with playing with the bobbles on the bottom of the tree.

They all had something to eat after the Jones family trimmed up from the buffet that Susan had done, then all sat down after to watch the soaps with just the fairy lights on and the fire lit. It was lovely and cosy. Michael and Susan cuddled up on the sofa, while Jason cuddled up to his granddad and Sarah cuddled up to her mum. Ashley, Antony and Diane sat by the fireplace. Feeling the heat from the fire, with another glass of mulled wine, it was lovely. Felix and Tabby sat by the fire too.

For that moment in time they were all happy and contented. Even the house was still and silent had a positive feel to it. Just the sound of the telly and the crackling of the warm fire, glowing brightly with the lights from tree and fairy place giving the living room a florescent multi coloured glow, the true meaning of Christmas.

Sarah did not have much going on in the build up to Christmas! The house was not too active. Just the footsteps which did not happen every day, just a couple of times, it was unnerving but it just the sound of footsteps. Sarah still felt at times that she was being watched at times and things in her room would be relocated and moved to a different part of her room. Sarah would at times speak to her friend but Anna didn't seem to want to talk that much to Sarah as Christmas got closer and closer.

Christmas day soon came around, with the build up to Christmas often did with the busy tasks of sorting out presents and other festive events. Christmas Eve came. It was still white with snow outside with blue skies but very cold, chilly day. It would be another white Christmas! It would be a lovely Christmas Eve.

Michael had to work half a day then Michael had a Christmas drink with his work colleagues afterwards, then home for Christmas for the next few days till after the New Year, as his factory closed for Christmas. Susan wrapped the last few presents for the family. Sarah and Jason still believed in Father Christmas, Sarah presents was in a secret place, along with Jason's 'Father Christmas would be on his way soon' Susan said to Sarah that night before Sarah went to bed. They had a lovely relaxing evening and just had a few little nibbles for tea as the next they would be eating a lot. They all had an early night.

Susan always told the kids near Christmas that 'they had to be really good as Father Christmas was watching them and knew when they were naughty' all her children growing up believed her every word and would be extra good around Christmas. They didn't want to be on the naughty list. Susan had way with words the kids took it as the gospel truth.

The day had arrived it was Christmas day! It was the usual a hectic day. Susan prepared the veggies the night before and put the turkey in the oven for a couple of hours the night before too. She had the potatoes on and put the oven on again for the turkey.

Sarah as normal was up early that morning! She had gone into her mum and dad's room to get her mum and dad up. Susan never really minded as Sarah was no different from any other kid Christmas morning! She got up and went downstairs Sarah about half 6am. When Michael and Diane got up about ten minutes after Sarah, Diane their mum and dad sat round the tree to unwrap the presents, all taking it in turns to unwrap a present, so they could see what other had got for Christmas, Susan and Michael had brought their kids up that way, it was really special.

Christmas was about giving not receiving and that it was about giving and seeing the pleasure on the person face when they have unwrapped a present. They all had a nice time it was joyful and special, they had a big hug, wished each other happy Christmas.

Sarah and Diane took their presents up to their rooms. Michael took his and Susan stuff upstairs, then came downstairs into the kitchen to put the kettle on, while Susan got some toast on the go. It was to be a light breakfast, after breakfast Susan would have to make a start on preparing the Christmas feast.

Around about ten Ashley and Terry with Jason, Antony and Susie came over baring gifts apparently that Father Christmas had dropped off in their house at night. Jason could see some presents under the tree for him being a typical kid he dived straight in. it was a full house and what was a quiet house had now the usual sounds and smells of Christmas.

Sarah wanted to say "Happy Christmas Anna" Sarah whispered to her friend Anna. She could not feel her in the room this made her feel sad. But she took her mind off it by sorting her presents out. That day Anna did not speak to Sarah, like she didn't want to or maybe Anna could not speak. 'After all it must be upsetting for Anna. She desperately wanted to be with her mum and could not! This time of year was for families' at least that what Sarah thought might be the case.

63

The Christmas dinner was lovely prawn cocktail to start, but no prawn cocktail for Jason, followed by traditional turkey dinner with the trimmings, with lashes of gravy then to finish homemade Christmas pudding with brandy cream. It was amazing and smelt as good as it tasted.

It was a nice day Susan's sister Emily with their family popped round for a Christmas drink after the Christmas dinner. Mark popped round with his mum and dad to drop off present and to have a Christmas drink with his sister and so Susan could see her mum and dad too.

Then later just before tea Ashley had invited her mum and dad back to her house along with Sarah, Diane, Antony and Susie for tea. Antony had already been invited up to Susie's mum and dad's house for tea. Antony offered to drop his mum and dad up there, as there was not enough room in just one car for them all, which was Terry's car.

Later that day when Mark went home after dropping his mum and dad home, Antony and Susie took his mum, dad and Sarah up to Ashley's house. Terry and Ashley, Diane and Jason followed in terry's car.

Antony dropped his mum and dad off then, went to Susie's mum and dad for tea. The kids played while the adults listened to music, chatted and drank. Lucky enough for Susan, Michael, Diane and Sarah they were staying over and going back home in the morning. It was great everyone enjoyed themselves it was a really good evening.

Sarah was enjoying herself too and Jason but for Sarah it was taking her mind off things in the house. However she did miss her friend Anna. Jason had lots of toys to play with. So while the adults had their grown up chats Sarah and Jason played in his room.

Ashley, Antony and Diane enjoyed it too! Ashley's boyfriend and Antony's girlfriend were invited too. Poor Ashley she had to cater for quite a few family members. She had also invited her Auntie Emily and her family, Mark and his family also her Nan and granddad but it was nice for her to have a full house.

It was her mum, dad and Ashley's boyfriend also Jason, Emily, Peter and Jessica, Mark, Vivian, Nicole and Natasha, Antony and his girlfriend Susie, Diane, Sarah, also Michael and Susan's mum and dad. Lucky enough Susan was there to lead a hand. It was all hands on deck, to get things ready before the rest of the family descended.

It was a great Christmas party everyone enjoyed it, plenty of food and drink. It started at 7pm and finished, when the last person left which by the time the family left about one in the morning.

Susan and Michael were glad that they stayed over with Diane and Sarah. For Susan and Michael it was nice to have a night somewhere else for just one night, they had a bit own personal festive fun that night too. Sarah and Diane had to share with Jason, it was ok, they were both so tired and they both went straight to sleep. Sarah had a lovely deep sleep, the bed were really comfortable.

The next day Sarah woke up fine. It was Boxing Day! Christmas day was all over. The snow was still thick like a white blanket on the ground. The sun was shinny with cold fresh crisp air. For Sarah it felt like her first proper sleep in ages. The poor adults woke up not so good, bad heads all round. Michael and Susan dragged themselves out of bed and went downstairs were Terry and Ashley was in the kitchen making some toast and strong coffee. Diane rolled out of bed a half an hour later, looking like how her parents felt. Then Sarah and Jason arose from their slumber.

"Thank you for having us overnight Ashley and Terry I really had a great time last night it was a fun, got the sore head to prove it!" Susan said with her head not feeling to clever rubbing her forehead. Terry passed Michael and Susan a glass of Andrews to take the edge off the hang over.

"No worries it was nice to have you guys round with Sarah and Diane" Ashley replied, it was nice for Ashley to have her family over for a change. Normally, it was just up to her mum's at Christmas but it nice to have Sarah and her sister up as well as her mum and dad. Ashley loved Christmas it was a lovely time of the year.

"Yeah it was pretty good, just what we needed" Michael added, also not feeling too clever but he had enjoyed his time with his daughter's and grandson.

Susan and Michael stayed till late morning to give Sarah and Jason a chance to have a play. Susan and Michael to feel more like themselves. Diane stayed down stairs with her sister, mum and dad for a chat.

Susan had planned to do a joint of beef for their tea, so they only had the morning there. Susan had to get back to prepare the veggies and meat. But they had really enjoyed themselves! It was what they all needed. They said their goodbyes and off they went back home. It would be a little bit of a walk home, there were no buses. Terry did offer to take them home but Michael said no that's ok. The roads and streets were quiet not a soul about. No shops were open, just the odd person. They walked through the crisp white fluffy snow. It was about a 20 minute walk home but the sun was shinning with the crisp fresh air.

Boxing Day was a quiet day, Michael helped Susan prepare tea while Sarah and Diane watched the telly, the usual Boxing Day films like Sinbad eye of the tiger and the wizard of oz. Tea was lovely they all sat together, Michael had lit the fire, so it was warm and cosy. The evening went by slow and it was really nice night.

Christmas Day and Boxing Day flew round and before you could blink. Christmas was gone for another year, out with the old in with the new. It was now a new year.

It was a quiet New Years which after the hectic Christmas was good. It was just the four of them for the New Years, Susan, Michael, Diane and Sarah. Ashley was spending her time with her boyfriend and son, Antony was spending it with his girlfriend and her parents. Michael had a few beers and Susan had a few glasses of wine, she let Diane have a small glass too as it was New Years Eve and Diane was nearly 17 years old.

No one knew at the time but Ashley was not getting on with Terry, the pre family package that he walked into when he started this relationship with Ashley was not really what he wanted. It was not like he thought it would be! He was ok with it at first. If it was just Ashley that was fine but it was Ashley +1, this was the problem and he started to get a bit jealous of Ashley affections to her son rather than him all the time.

It was a few weeks before Sarah's mum and dad birthday, mid January and Diane's 17th birthday end of January. When it came to Susan and Michael's birthday they went out for a family meal. It was nice being out as a family. They never had loads of money. So they all appreciated it, when they could go out, but Sarah's thoughts were never to far away about the house. After Diane's birthday it would just Sarah her mum and dad. Diane was moving in with her brother Antony and Sister Ashley and Ashley's boyfriend and Jason.

Terry did not like the fact that Diane was going to move in as well, Ashley's brother was already living there. Terry was not happy about this but Ashley just said tough luck, it was her and her brother

Antony's house, so it was up to them. Terry did not pay his way like that, more or less living there for free. At the time he was not working, he not long lost his job.

Diane just went out with friends on her birthday to the cinema. She was now 17 years old. Diane moved her stuff into her brother and sister house about a mouth after her birthday, so Susan and Michael had the small bedroom as a spare room.

Ashley lived in a three bedroom terrace house. Diane was enjoying her independence from her parents even though she would have to share a room for now with her Nephew, also she was with her older brother and sister! It was not the same as living with parents. Diane had also managed to pass her exams and was working in a kitchen in an Italian restaurant as one of the chefs, so she too could pay her way.

The next few months were as strange as ever in Sarah's home, it seemed to be a little bit more paranormal activity when Diane had moved out. The footsteps most nights now, not just now and again! The footsteps that once did not bother her but now they seemed more prominent, Sarah felt alone who could she turn too!

It felt safer when her big sister was around but now her sister was gone Sarah felt more afraid. She did not want to go asleep at times but the voice of her friend Anna would comfort her, this made her feel safe again. So she was hoping that every night it would be the end of it.

As normal Sarah hated school. With everything that was going on at home, she felt more different than ever. Sarah was different from the other children! She could see and here things or sense things that no one else could. But she coped just about, as soon it would be Easter and then her birthday something to look forward to!

Quite often in the Easter half term the Jones family would go for a picnic in the park, Susan would pick a lovely warm spring day. It was also good fun, after the kids had their time at the park with the swings and sliders they would all take a walk down to the river, the kids and the big kids at heart could have a paddle. They would do this a few times in the year, when the weather was good. This part always seemed filmier like a feeling like she use to play their before, like a different childhood. This confused Sarah at times, memories of a childhood that she did not have!!

It would be Ashley's 21st birthday in June, a special birthday. Ashley was going to spend one weekend with her family and another with Terry, her birthday was half way through the week. Ashley and Terry was still not getting on brilliantly but ok.

It would be a new school after the summer holidays junior school St Bells junior school as her birthday was in May, it would work out that she would be one of the youngest in her class. It would be further away than her school that she was in now, about 15 minute walk. The children would be older she was not looking forward to it as she knew probably the bullying would be worse than in the school, that she was in at the moment!

The house was starting to come together by this time. Michael had given the house a fresh lick of paint though out the house, in the bedroom's, the living/dinning room and landing a magnolia paint, as it would go with anything and beige carpets. It looked much better and well over due.

It was nice that Sarah saw her real mum Ashley and half brother Jason and older brother or sister most weekends, they could catch up. That was one thing now they were now a close family. Their mum Susan was the glue and their dad Michael had become the Rock of the family. As Susan and Michael had been together for nearly 30 years, they had had their ups and a lot of downs just like most couples and stressful marriage at times. Although Ashley and her dad were still not that close, Diane and Antony were close to their dad. However Diane was a mummy's girl.

Easter time soon arrived! It was a lovely time of the year. Spring time was here once again, fresh and crisp air in the mornings, with the warmth of sun shinning through in the afternoons with the odd shower here and there. All the flowers and blossom trees in bloom, the sounds of birds with the young chicks, chirping away for food from their mother's, the sounds and smells of spring that you could hear all around!

Sarah and Jason were also looking forward to Easter too, lots of chocolate eggs and an Easter hunt that they always did. Easter was good as they had ten eggs each plus egg's from the Easter egg hunt, again a family tradition. Also two weeks off of school, great for the kids. Susan, Michael and rest of the family would all meet up for a big family picnic in the park and the kids would go paddling in the stream with their scandals or wellington boots that went through the park.

They would pick a nice warm day in Easter half term, it was great. The whole family enjoyed it with plenty of food and drink for everyone. All of adults of family brought something along to eat and drink.

Michael, Susan, Sarah, Ashley, Jason, Antony, and Diane and sometimes Susan's mum and dad would come. Easter was a brilliant time. Antony by this time was getting more confident driving his car, it was a bit of a banger but it was cheap. It was good enough for his first car as he was 18 years now, it only took a mouth for him pass his test.

Sarah's 7th birthday was coming up but it would be a small thing this year. Just her mum, dad, her real mum, brothers and her sister, as they spent a lot at Christmas, plus buying things for the house, to redecorate. Which Sarah didn't really mind as long as her family was there, that was the main thing. That was more important to Sarah. Then it would be her real mum Ashley's birthday third week in June.

They were ok for money but at times it was a struggle having only one wage, Susan had always wanted to stay home. She had been a housewife and mother to her 3 children, then Sarah came along, Susan wanted to be there for all of them. Which Michael did not mind, it was quiet common for it to be that way in the 80's, which was nice that they always knew that their mum was there for them.

It was nice Sarah's 7th birthday just the seven of them. Her mum, dad, Ashley, Jason, Diane, Antony and Sarah, they went out for a nice meal as a treat at the harvester, it was yummy especially the rocky horror desert for afters. Ashley, Antony and Diane had all chipped in to put something towards the meal, they knew their mum and dad were struggling a bit. After the meal they all came back to the house for a catch up.

Sarah had got a new bike for her birthday from her mum and dad, Ashley had brought her outdoor games and Antony and Diane got her some tapes. Auntie Emily brought her a little portable stereo so Sarah could play her music tapes. The rest of the family had given her money. It was a good day, Ashley with Jason, Antony and Diane stayed till about 9 in the evening then the four of them went home in Antony's car. Jason was starting to get tired too.

After her birthday things went a little quiet. Not for long though as things were never that quiet for long. Sarah decided that maybe if she did not talk about things that went on in the house, to Anna or anyone else, the bad presence would go away and leave her alone, for a short while this seemed to work.

But the ghost of Edward Anna's father was not the sort of presence to just give up. Anna's father had other ideas. This presence wanted to make everyone, who felt his spirit, feel uneasy and afraid. That was his power over people, after all he was dead. So he time on his side, he had all the time in world in fact, to bleed his negative poison into this family slowly over time.

In life this bad spirit could charm his way around people in a very slight and devious manor, which gave him a sense of power and control! He was also corrupted by greed. The more successful he became, the more money and power he wanted. He had a lust for controlling everything and everyone around him. Like a hunger that had to satisfy but in death he could not do this. So he used fear that people had for him in the same way, to make himself feel a sense of power.

Up until now that was not challenged, for whom ever stayed in the house, would never stay for long! This house had a few family's that owe it before the Jones did but he would threaten and frighten everyone out of what he felt 'that this was his house', But this family was different. They would not scare as easy, Sarah did not realise at this point that, she had strength that no one else had. As she in her subconscious mind, she knew the truth and in this case truth was power.

The house was not all bad though Sarah and her family did have also good times in the house. Like birthdays, Christmases and summer holidays or other half terms from school. The summer was always hot so when they were home Sarah played a lot in the garden with her brother or the next door neighbours kids would come around to have a play in their little swimming pool. They also had a swing in the back garden, with different out door games. In fact they had a lot of fun at times. It was always a busy house in the day.

Michael was a keen gardener he planted running beans. They had a strawberry and gooseberry bush too. His runner bean plant was off limits as he kept those, when they did their roost dinner. The strawberry and gooseberry bush was fine for the kids to help themselves.

Michael would come out to his prize runner bean plant and would notice that his runner beans had been picked, not all but some. He was always annoyed by this. Sarah and Jason would be hiding and would laugh quietly, to their dad/granddad reaction of annoyance. As they would be munching on his runner beans, Sarah and Jason could not help it they were nice. Fresh and crunchy a taste of late spring. But then Ashley, Antony and Diane did the same when they were kids too. Again another family tradition at least for the kids! It had to be done.

They would get a telling off by their dad, but was soon forgotten. They could do it all over again! Susan would always see the funny side to it but would not show it, instead try to pretend to be disappointed with her kids about it, shaking her head in disappointment. Sarah would sometimes get a few for Lucy and tom when they came over. It was a secret mission to get them without being seen, doing the dastardly deed.

Then when he came out and noticed that more had gone a couple of days later. There would be four of them hiding and giggling to see him annoyed once again, but fun for the kids.

Their days out were fun too picnics in the park to play on the swing and sliders or have a paddle with in the river or off to Weston for a day at the seaside, with a bag a chips, lashing of salt and vinegar and sweet candy floss on a stick, with a can of coke or lemonade to wash it down. A donkey ride and then spend some change on the amusements to finish off the day. Simple, inexpensive, fun, brilliant memories that Sarah and rest of the family would remember growing up!

It was Ashley's Birthday by this time and Ashley would be 21 years old, still young. She had planned three things one day with her boyfriend, which her mum and dad would baby sit and another day with her family, also one night out with her friends.

Ashley's night out with brother, sister and her friends she planned on her birthday as it fell on a sat night, THE night for going out for a young 21 year old. The following in the week Ashley was going to have a birthday tea with her mum, dad, Jason and Sarah. Ashley was going out for a meal with Terry. Diane had offered to babysit. Ashley had a nice time, it was a good 21st.

Sarah just kept her had down at school it was soon to be the summer holidays again. Sarah's parents had planned a few days out and a family break to Devon. This time it would just the three of them her mum, dad and herself.

The weather was warming up. Back then the summer were summers and seasons were seasons. It was going to be another hot summer. Sarah always liked the summer holidays normally but living in this house, it made every day a challenge for Sarah! At the time she did not know how strong she really was, even at only 7 years.

The weeks went by fast and before they knew it, it was back to school for Sarah. Jason started school at the local Infants school. It would be a different year with Jason also at school, well at nursery. For Sarah it was also the start of her new school St Bell's junior school.

Antony had his birthday in August, he just went out with his friends in town to spend his birthday money; he was 19 years old now. He was working full time now and he was getting on really well with his girlfriend too. Antony had to save hard for their wedding.

The summer holiday flew by, as they often did. It was back to school for Sarah. Sarah's mum had walked her to school and she was going to pick her up as she did every day from her old school and would do this in her new school.

It was her first day! Sarah just smiled at her mum to make Susan think that her daughter would be ok. A false smile to hide discontentment and said to mum she would fine. Susan left as the door to Sarah's new classroom opened.

Sarah was so nervous and shy, kept herself to herself. The fill of dread once more, what could she except for this year. Maybe the kids would find someone else to tease. Maybe this school would different but she knew in her heart it be no different she could tell by how the kids were, towards other kids.

Sarah's school through the coming weeks was just as bad as her other school. In fact worse, the other kids would stare at her or say "God, she is ugly!" And "She is weird" again Sarah would try not to take any notice and just consecrate on her school work.

The school children were older so their words were more harsh and spiteful. This made her feel more abnormal than she felt before but she did try and be strong, kept it to herself. Trying to handle it by herself in any case if she said anything to her parents it would only make things a lot worse for herself, they would bully her even more.

The house or at least this bad presence was beginning to make Sarah feel very uneasy in the house. It was getting hard for this little girl of 7 to bear on her own but this was the way! It had to be. In the other school she did have the next door neighbour's daughter at the same school Lucy Chapel but at school Lucy was different and only played with Sarah when she had no one else to play with.

Lucy wanted to be round the girl's that were popular, not Sarah. Sarah was not popular at all at her old school and neither was she popular at this school but she never wanted to be popular, it would have been nice though, if she was at least liked but she did have her special friend at home.

CHAPTER 10

Meanwhile Ashley was taking Jason to his new school, Jason had started back a few weeks later than Sarah and for the first few months, it would just be part time. Jason's was confident for his first day at his Infants school, unlike his sister Sarah. When she first started her primary and junior school! Jason was nervous but this did not stop him making friends straight away. He had a lot to say, a bit cheeky but in a cute way. It was about 3 weeks before his 4th birthday.

But little did Jason's family know or suspected that Jason was being contacted from beyond the grave by Anna's father. He was coming to him in his dreams. It was another way Edward used his mind games, it had only started to happen in the last few weeks! But it nothing that bad, just Anna's or Edward's image; with not much detail very vague images.

At school for the next coming weeks, Jason appeared to be a normal and innocent little nearly 4 year old, at nursery at the local school before he started properly the following September at school and home but things were about to change.

Susan was getting on really well with her mum and dad, older younger sister and brother they visited each other quite often even if it was for a quick coffee just to catch up. They had finally put the past behind them and were also getting on well with Michael, Emily and Mark's children Jessica, Nicole and Natasha also became close too with Jason and Sarah. Which was good as it was coming up for Jason's 4th birthday and Ashley wanted it to be special.

It was Jason's 4th birthday! They held it at Susan and Michael's house. The family had a little birthday party for him around teatime, they did the year before. Ashley had invited the whole family again, Susan's family and Ashley's brother and sister, a big event for a four year old!

All the family had helped to make Jason's fourth birthday special. There were loads of balloons, party poppers and lots of really yummy things to eat and drink. A proper fourth birthday party! Jason had a nice birthday 'it was cool' Jason thought some really good presents, kids tool bench, a kids garage, more colouring stuff, some films and money. The kids played party games, like pass the parcel and musical chairs and lots of food also a cake in the shape of a transformer, the party went quick.

It was time for the family to go the end of the party, the time pasted by very quickly. Michael helped Susan and Ashley to tidy up while Sarah helped her brother take his toys upstairs to the spare room. He was going to leave some toys there so he would have something to play with when he visited next. Jason loved his grandparents, they were great. He liked his great grandparents too but they were getting older and could not play so much with their great grandchildren.

Jason great Nan enjoyed the wrestling and watching big daddy, she would give a few punches too at the television screen. His great granddad could make all strange faces, so the kids found them amusing in other ways, they both were characters. By this time there great granddad had retired from the navy for quiet some time but he full of stories, of his time at sea.

Sarah was happy seeing her Nan getting on well with her family and seeing her real mum Ashley getting on well with her Great Nan and granddad. Sarah was enjoying the party too but she could help have her mind on the house, the thoughts were never far away, Sarah was a thinker.

That night Jason was tired from his big party and excitement, that night he stayed up his Grandparents house. His head hit the pillow, he was so very tired but in his dreams he was not alone, once again. The dark figure that Sarah had felt was in his dreams once again. He woke up in the middle of the dream and called out to his mum he did not like this dark figure it was not a nice person. "Nan" Jason shouted out. Susan went rushing in to him. Susan and Michael just thought it was because he had been watching Dr Who after his party had finished. Susan just gave him a cuddle and Jason drifted back off into a deep sleep, no really thought much of it. It was just a child's normal nightmare. The house that was quiet and still apart from Jason's bad dream. Nothing stirring in the house that night for a change!

The next day at Jason's school it was arts week! The teacher had noticed Jason's picture of a tall, dark hair man in a black suit with a pocket watch and cane. Also a pretty little girl about 9 years old, shoulder length straight blonde hair and sky blue eyes, in a long white flowing nightdress, as a teacher would Mrs Woods asked "Who's that a picture of? Is it your Granddad and sister!" she asked out of curiosity.

"No, that's the little girl and her dad that lives in my Grandparent's house. I don't like the little girl's dad! He is not very nice. Anna dad lives in the cupboard" Jason explained with innocent.

The teacher was slightly taken back by this little 4 year olds statement! A bit confused about this story and thought it was a strange thing to come out with but as he was only 4 years old, maybe it was just the tells of a little boy with a big imagination.

Mrs Woods thought she would try and find out more about this man in the cupboard and his daughter. Jason mentioned about the little girl, that her name was Anna. But not much else as it was only an image, in his dreams, nothing more.

The teacher was getting a bit concerned and very much intrigued about this. This story was quite detailed for a 4 years plus, Jason would also in general conversation with his friends mention things, just random sentences about the little girl or this dark figure.

Jason's mum and Grandparents had no idea about what Jason was talking about at school? He would never mention these things to them. Jason's mum would ask about his day at school. Jason would just say everything was fine, that he had made lots of friends and he liked his teacher Mrs Woods.

Jason's was getting on well in school, so Mrs Woods was only a little worried but not overly concerned. He seemed a normal, confident little boy and most children that had some sort of problem would generally be withdrawn and quiet.

CHAPTER 11

It was coming on now for that time of year, Christmas was once again, round the corner for the Jones family. As most families, the Jones enjoyed their Christmases together. Also it was nice to see the whole family together. It was the traditional Christmas once again! It was a lovely time of the year.

Michael and Susan could never afford loads of presents for their kids! It was one main present, with little things that didn't cost much. The kids never minded that growing up as it was the time and quality of that time they spent together as a family, which was more important.

Susan, Michael and Sarah, Jason, Ashley with Sarah's older brother and Sister all helped to trim up. They did their usual and special Christmas making a decoration for the tree or house. Susan and Michael had invited Ashley's boyfriend Terry along with Antony's girlfriend Susie and by now Diane was 17 years old and had her first boyfriend too his name was Sean Collins.

At this time Ashley and Terry was not getting on so well but Ashley hid this from her mum and dad. Terry was still jealous of Jason and now it was being to show, he was always telling Jason of for something or putting Jason down. Which Ashley would have to pull Terry back into line after all that was her son. If it was a problem about Jason well Terry knew where the door was. Ashley and her son came as a package!

Ashley and Terry tried to hide the fact that they were not getting on well from everyone including Antony and Diane but they knew something was up between their sister and her boyfriend plus they also started to notice how Terry was around Jason. Susan noticed that day that her daughter and partner were quiet towards each other.

For this Christmas things would be a stirring in the Jones household. Relationship wise and in this creepy old house! This time the ghostly nasty appropriation wanted to add a little drama to the festivities; he did not like these happy times!

The house at night always had it eerie and strange noises, old houses often did but Sarah and the rest of the family knew the difference between normal noises that house would make the sounds that did not fit or belong in an old house.

Leading up to Christmas the footsteps at night would still be there, also this bad entity would make himself known but only to Sarah to keep her fearing him and was clever enough to do this when the rest of the family were not around if he wanted to do something that was more intense. In other words no witnesses to cooperate to what Sarah was and will go through as time went by.

The weeks leading up to Christmas past by fairly quick, this time Anna was talking to her friend Sarah. They would talk as they normally did at night when Sarah was in bed. Anna said about the last Christmases she could remember with mother and how special her mother made them. Anna always felt loved and safe with her mother. Anna would love to be with her mother again, Anna missed her mother Helena so much.

One night on Christmas Eve as most nights Sarah spoke to Anna to wish her a happy Christmas but this time Anna did not speak. This would happen for one reason only, her father was there. Anna was indeed scared of her father for a good reason. This time there were no footsteps up the stairs, just the feeling that she was not alone in her room.

That night Sarah went to sleep as normal, although her instinct was telling her not to go asleep! But Sarah was so tired and she knew that it was Christmas the next day, so she finally went to sleep, only to wake up in the middle of the night, knowing she was not alone still and it was not Anna.

"Please just leave me alone" Sarah said in a quiet and shaky voice. Sarah was terrified she knew what this spirit was capable of! The temperature of the room was like ice. She could see her own breath.

Sarah felt one side of the bottom of her bed dip down, as if someone was sat on the end of the bed. She felt pressure on the bottom of her bed but there was no one there, at least that she could see! Sarah felt piercing green eyes staring right at her through the darkness of the room.

Then she felt this unseen spirit leave, almost for this time, he did want to harm. Edward just wanted her to know he was watching her at all times. Sarah did find it hard to make herself go to asleep but she knew she had to. It was Christmas day in the morning. In the end Sarah was so tired, she fell asleep. Nothing more happened that night.

In the morning Sarah was the first one up, excited to see if Father Christmas had been during the night. Sarah had not forgotten what had happened, she was not going to let it spoil Christmas day with her family, so put it to the back of her mind.

Sarah could not help feel excited after all she was a 7 year old little girl. Sarah ran into her mum and dad shouting "He's been" Sarah jumped on her parent's bed, holding her stocking in her hands "My stocking is full" she added.

"OH RIGHT! You must have been a good girl then." Susan said looking at Sarah then turning to her husband and smiled. "Your dad and I going to get dressed" Susan said, both Michael and Susan feeling that it is too early but they both were wide awake thanks to their lovely daughter jumping on their bed. It was about half 6 in the morning and still dark outside just the lights coming into the house from the street lights.

Sarah went into her room and put her lovely warm fluffy pink house coat and pink fluffy slippers, on top of her warm thick pyjamas that she had the year before at Christmas from Ashley, Diane and Antony. Sarah waited for her mum and dad to get dressed. Sarah was going to get dressed after her presents, just in case she had something new to wear as one of her presents, which sometimes she did.

Michael and Susan got up and dressed, as they did every year in festive clothes. Susan with a long sleeves sparkly red dress black thick tights and Michael black chinos and black shirt, they both looked really smart. Then went downstairs with Sarah, the house was in complete darkness only the fairy lights on, Susan put a dim light on while Michael put the kettle on. Susan sorted the presents into piles a pile for Sarah, a pile for Jason, a pile for Ashley, a pile for Antony, a pile for Diane, a pile for Michael and a pile for herself.

Michael brought a cup of coffee for himself and his wife as he lit the fire. Knowing what their others kids were like even though it was early, they would also soon be round. Even at their age they still got excited about Christmas and it was the family tradition to open the presents together round the Christmas tree with the warmth of fire burning.

Sarah was looking forward to Christmas day but each day she woke, she always was afraid of might the next night might bring. But this was a special day that nothing was going to spoil this day. Sarah was determined to have a wonderful day! No matter what! Sarah did still believe in Father Christmas at that time, she was still 7 years old. She did feel a bit excited as her stocking was full! She always had in the back of her mind, what would happen next.

By the time Sarah had opened her stocking and her parents had got dressed. Then went down stairs it was just before 7am in the morning, Susan didn't really mind. She had a big day ahead of her, as Christmas was always a busy day!

Sarah's face lit up with joy as she seen his nice pile of presents. Sarah smiled even though she was worried about what the day could bring! She could not help get a warm feeling from her heart, as she seen the presents with the fire glowing bright and the fairy lights on, her mum and dad sat by the tree. The snow was still thick on the ground it looked very pretty but bitterly cold.

About five minutes later the rest of the family descended, their Grandson, son and daughters with their partner's Terry, Susie and Sean, along with more presents from Father Christmas, it was going to be a full house. Poor Susan was cooking for ten but Susan loved it, it was hectic but wonderful.

Jason was ascetic the tree was full of presents. The presents were for them all. Susan put the kettle on, while Michael sorted the presents out into groups of his wife, his, Jason and Sarah. The kids started opening their presents. This was a good distraction for Sarah! She could not help but think about things that had happened in the house.

Sarah had a pretty smart red new sparkly dress to wear with pretty black tights and red little cardigan to match. After the presents were opened Jason played with his new toys and Sarah went up stairs to change into her new clothes and came down stairs to play with hers new things. Ashley, Antony and Diane helped their younger brother and sister open more presents. Susan started to sort out the Christmas dinner, while Michael took Susan's and his stuff upstairs. They were all pleased with what they had.

Ashley put the telly on for the kids and for the rest of them as normal there was some sort of family Christmas film on. Michael got the family a hot drink. It was really lovely, as most years the snow had fallen thick and heavy on Christmas Eve. There was a blanket of thick white pretty but cold snow. A real traditional Christmas!

Michael went into the kitchen, after he got them all a drink and had put his and Susan's things upstairs, he came down stairs into the kitchen just to see if he could help and to see his wife. Susan was in the middle of cooking, when Michael up from behind her and put his arms around her. He gave her a kiss on the neck, tenderly.

"Happy Christmas love, love you." Michael said as Susan turned round to give her husband a proper cuddle and kiss.

"Thank you, Happy Christmas and I love you too" Susan replied gazing lovingly into her husbands eyes.

About 9ish in the morning he gave them all a home made mince pie with a glass of Asti for the adults and warm berry juice for Sarah and Jason. That day was a lovely day. It happened to be a lovely crisp white Christmas. Snow all around with blues skies but cold. Like the sort of Christmas day, that you see on Christmas cards. Later that morning Michael took the kids and the big kids out to play snow balls fights. It was really great fun.

Susan had everything under control with the food. She was use to cooking a lot of food; in fact no one would starve with Susan cooking. She always did too much and gave everyone a mountain of food.

Then a bit later it was time for Christmas turkey dinner. It was lovely with homemade Christmas pudding for afters, they all had full tummies! Susan was very good cook, it was never anything fancy but it proper home cooked food, which she had got a lot of her colour skills from her dad. as he was a very good cook too. Susan's dad use to make his own sweets and baking himself. Although Michael would always make the gravy for the Christmas dinner that was his contribution to the Christmas dinner and would always do the dishes after!

The rest of the family popped over after Christmas dinner. It was a really nice Christmas day, a proper traditional family Christmas. The day went by so quick though as Christmas always did.

Lucky enough for Sarah not much happened on Christmas Day no footsteps. Anna's father seemed to leave them alone for once. However Edward Anna's father was just biding his time, the calm before the storm. There was plenty of time for that.

CHAPTER 12

It was the New Year 'hopefully this year would be more calm;' Sarah thought or at least that's what Sarah wanted. It was her mum and dad birthday in three weeks, then Diane 18th birthday a week later and Sarah wanted to make it special for her parents Jason wanted to help as well and make his grandparents have a lovely day. They had always put Sarah and Jason first rather than themselves.

Susan's dad was not very well at this time, he was 73 years old. He been having a few heart problems, he had been sent for a few tests. Which shown that he had a heart condition angina. So he had to take care of himself and try not to get stressed, which was a bit of a worry to his sons, daughters and his wife. Mark, Emily, Susan and Hilary were very worried about him.

Another year had gone now a year begun! Hopefully it would be a good one. It was back to school, 'oh joy' Sarah thought to herself. Sarah really did not like school. Jason excited about school, he loved Christmas but he missed his friends. Sarah missed nothing about school! She hated it but nothing she could do, just something she had to put up with.

Jason was 4 years now and wanted to help make his Nan and granddad birthday nice. Jason made their birthday cards. For Sarah this was also a way to keep her mind off things.

That day after school Jason came over for tea with Ashley, like sometimes they would, they had their tea as soon as they got there, it was teatime by now. Sarah and Jason went upstairs to write some ideas down on paper for Susan and Michael's birthday. Sarah could feel Anna's presence. Anna was watching Sarah and her brother as sometimes she would. Then the temperature went down and the atmosphere changed from a nice warm feeling to an uncomfortable feeling. Jason did not notice or at least he did not react but Sarah did.

The door in Sarah's room was closed too, but then it opened by itself. At first they thought it was Felix or Tabby coming in but Sarah was pretty sure that she had seen both of them go out, they often did after they had something to eat.

Sarah was hoping that it was one of the cats! Then Sarah felt a cold draft glide past her and felt something touch her hair. Sarah looked across to Jason. She saw a dark sincere shadow hovering above him. She could not tell what it looked like, it was just like a dark mass but it did look like a shape of a man.

This entity she knew was Anna's father, Sarah felt it was taunting her, Jason did not say anything. He didn't even seem to notice or sense this dark shadow elevating above him or the temperature change. Sarah wanted to say something but she knew that this could lead to her and her family being terrorised by this menacing spirit and it would terrify her brother, it would give him nightmares. Sarah had to protect her brother, at this point Sarah had no idea that her brother was already being contacted by this presence in his dreams.

Sarah natural instinct was to protect all her family, what they didn't know could not hurt them! At least that what she convinced herself even though she knew that it was not as simple as that and that it would never be!

Sarah said nothing and just tried to hide her worry, hoping he would leave her brother alone if she did not speak. Then the dark figure vanished and the temperature returned to normal. That night Jason and Sarah planned to make a special night for their parents, this would give Sarah something else to think about but at the same time Sarah mind was on the house and this dark presence, Sarah did not know what to do for the best!

In the day things were better than at night, Sarah had the next door neighbours kids, Tom and Lucy to keep her amused sometimes, but she didn't see them as much now as they had a little baby brother his name was Oliver.

Michael and Susan birthday had come around. Then it would be Diane's birthday. Sarah had told her mum and dad to sit down, put their feet up. Ashley with Jason had popped round with food to help Sarah and Jason to give Susan and Michael a treat. Susan always cooked, cleaned and tidy up for her family. Michael would work hard in his job for his family, so it was their night off from all that.

Sarah came up to her mum and dad after they had their meal with the card, that Jason had made from him and his sister to give to them for their birthday's with a box of chocolates that Sarah had brought, with pocket money she had saved. Ashley stayed for a little bit, just to give her mum and dad Susan, Michael and her Daughter and her son their tea and to tidy up. Then she left with Jason, he had school the next day like Sarah. Susan and Michael had a lovely evening. It was nice to be fussed over for a change.

Their birthdays happened to fall mid week! Sarah had to be in bed her normal time at 8pm. So at about quarter to Susan went upstairs and got Sarah ready for bed. Then she said goodnight to her dad before they went to bed, Sarah was tired that night so it didn't take long for her to drop off.

This was Michael and Susan's time, adult time. It had been a nice evening, so far. Michael and Susan cuddled up on the sofa, to watch some telly before bed. It was warm and cosy. Michael had lit the fire, while Susan had put Sarah to bed. Now the fire burning well! Giving out lovely amount of heat, it was lovely warm, cosy and romantic.

"You looked beautiful tonight, love!" Michael said giving her a passionate kiss.

"Thank you, I do love you so very much" Susan added, Susan had made an effort to look nice, that evening.

Michael and Susan embraced and kissed passionately. Michael and Susan was a loving couple, that night as many nights. They were loving but passionate by the warmth of the fire as after even nearly 30 years. Those feelings were still burning, the spark; as strong as ever. Still managed to turn each other on!

There were no footsteps that night, just sounds of a loving couple, after Michael put out the fire and they both went to bed. Sarah was still sound a sleep.

The next day everyone was up, their normal routine, it was work for Michael and school for Sarah. Sarah felt that something had change or been moved when she awoke. At first she not noticed, she was still sleepy but then she saw that a few of her tapes were on the floor by her bed. Which she did think was odd as she knew that she tidy up her room, before she went to sleep and put them neatly on the shelf in corner of her room, next to her stereo but didn't really think much about it. Sarah was just a bemused by this.

Susan had her brother Mark popped round for coffee and chat after Susan had dropped Sarah off to school. It was nice to see her brother. He had the day off and was popping into see his sister, before he popped round to see his mum and dad.

Susan made breakfast for Sarah, while Michael popped the kettle on. Susan had done her usual packed lunch for her husband and Sarah. Michael had a coffee said goodbye to Sarah and a hug, then hugged his wife then went of to work. Sarah sorted out her bag.

Sarah's junior School was about 15 minutes away. Normally Sarah would walk to school with her mum, even if it was bad weather as Michael never learnt to drive. It was something he just never got round to, plus he like walking in fact he walked everywhere.

Sarah was ready so off she went with her mum. Sarah would always be a bit quiet going to school, she knew that she would be teased at school but Sarah was always a quiet girl, so at first her mum never was suspicious and really did not think anything of it.

Sarah had started to feel like she was being following with her mum to school. Sarah would feel this quite a few times going to school but not so much coming back. Sarah could never see anyone following them, just had strong feeling and normally! The feelings that she got was always accurate. It didn't feel like Anna, plus she felt that Anna could never leave the house! Anna's father would never let her leave! She was trapped by her father in the house for infinity.

Susan started to notice over the coming weeks that her daughter was starting to be very quiet on her way to school, quieter than normal. Susan would ask if everything was ok but Sarah would not say anything about how she really felt and just say she was ok, everything was fine.

The worse news was yet to come. Henry Susan's dad that had been unwell for sometime was getting worse. The medication was not working that well anymore, he became more and more unwell, this made him stressed which in turn effected his health even more, a catch 22 situation!

A few weeks later Emily had found her dad on the floor in his living room. He had collapse and had a heart attack, the ambulance came but by then it was too late. The paramedics were unable to resuscitate him, he had died. Emily had been banging on the door but there was no answer which was strange, in the end lucky enough Emily had a spare key and had let herself in. Her mum was no where to be seen? Emily did not realise that her mum had gone out to get her husband new medication, that the doctor had prescribed him, to try him on to see if it would help him more than his old medication.

Hilary came back with her husband new medication to find the corona and ambulance outside their home. She was horrified and collapsed with shock. Hilary had only been gone about 15 minutes, later she came too and her son Mark was there so was Susan. Mark had picked Susan up on his way over as Emily had informed them of the bad news. Emily had also managed to get hold of Harry in New Zealand to tell him the bad news.

This was upsetting for the whole family, they were all grief stricken. After he was told he had angina, he was never a really well man but he kept going and fighting. In the end his fight was not good enough.

His wife Hilary, his kids Emily, Mark, Susan and Harry were really devastated. They had lost their dad but even more for Emily, she still could not get the image of finding her dad dead on the floor of her mum and dad's flat. As by that time Hilary and Henry had moved into a bungalow due to Henry's angina. The house that they had was too much for him. He could not walk up the stairs of their house very easily and he would be short of breathe or in pain. The rest of the family were upset too they had lost their granddad.

Susan helped her mum clear Susan's dad things out, with the help of her brother and sister. They also had the task of sorting out the funeral, going through their dad's things. It was hard and very upsetting. Michael and Susan's kids helped Ashley, Antony and Diane all did their bit to help. Hilary did try but she always found it too upsetting and burst into tears, so the family sorted Henry's things out.

Henry's funeral was for a week's time. He would be sorely missed, not just by his family but friends that had made through the years; he was a reserved type of person but kind and witty all the same. He had lots of friends that were coming to pay their respects from the navy as he served in both world wars. Harry was flying back for the funeral too and would go back home a week after the funeral.

The week leading up to his funeral went quick. There was a load of stuff to sort out and arrangements to be made. The wake was to be held at Mark's house, he had the most downstairs space. The night before Michael, Susan and Sarah stayed at Mark's house, so they could be there early in the morning.

That night they all remised about memories of Henry. It was sad but at the same time comforting to remember the good times. Day trips, holidays and Christmases gone by. Of course the funny faces that he used to pull. That he could make everyone laugh!

Mark had offered Susan and his mum to stay over too. The family felt it was not a good idea for their mum to be on her own, Emily popped round to help with the food.

That evening before bed Ashley and Diane popped over to help their mum with preparing some food for the wake as well, Sarah wanted to help too. Ashley, Diane and Antony offered to do the food to give their great granddad's family so that they could have some time to reflect, to help with the grief. Susan said ok, she knew that her kids wanted to help in some way.

But it was not all tears a few laughs remembering their beloved dad. After the food was prepared Ashley and Diane gave their mum, dad and uncle a hug goodbye and went home, they all had an early night.

Sarah and Jason did not go to the funeral, the family thought that they were too young at the time, they could say goodbye to him in their own way. Something more personal, Maggie Barns Susan's best friend stayed behind to look after Sarah, Jason and Jessica.

Maggie had put a framed picture of their Great granddad and said they say a pray for him and light a candle to say their goodbyes to him. This was nice for them, they could say goodbye in own way with their own thoughts.

The next day it was time to bind farewell to Henry Walsh. The service was nice but emotional! He had a good send off. The flowers and cards that people had sent were lovely with kind thoughts. He was well respected member of the community. He had served his queen and country with gallantry and honour.

The wake was nice too all remembering Henry in their own way, tears of laughter and pain for his family and friends. Laughter to the man that was, tears of pain for lose of the man, the husband, the dad, the Granddad, the Great granddad and the friend.

The day came to a close, a busy and an emotional day for all. The family had gone home. Michael thought that at that time, maybe Susan's mum should not be alone and invited her to stay at their house. Hilary agreed with Michael, she didn't want to be on her own either. Susan thought that it was a good idea too.

Harry stayed with his brother for the week that he was there, he would returned home to New Zealand a week later, to his wife to be and business.

The next day Hilary returned home, later that day. Through the coming weeks, Mark and Emily went through their dad's things and sorted out their dad's finances. Their dad didn't ever have loads of money but he did put a little something for each of his kids and his wife. This was after the funeral and expenses were paid. Between four of them it was not a huge amount but it was nice to have something set aside for a rainy day. Henry was going to be well missed most of all by his family but also to a lot of other people.

CHAPTER 13

Jason was doing well at school and really enjoyed it, a bit sad with the passing of his Great granddad, but at the time he was still a bit young to understand about death and was just told that his great granddad had gone to heaven but he still had his Great Nan, Nan and Granddad alive, so his teachers did not take much notice of his pictures that did when they had art.

Jason seemed still a happy and confident boy. Normally for most children if there was something going on he would act different, not quite themselves also not wanting to join in with others. Jason was none of these things, however the teachers did find the pictures strange, his story of a man in a cupboard and the little girl was odd. Jason teachers, just let him know that if he ever wanted to talk about anything they would be there, anytime.

Sarah had one friend at school by this time her name was Tracy Kindle she was nice and she was on the shy side like Sarah, they stuck together at school as she did not have any friends either, the children would call Tracy names too.

So Sarah did have a few friends like Lucy and Tom Chapel from next door also a few doors down. She played with Charlie and Lorna Carlton not close friends just someone to play with, but they were not Anna. Anna was still Sarah best friend, she felt that she could be more herself and could talk about anything with Anna.

Sarah was getting on well at school in terms of work, as to take her mind off the bad things at home or her great granddad's death, she would throw herself into her school work. But it was everything else that was the problem with school, mainly the other pupils.

The name calling, Sarah had to put up with it most days and not just in break time in lessons too. She had Tracy but she was a joke too for the other pupils. It was still more Sarah as Tracy would answer back to the cruel kids. The teachers would always stick up for Sarah and tell the pupils off, it wouldn't stop them. It might stop them for a while, not for long. Sarah found it hard. Sometimes telling them off made things worse for Sarah, then she was called "a teachers pet".

Sarah talked to Tracy about most things but not about Anna or her nasty father, she felt the less people that knew about him the better, plus everyone would think that she was a freak. Sarah would talk about other things that two 7 year olds would talk about. Tracy came over for tea a few times, she was always very polite.

One lovely warm Saturday morning, Sarah went over to see her friends next door. She had been invited over for a bit in the morning, the weekend had arrived; no school! Lucy asked if Sarah wanted to come over and play for a little bit. Their little brother was still fast asleep they could not make too much noise. Oliver had been restless through the night.

Heather and timothy was the names of Tom and Lucy parents they were really nice people. Heather had some biscuits out and had made some hot chocolate with marshmallows for the three of them while she sorted out her little boy, as he was due to wake up.

When all of a sudden Heather screamed! Lucy and Tom ran into their mum followed by Sarah, then her husband. Who was at the time cleaning the car but heard his wife terrible cry from outside, he knew that something was very wrong.

Heather was in her little boy's room, there was a deadly eerie sort of silence in the room. Timothy ran in his little son's bedroom Lucy, Tom and Sarah was staring in the cot, timothy pulled his kids away from the cot, this was not the sort of site for his 7 year old and 5 year old to see.

There little baby brother's Oliver body stiff and cold; He had past away in the night, a tragic cot death one those things that had no reason, just whys? Timothy took the children away from the scene, he was upset too but had to be strong for his wife and children. The three kids were in a state of shock the three of them, sat in the living room in silence. While Timothy ran next door to Sarah's house to get her mum, Lucy and Tom were mortified to see their precious little brother dead in his cot, Sarah was in shock too she never seen a dead baby, it was an haunting image she would not forget.

Susan came running in a few minutes later, just before Michael came in as well. Heather was still screaming and had brought her dead baby through to the living room for help, for someone to bring back her little boy. Michael decided at this time maybe it was best, that he took Tom and Lucy with him back to their house with Sarah, while Susan calmed down Heather. Timothy was just pacing up and down the living room. He just didn't know what to do! Understandably Tom and Lucy were upset too to see their little brother like that. Sarah had seen him too. It was not her little brother but Sarah was also quiet shaken.

It took a while that day to except that Heather's little boy had gone, even when the coroner took him away, she was convinced that boy was still alive, it took a long time for them to price her baby boy away from her. At first she though that they were trying to take her baby away, he was just sleeping. Even though his body was as cold as ice, no breath! But this at least he had not died in pain as sad as it was, he just peaceful slipped away in the night, time for one last dream.

That day was very busy, Michael and Susan helped with the arrangements for the funeral for little Oliver. Ashley, Antony and Diane wanted to help in any way that they could. Heather was in shock, she could not accept that Oliver was gone and her husband was full of guilt, he had convinced himself that somehow they had done something wrong with Oliver? Not that this was just a simple tragedy, no one was to blame!

That night Sarah did not sleep well, the haunting memory of Oliver, it had impaled in her mind. It was horrible to see this little baby boy lifeless, still and stiff, blue tainted lips. The Chapels had a few bad months a head of them but they would pull through in the end, with a little help from their friends! Time would be kind even though this was not a pain that would go away, it just would not be as painful as time went by, they would never forget.

Diane was getting on well in her sister and brother's house. Ashley with Jason, Antony and Diane would pop in quite often. They were a close family and they wanted to make sure their mum was ok, seeing the Chapels dead baby would probably bring back the memories of their mum. The loss of her child just after she had giving birth, also check on Sarah.

Ashley could remember her mum's pain, when she lost her little boy, Ashley's baby brother. She came over a lot for a few weeks, this was difficult for Susan. Diane was too young to remember much but she came round too also Antony to keep a check on their mum. Also to make sure that Sarah was ok, they knew that she had seen the baby Oliver dead in his cot too.

The funeral for little Oliver came and went. It was sad but it was a nice send off for such a short life, he was 2 years, when he died this was also upsetting for Susan. She remembered her little boy that she lost too; he only lasted a few minutes. It was heart retching for Susan.

After the funeral and the next few weeks, Michael had noticed as well as the rest of the family the death of Oliver had hit Susan hard. It brought back the raw pain and emotion of the death of Susan's little baby boy, that day that Oliver had died Susan had held Oliver in her arms too before he was taken away. He reminded her of her dead son, when held for the last few seconds of his life.

Susan was not coping well and was starting to show signs of depression that was a start of a break down. She was becoming irrational at times, mood swings and tearful, in the next breathe she would be fine. Susan was offered cancelling but she did not want it, she thought in her mind her asking for help was weak.

It would be Sarah birthday soon this maybe a good way of taking Susan's mind of her problems! Also a party would help Sarah too. Tom and Lucy had already been invited over before Oliver's death. They still were planning to go even though they did not feel like it. Heather and Timothy thought it would be good to give their kids something positive to look forward too.

There had been a lot to contend with in this family. Over the years they had seen deaths, weddings, bullying, adoption, teenage mum and of course living in haunted house! But this family was still going despite everything. Ashley, Diane, Antony and even Sarah were all strong in their own right, which help when it came to these hard events that seemed to plaque this family. They would get through it together, as they always did.

Hopefully the rest of the year maybe a little easier, but even though this family did have their fair share of tough times they all had good, funny and enjoyable times too. Memories that would last forever! The weeks leading up to Sarah 8th birthday came round quick. Easter came and went in a flash. The usual Easter egg hunt and Easter eggs from the family! Then it was few weeks to go till her birthday.

Susan was depressed and down, she had good and bad days, she was never quite herself after the death of the little boy. It was like she had lost something, like her spark of life had faded. Susan tried hard to be happy around her family but they could see through it. Their mum was valuable and not herself. She would not be for a while this made her family slightly worried. Their mum had always been the strong foundations for this family.

This birthday party would be good for Sarah too, losing her great granddad and seeing Baby Oliver dead was unsettling and upsetting experiences also all that was going on in the house, these would be bad memories she would never forget.

Sarah was looking forward to her birthday, her mum and dad had brought her a few things to play with in the garden that year. They had brought a new swimming pool as the other one they had was broken, she had some out door games and a couple of space hoppers. Hopefully the weather would be good. It was a busy couple of weeks. Then it would be Ashley's 22nd birthday a month later.

The house it self had it ups and down. The footsteps would be on and off, in a strange way the footsteps themselves Sarah got use to, she just didn't like who the footsteps belonged to? She enjoyed her talks to Anna.

The year had not started up that well, at least there were some happier times coming with wedding and other events that the family did every year. It would not take the bad memories away just help things feel a little more able to bare.

About a month after her birthday Sarah's brother and his girlfriend Susie were going to get married in the July. In a register office they didn't want a big wedding just family and a few friends. This would be good for Susan it would give her something else to focus on, for Sarah a way to take her mind off things, in the house plus with the death of her Granddad. It was nice to have something positive happening in the family.

The following year Diane and Sean were due to get married in the July. So there were a few things to look forward to. Also Sarah's birthday was coming up again. Diane had moved into her sister house for a while but she was concerned that there was no one to keep an eye on her mum.

Sarah's uncle Harry and Jane were getting married in the 2nd week of September in New Zealand. The family were invited but it would cost a huge amount of money. Uncle harry was just going to send the family a copy of the wedding photos, again just a register wedding but in her case, this was his second wedding. He had been married and then divorced before a few years back but it was not a good marriage Harry was a bit of a cheat, he had quite few affairs before his ex wife found out but now he seemed more settled, able to commit with Jane.

Hilary was still grieving for her husband but the family keep an eye on her, Antony, Susie and Diane would visit, when they were in between work and other comments. So did Ashley and Jason. Hilary daughter's Emily sometimes with Jessica would pop round. Susan would sometimes with Sarah and her son Mark sometimes with Nicole and Natasha.

They all monitored Hilary in turn. They would also sometimes take her out to make sure she was not stuck at home all the time. Sometimes just for shopping or a day out somewhere like the park or a day out to Weston or down to Devon or Dorset for the day.

Ashley and Terry relationship was not getting on at all by this time. Ashley did like Terry and loved him but just not enough to marry him. So when he asked to marry her, Ashley said no and was very honest for reason's why. They ended their relationship, which was sad but the right thing to do if the relationship was not going anywhere. Plus Ashley could see that Terry was not keen on her having a son.

Ashley was single once more but this did not really bother her that much. She was young still had plenty of time to find the one right for her, also someone who would treat her son better, would except that Ashley and Jason came as package.

This year was to be an eventful year for many reason; the events of the last year. Some very bad events had brought all the family closer and closer together year by year. This strong family would need this in the coming years too! Things were stirring in this house of secrets!

CHAPTER 14

It was Sarah 8th birthday! Her birthday was in mid May. They had not done much for her 7th as it was their first year that they done something to change the décor of the house in years, money had been tight. It was just the seven of them on her 7th, mum, dad, Ashley, Antony, Diane, Jason and her. Sarah had hoped being mid May. It would be a lovely warm spring day! Instead it was wet day, sunshine and showers.

Sarah was going to have a birthday party to make up for the birthday of year before it was just family. That was ok but she would like a few more people around for her 8th. So her mum invited the next door kids tom and Lucy chapel from next door, also some of Sarah's mum and dad's family.

Lucy and Tom did not feel like a party but their mum and dad insisted they go. It would give them something else to think about, a chance to have a little bit of fun, it would take their mind of the death of their little brother.

Lucy and Tom Chapel had always played outside with Sarah and Jason, unknowing to Sarah. Lucy and Tom never felt that comfortable in the house, they didn't understand why! But it was just how they felt about the house.

Sarah's friend Tracy from school was invited too, Lucy was going to a different junior school to Sarah. At least this time Sarah had a few friends round. The British weather was not too good, so they had the party inside. As for most birthday party's, there was lots of food and drink also party games, with lots of party themed music. In a house of horrors is not a good place to play games, however Anna's father had a few ideas for his own party games . . . .

Ashley, Antony and Diane sorted out the games for the kids, as they were big kids themselves at heart. They were all having a whale of a time and making lots of noise to show for it too. Screaming, shouting and laughing a lot of noise for just five children.

It was a good party so far music playing lots of yummy food and drink. Sarah also had a new bike and some music tapes for her stereo just what she wanted! Sarah mum worked hard all that day to make the house look nice for her daughter 8th birthday party, birthday banners and lots of balloons. They were all having a great time. Then it was party game time, Simon says, pass the parcel went well and so did musical chairs.

Tom had a great idea for a game Hide and Seek, Sarah was not too sure of this but it seemed a good idea at the time. What harm could it do! Sarah, Jason, Tracy, tom and Lucy took it in turns to hide and to seek. Ashley, Antony and Diane didn't play with their sister for this game! They were getting a bit big to play Hide and Seek. Ashley, Antony and Diane just chatted to their mum and dad. The adults catch up on each others latest news.

Lucy and Tom were enjoying themselves and just for a short time they had been able to put, what had happened to their family out of their mind both of them were having fun. The game of hide and seek had started, this would be no ordinary game of hide and seek. There was a presence in the house, an evil presence that was watching their game with interest. Sarah at first did not sense him, she was too busy hiding, having fun.

It was Sarah turn first to seek, Jason and tom picked the same place in the bathroom, Tracy picked under the spare bed in the spare room. Jason and Tom were easy to find, they were not very inventive, when it came to hiding places. Lucy was also easy to find as she hid behind the bathroom door. When it was Lucy turn to seek, Sarah went behind sofa or other places downstairs. Sarah was not hard to find, neither was Tracy, she had hid behind the kitchen door and Jason was in his usual hiding place. Sarah felt uneasy picking a hiding place upstairs! Lucy was good at seeking she found them all easily.

It was Tom Lucy's brother next to count. As they all hid tom started counting. As usual Jason picked the bathroom. Tracy picked behind the armchair in the living room and Sarah hid in her mum and dad's room, she noticed Lucy go upstairs. She thought just in case anything strange was to happen! Sarah would be close if Lucy needed help in any way! Then she felt Anna's father close, Sarah had a strong sense of danger, something fiendish was about to happen!

Lucy decided she had to think of a really good hiding place and then she had what she thought was a brilliant idea! She had a really good hiding place to hide in the cupboard in Sarah's room "No one will find me here" Lucy grinned to herself. Sarah heard her cupboard door open then close. 'Oh no' Sarah thought to herself 'of ALL the places Lucy could hide why there, THIS IS NOT GOOD!' Sarah knew that her friend would be in trouble.

Then tom said "10 coming ready or not". They all kept very quiet and still.

Lucy was pleased with herself in the darkness of the eerie cupboard. So was something else pleased that she had picked that cupboard, 'let the games begin', the dark force thought to himself, 'my turn' all of a sudden the temperature dropped and the atmosphere in the cupboard drastically changed so much that even Lucy felt it and she was never a sensitive girl! The negative energy was overwhelming! And Lucy felt cold hands on her shoulders. Then a deep voice said right into her ear "You will die, Lucy". Lucy tried to get out but she could not open the door.

Anna's father Edward would not let Lucy out, at least not yet! He could feel her fear which made him feel stronger, with that negative vibe from Lucy's fear. Lucy screamed "Help! I can't get out". She was shaking when Sarah finally managed to open the door. Lucy explained what had happened to her.

This was not good Lucy was in a state. This party was suppose to take Lucy's mind of losing her brother but now it had traumatised her, in the process had brought her memories of losing her brother flooding back.

Tom, Jason and Tracy came running in to see what was going on. They too heard Lucy scream in fear. Lucy told them as well about what had just happened, Jason and Tom were a bit young to understand and just thought that it was Lucy joking as she was a bit of a fibber. Often made up wild stories and joked around but Tracy was older. She didn't really know what Lucy was like, so she kind of believed her, she was a little freaked out by what had happened.

"Oh no, that's terrible!" Sarah said. Sarah did not know what to say to Lucy? She was in shock herself! Anna's father had always done that sort of thing to her but no one else, at least certainly not telling someone that they were going to die.

Sarah's mum and dad came up to see what was wrong? Along with Ashley, Antony and Diane "What is it?" they asked wondering what on earth made Lucy scream like that! Lucy explained but they didn't want to believe her. Ashley, Antony and Diane did not say much, just looked at each other. This brought back to the three of them their own personal memories of the house and the strange things that would happen to them growing up!

As Lucy had not long lost brother and probably in the grieving process just boiled it down to that' that what Michael thought. The rest of the family it probably was partly the grieving for her brother coming out but they knew that there was something not nice in the house.

They all went down stairs, Tracy was still pretty freak out and was looking forward to going home, not long after Tracy's mum came to collect Tracy to her relief. Tracy did not say anything about what had happened to Lucy, she knew that her mum would not believe her story. Tracy just told her parents that she had a great time. In one way she did, up until Lucy had her bad ordeal, Tracy was in fact having a really good time.

Ashley, Antony and Diane also unknowing to anyone else believed Lucy, the three of them had all felt this presence as children themselves, knew it was wicked. It had never really done much when they were children growing up in that house. It seemed to start more with Sarah for some reason, she seemed to be the main target for his haunting, as Sarah grew up but no one had any idea of this as yet, her family had their own haunting memories too. Sarah never said anything in the fear that something would happen to her family if she told.

Lucy went home after that with her brother. She could no longer stay in that house any longer understandably. Little did Lucy know but Sarah did believe her and unknowing to Sarah so did her mum Susan, Ashley, Antony and Diane. Lucy needed to be with her mum and dad. Lucy did not tell her parents, her mum and dad had enough on their plate. Lucy said that she was missing her baby brother, that's why she was upset.

Ashley could tell by the look on Sarah's face, she could see that Sarah was freaked out by the events that had accrued to her friend Lucy. Sarah was trying to hide it as best she could but she was already emotional about the house with dealing with her own countless experiences.

Antony tried to take Sarah mind off things by talking about his wedding coming up, he could also see that his little sister was shaken up. Antony had found a flat for him and Susie to move into. The flat was not that far away about five minutes drive away. It was exciting news but Sarah could not forget about that day.

Later that evening Ashley, Antony and Diane went home. They were slightly concerned for Sarah and their mum. They didn't know what could happen next, the house was not right and had never been right but they never heard anyone have a bad experience like that, that threatening!

After what had happened that day, it was not going to be the same. That night when Sarah went to bed, she called on her ghostly friend, she could not sleep! How ever hard she tried. It was not the sort of memorable birthday she was hoping for. "Anna, its Sarah." she said needing Anna's help, trying to make sense of what had gone on that day, with emotional effect of that day and still grieved by the memory of the baby Oliver death, tears welling up in her eyes, Sarah was lost.

She heard Anna voice but it sounded different quiet! Almost as if she was afraid to talk "Yes" Anna said in a whisper. Sarah knew that Anna's father was around by the tone of her voice.

"I need to talk to you, my friend Lucy got stuck in the cupboard and heard a man's voice! It told her she was going to die! Was that your father?" Sarah asked. Anna did not answer or could not answer! It went deadly silent through the dark house and it became cold as ice as if something was coming.

Sarah hairs stood on end at the back of her neck, she felt afraid she felt darkness was coming! She had a heavy feeling! Sarah knew what this meant but this was the last thing she felt like dealing with. Then heard footsteps up the stairs once again, heavy footsteps, even though she felt uneasy. She told herself maybe it was her dad going a bed, at least that's what Sarah made herself believe! She knew her mum and dad had already gone a bed as it was late at night. Sarah was determined to face whatever it was! Sarah had enough.

Sarah got up very sheepish and checked, Sarah foolishly thought she had to face her fear. Sarah was always too afraid to check the footsteps but she needed to know what was doing this and make a stand! That she was not going to let him rule her life or anyone else. So she got up, hoping to catch something or someone coming up the stairs, in her heart feeling terrified, shaking to her very bones.

Sarah went to the top of the stairs but the footsteps had stopped by then as if it knew Sarah was coming, this entity was toying with her. The landing light was on but not the hallway light; Sarah gazed into the darkness of the stairs into the dark abyss of the hallway but there was nobody.

Sarah knew something was wrong, she felt those piercing dark green eyes stare straight through her in the dark. Sarah ran back into her bedroom and to bed, she felt like someone wanted to harm her. She had always felt this entity all her life. She knew it was bad but she never felt as if it wanted to hurt her, just haunt and watch her. To toy with her emotions!

Sarah could not sleep that night, she could not help it. All she could think about those footsteps, she wondered would these footsteps keep happening again and again, she didn't like the way it made her feel. There were no footsteps that night.

For the next few weeks it had all stopped the footsteps, why did they keep happening, plus Anna was not speaking to Sarah. Sarah had all these questions but no one to answer them! Sarah was confused why was Anna not speaking to her? What did these footsteps really mean?

At school Tracy never brought up what accrued at her birthday party. Sarah could tell that it scared her friend too much. Tracy felt uncomfortable talking about it. She still remained Sarah's friend but after that birthday party. Tracy was not that close to Sarah anymore, which for Sarah was a shame, as she had thought at last she had a close friend at school.

Sarah had started to have bullying outside school too by the kids in the neighbourhood. They had always called her the odd name because she was quiet and kept herself to herself. This one particular time after school, there was a group of kids about Sarah's age and some older mixture of boys and girls. They were sat on a wall just down from Sarah's house. She was just on her way back from the corner shop. These kids notice and started the name calling and this time decided they wanted for no reason to chase her, to intimate her and make her feel afraid. It worked Sarah ran the rest the way home, with kids chasing behind her till she got to her front gate to her house. They stopped just laughed at her calling her a scared cat, Sarah could feel the tears building up but she had to hide them, she could not tell her mum, this would upset her and mum already had a lot to deal with. So she went in and put a false smile and a brave face.

Later that night when everyone was a sleep, Sarah finally let the tears flow. She could almost feel like this bad entity and witness what had happened to her and was laughing at this misfortune of this little 8 year old with the weight of the world on her shoulders. The next day was a Saturday and was quiet with the house but the next day was to be a Sunday, this menacing presence had plans for little Sarah. Sunday in the day was pretty normal and an ordinary day with a lovely Sunday roast and just watching telly.

The entity that made these footsteps had another plans to scare and taunt his victim. This apparition would not stop or cower for anything. It had a dark propose in mind. To what this propose was at the moment Sarah had no idea!

As normal on a Sunday was a bath day. She had a bath every other day. On a Sunday, it was so that Sarah would be fresh for school the next day and for the start of the week. Susan had done their tea, just some sandwiches and a cake for after Sarah's bath. Michael did a bit of gardening, pottering around doing some things in the garden before it got too dark.

Susan had run Sarah's bath for her, when it was ready Susan came in the bathroom with Sarah to wash her hair. Sarah was 8 years now, after her mum had done her hair, Susan left Sarah to wash herself and have a bit of play time in the bath.

Sarah had washed herself and was just relaxing, laying down in the bath for ten minutes before she had to come out. Sarah closed her eyes just for a moment to empty her mind of all the stresses of the house and school. Then she opened them a dark shadow was in the corner of the bathroom, it was not dark it was still daylight so it noticed, it was only there for a slit second then gone. This freaked Sarah out and for a moment she too frightened to move, this was not the first time she had seen a figure in the bathroom with her. Sarah just told herself that it was just her imagination but she knew it wasn't! She was unsure what would happen next!

Sarah was hoping her mum would come in but she didn't or her ghostly friend Anna would come to her aid. She had also noticed that the temperature had dropped. This only normally meant one thing, she was not alone! Sarah got the courage to get up.

However when Sarah went to get up she could not, she felt something push her head into the water. She could feel a tight grip around her neck, Sarah tried to struggle and break away by kicking but the more she struggled the more she felt herself being pushed under the water in the bath. She could not breathe! Sarah could not see anyone that could be doing this to her but she felt an evil force!

Sarah tried to scream but nothing came out. She could feel herself chocking on the water from the bath. Then she felt the grip loosen, whatever had her was letting her go. Sarah could sit up finally. A couple of minutes later, Susan came in, Sarah came out of the bath coughing and choking.

Sarah quickly put the towel around herself covering her neck; she had seen marks on her neck from whatever was pushing her into the water in the bathroom mirror. This entity had tried to strangle and drown her in the water, this scared Sarah, for a moment she could not breathe properly gasping for air.

"Is everything ok, Sarah? I heard you coughing?" Susan said looking very worried Sarah looked pale in colour and not herself.

"Yes mum, IM FINE, just swallowed some of the water, playing in the bath that's all" Sarah could feel the tears swelling up but she could not tell her mum the truth, if this entity could do this to her what could it do to her mum or dad. Plus her mum was not coping with things in her life already. Sarah could not burden her mum with this!

"Ok as long you are ok! I carry on with tea but if you need me just call" Susan said her motherly instincts was telling her that something was not quite right Sarah was being cagey. Susan left and went back into the kitchen.

"Please leave me alone" Sarah asked but there was no reply the entity had gone for now. Sarah got dressed quickly in her pyjamas and put her house coat on to hide the scar on both sides of her neck. After tea Sarah went to her room.

Sarah looked in her dressing table mirror the scar was not so red, the scar inside was more painful. She didn't know how to deal with what she was faced with after all Sarah was just an 8 year old little girl! She felt meek and so alone, 'what on earth would be the next thing?' Sarah asked herself. Things were getting noticeably gruesome for Sarah!

It seemed from her 8th birthday too, things were increasing at least the Paranormal Activity for her. It was not just inside the house now, things were starting else where. Like the garden at night or when she went to school sometime, the feeling of not being alone.

Sarah was starting to become afraid of outside at night. A deep feeling of dread if she wanted to go into the kitchen at night! Something was waiting for her, on the porch from the kitchen that went into the back garden. The garden was fine in the day but it was at night, their garden would take on a whole new ambience. Edward had other tricks up his sleeve. He too had friends that he could call upon to do his bidding. His friends were not good just like him! They too had dark intent purpose, whatever their leader dictated.

This never felt like Anna. Anna never made her feel afraid or unsafe. She knew that Anna would not harm her or anyone else. This thing did not feel like Anna's father Edward either but this was or felt bizarrely like a creature of the night! Which Sarah could not believe what her gut feeling was telling her, it seemed unconceivable! 'Things like that are not real' she thought. It was however she felt controlled by Anna's father. Sarah would have to be strong now, especially as she was not going to tell anyone and was determined to go through this alone.

How could Anna's father conjure up a creature after all, Anna's father was just a ghost like Anna, a bad ghost but never the less a ghost. But she felt something else was there in dead of night in the garden waiting! How ever much she tried to figure it out, she could not!

As Sarah felt so threatened by this she could not push it aside and forget about it, this was getting serious. This was not her imagination gone wild, with everything else that was going on, it was not a surprise that her imagination was running riot but her instincts were telling that this not just a creation of her mind!! Sarah could sometimes see red glow from outside in the garden! She stared out through the darkness of the night. A shadow seemed to move outside, in the dead of night, a dark shadow in near distance!

If the wind blew, the porch door would rattle and shake, it was not only the wind. Something else that was evil had been awoken from his long deep sleep at its master's call and bidding! Sarah could not go outside at night she was too afraid. This creature was lying in wait for her to come out. This was becoming more and more freaky, 'WHAT was it that?' What was she feeling?' Sarah would think to herself.

One night Sarah did not feel alone, the window happened to be slightly open. She was too tired to close it and feel asleep, but this time it was not Anna or indeed her father, something else had entered into the room that night. Edward's hound had come to call on Sarah.

Sarah awoke from her sleep. She had a strange feeling that feel uneasy, so scared, Sarah felt something heavy on the bottom of her bed! She could feel pressure on her legs like something was on them; Sarah put her covers over her face, she could not see anything and she didn't want to see it either.

What ever this was she felt like it crawled up her bed! She knew now this was not Anna or her father, it was the creature. She could feel it red eyes piercing through her skin. It was looking straight at her. You could not see this creature but it was there, you tell by the impressions on the bed as if something was moving up from the bottom of the bed to the top by where Sarah's face was.

Sarah tried to scream but nothing came out, it was her fear. Edward was trying another way to taunt and scare her, this freak her out. So much so that it brought her to tears. Then strangely enough after about what felt like a very long five minutes. Edward had called his beast off her for now.

The footsteps continued getting more frequent and this insight about the back garden but still Anna would not speak in coming weeks as if she was scared off. Things would also move in her room, this not just a little bit but with more vigour. It was moved with anger, something annoyed or frustrated.

Sarah would come back from school and her toys that she put away neatly before going a school would be on the floor or her books would be stacked in the middle of her room. She never mentioned it to her mum about anything. She was too scared of what might happen if she started to talk about everything!

Sarah had noticed also that her mum and dad were not getting on as well. They didn't say anything to Sarah but she knew they would never row but cracks were starting to form only just slightly. The house and her mum's break down and past events with how Michael's temper was in the beginning of their marriage had started to damaged, her mum and dad's marriage.

Sarah started to see shadows appear in her room at night, the shadows seemed to be a figure; sometimes more than one would appear! The next evening Sarah was determined that she was going to talk to Anna about her latest experiences. Sarah needed some sort of answer.

Anna came to her that night without Sarah even calling her name but this time Sarah could see her like she did once before, when she was half asleep. Anna could feel Sarah's fear and how scared she was.

"I'm here Sarah, you are not alone!" Anna said in a soft and kind voice.

"It is good to see you, I have been really scared! There is something in the dark; it only comes out at night. It hides there, it terrifies me" Sarah said near to tears.

"Yes, I know but you must not talk about it or it come for you again" Anna replied almost as this was a warning from Anna, a concerned friend trying to keep Sarah safe.

"I will try my best, it is hard as it ALWAYS seems to be there" Sarah said the image of the red eyes burned in her mind and the shadows through the darkness of the night. "Why does your father do this to me, I don't understand?" Sarah added.

"I don't know, I will stay with you for a little bit" Anna said in return which gave Sarah a little bit of comfort knowing that Anna was there and she was not alone, someone that understood. Anna did know why but could not say. It was one of reasons Sarah came to her. Sarah drifted off to sleep. Nothing evil came to her that night. Anna did not leave her side as she promised and watched over Sarah, like an angel as she floated over and floated around her room with fluorescent blue light all around her!

The next day Antony and Susie popped round that morning before work to arrange with his mum and dad the wedding arrangements, there was a lot to discuss and Antony was going to give Sarah a lift to school on his way to work.

Antony and Susie popped round about half 7 in the morning. Sarah did not say anything about her experiences. Sarah was determined to keep her family safe. Sarah just carried on getting ready for school while her parents discussed the wedding plans with the happy couple. This was hard she had felt this creature on her bed she felt it's breathe on her face.

It was nearly time for school, Antony and Susie gave Sarah a lift. Antony could sense there was some thing bothering his little sister. She was quiet more than normal.

"Are you ok, Sarah?" Antony asked a little worried about Sarah.

"Yeah I'm fine just a little tired a bit, that's all" Sarah replied she was too frightened to tell the truth, plus would they believe her? Sarah thought to herself. Antony did not push her. He was not convinced it was just tiredness. Sarah was dropped off to school but her mind would wonder in a day dream.

Sarah really tried her best to do her work. She could not get the last few experiences out of her head. Sarah was so scared it seemed there was no one she could speak too.

It was coming up to Antony and Susie's wedding, it was a quiet affair just family but a nice day, a friend of Antony's did the photos for the big day. This was something nice to happen to the family and for a day, Sarah could think about something else. As most wedding's it was a hectic day but a lovely day. They had the reception in a function room of a pub that was Antony and Susie's local.

It was a nice day a chance for everyone to enjoy themselves and for Sarah a nice, welcomed distraction. It was a lovely warm summer's day, not a cloud in the sky.

Summer holiday's came along. Sarah and Jason had a good summer holiday with their family. They always had a summer holiday together, even though now 3 of Susan and Michael's children had grow up and got their own partners, they still went away with their mum and dad.

Sarah she liked the summer holidays but her mind was always on the house. She looking forward to it, well as can be expected! As something was happening most nights now, sometimes just the feeling of being followed to the footsteps, things being moved or something on Sarah's bed!

Anna was there for her at times but it was getting harder and harder not to tell any one about the things that were happening to her.

They all went on holiday to Devon for a week, at the end of July. It was nice to have a bit of fun. It was nice that her older brother and sister's came too. Sarah thought. For the rest of the holidays Sarah and Jason had days like to the park or to the seaside. Anna and those footsteps, still was always on her mind however it was fun. The summer holiday had ended and now back to school for Sarah and Jason.

Before the end of the summer holidays Auntie Emily had an idea for a day trip, she could see that her sister was still having a bad time of things. Mark was going to arrange to hire a van for a day. They could take a trip to Weymouth. It would be Hilary, Susan, Michael, Sarah, Diane, Emily, Jessica, mark and Nicole.

With all that was going on it was a nice welcome break away, even if it was just for a day, also in the middle of the summer holidays. Ashley took Sarah on a short break to Sandy bay in Exmouth with Jason and Diane, these were good days. Sarah enjoyed her little holidays, even though they were in England. The weather never let them down, so it always plenty beach days on their holidays or breaks away.

The holidays were now over and would be back to school. Jason always loved his time off school, also loved his holidays too, always looking forward to going to school to see his friends. Sarah was the opposite hated it once again go back to school to the name calling and feeling an outcast. Jason was in school full time now and was doing well.

One night after a long and hard first day back at school, Sarah felt the creature once again. This time she saw it, at least the outline of it in the corner of her room. Sarah felt that she had caught the creature by surprise that she was not meant to see it. Having said that she did not see it properly, it was dark in the corner of her room were this thing was. Sarah was a sleep at the time, it was in the middle of the night but for some reason, Sarah had stirred in her sleep and knew instantly, she was not alone.

It was hard to tell what it look like as it dark in her room but it was not a person, big red eyes that glowed in the dark, it was a dark figure of some sort of strange creature like nothing she had ever seen, Sarah was so scared she felt like crying, she tried to scream, nothing came out of her mouth.

Whatever it was it had long thin fingers with long nails or claws, it looked like something out of science fiction book oval shaped face big eyes, tallish about 4 feet, it seemed to be able to on all four or stand up right on two, it was hard to tell. It was only there for a few minutes then vanished.

Sarah could not sleep that night in fear that it might come back! She had never seen anything like it at all, not ever. What ever it was it was evil she felt that much but it also she felt controlled by someone, it could easily hurt her but it didn't like it was waiting for its orders.

Sarah once again did not say anything to her parents, this was her problem. Sarah felt that she had to be strong this was getting serious, she feared for her family if she started to talk.

After the weeks went by and Sarah would wake up in the morning, she would see a few scratches on her body or a bruise. She had no idea were it came from. It would not have been there before she went to bed. They would always appear by her ankles or tops of her arms, chest or ribs. They wouldn't be really deep scratches, or big bruises. Sarah would think much of it. Maybe she scratched or bumped herself in the night;

Michael and Susan's Anniversary was looming, talking about and arranging their Son's wedding brought back fond memories of when they arranged their wedding all those years ago!

Susan had no idea how bad things were for Sarah, she sometimes feel that Sarah was not happy, if Susan asked how her daughter was. Sarah would just say everything is fine, just that she didn't have a lot of friends. Sarah dare not say anything more. Susan did not try to force the problems out just said that she was there for her daughter.

Michael and Susan anniversary was not far away again and Jason's 5th birthday, in the October. Michael and Susan had not planned much for their anniversary. Just a meal out in their favourite country pub which for a country pub did really lovely, star quality food; which was fine for them! It would also be nice for Sarah to stay with her real mum at least nothing could get her there.

Michael had booked for the night, Ashley offered for Sarah to stay up her house. It would also be nice for Jason to have his big sister to stay, Antony offered to take his mum and dad to the pub.

Antony had arranged to pick up Sarah too and drop her round to his sister's on route to dropping his mum and dad off. Ashley was going to go over to her mum's the next day anyway. She could bring Sarah back home at the same time. Ashley would come up about mid morning the next day, with Sarah and Jason as it would fall on a Friday that they went out which meant no school for Sarah. That was even better for Sarah. Ashley would not have to rush to bring Sarah back.

Sarah loved the thought of staying over her real mum's Ashley, they got on well. It was great being with her brother too and at this time it was a chance to get away, from everything bad in the house. It was great, a lot of fun. For Ashley this was a chance of getting to know her daughter and try and built on some sort of bond between them. Maybe one day call her mum rather than Ashley but she knew that this would take a long time, years rather than mouths! Ashley was prepared to wait for that magical moment.

Sarah leading up to her mum and dad's meal had more experiences. She never saw the creature again in her room but never was alone in her room, most nights. It would Anna, Anna's father Edward or the creature; sometimes, if she was alone any time at night. Then in the day she felt that something was watching her from the top of the stairs or things would be moved in her room, when she was not there!

The day of Michael and Susan's anniversary came round. Michael was home a little earlier than normal, to give him time to get ready and to give them time to drop off Sarah before, they went out for their meal. Michael and Susan were really looking forward to their meal. Susan thought it might be good for Sarah to spend a bit of time with her real mum.

By the time Michael had come back Sarah had already, had an overnight bag packed and was raring to go. Susan was upstairs just finishing getting ready for their night out. She had decided on the classic little black shinny dress. She looked as stunning as ever, Michael thought as he walked in the bedroom.

"WOW! You look amazing as every my love" Michael said. He gave her a huge hug and kissed her wrapping his arms around her.

"Thank you hope so for a 46 year old" Susan sighed feeling her age, knowing she was not as slender as she was when she was in her late teens. She had a curvy figure, womanly shape but tall with slender legs.

"You still look as good as when I meet you all those years ago" Michael said, as he got ready himself, which of course being a man, he took about 15 minutes.

Then after they had finished getting ready, their son Antony came round to pick them up and drop Sarah over to Ashley's house. Antony dropped Sarah off first then his mum and dad. Antony had also dressed nice as he too was going to be going out for a few drinks and a meal with Susie up their local pub, after he had dropped them off. This was good idea to have someone take them as taxi would have been costly both there and back as they were all dressed up a bus would not be suited. That was still a distance for Susan being in high heels.

For Sarah this was a nice welcomed detraction for the problems at home and school, also the chance to play with her brother, with his stuff. Sarah had a wicked night plenty to do. But Sarah always thought of Anna, when she was away from home.

Antony after he dropped off his parents and Sarah went off, he went out to have his meal with Susie. Michael and Susan had a lovely time. After the meal Michael and Susan got a taxi home. Ashley would bring Sarah back about half ten in the morning by the time they got the bus up.

Meanwhile as Michael and Susan were having their meal, Ashley had done a really nice meal for Sarah, Jason and herself with a double chocolate cake for afters with clotted cream. It was lovely!

Ashley had got a movie in for them to watch, it was E.T which was a really good film but as Sarah had her own little creature watching and following her. This film freaked her out a little, she try to tell herself it's just a film and hid how she was feeling very well from her real mum.

After Sarah played on her game boy that she had brought up with her, she had it for Christmas and watched a cartoon before she went to bed. The film still playing on her mind, even though she still kept telling herself it was just a film. Even Jason her younger brother was not freaked out by this film.

"How are things with you Sarah? How is school?" Ashley inquired as Susan had mentioned to her that something was up with Sarah, she was not talking about what was bothering her. Ashley thought as she was not her mum or dad in Sarah eyes, maybe Sarah would find it easier to talk to her.

"Yes I'm ok, I don't like school, not easy making friends" Sarah replied she did not say anything more.

"Yes school can be tough! It is hard making friends but along as you got one really good friend, that's there for you that what counts" Ashley said giving her daughter a bit of comfort.

Sarah smiled at the time. Yes she did have a good friend but not at school and she just happened to be a ghost. She was always there for her and Anna was always kind to her. Jason didn't say much as he was getting very tired and sleepy by this time. Ashley lifted up Jason and put him up to bed, as he had fallen asleep on the sofa.

Sarah went asleep after. Sarah had a nice time though, although she was a little restless that night. It was hard to keep her mind off things enough so she could get a decent night sleep. She slept in the same room as her brother.

That night Antony had come back to his sister's flat for a drink, they did not live that far from each other, after Antony and Susie had their meal. Sarah got well with Susie. She was really nice to Sarah and took her out sometimes to the cinema or the park with Susie's niece Sheena. Antony and Susie were married now so Susie's niece became Sarah's cousin through marriage. Later on that night Antony and Susie went back to their house and Diane came in from working a late shift.

The next morning Sarah got up and got dressed, than went downstairs to the kitchen. Ashley and Diane were making pancakes with blueberries and maple syrup, it was scrummy! Then just watched a bit of children's telly before Ashley and Diane with the kids Sarah and Jason, went back to Sarah's mum and dad's house about 10ish.

When she got home at ten her mum and dad were up and dressed. Her dad was doing some gardening and her mum was having a coffee before she did the housework.

Susan asked how Sarah night was as Sarah gave her mum a big hug. She had missed her mum and dad lots. Sarah said she had a nice time then Susan told Ashley, Diane, Jason and Sarah about their night, Sarah was really close to her mum.

Then it was getting close to Jason's birthday once again, his 5th birthday! Ashley was going to have a birthday party at her mum and dad's house for some reason. Jason would not say but he wanted his birthday at his Nan and Granddad's house for this year. Susan and Michael said that was fine.

Ashley said that Jason could have a few friends over from school, if that was ok with his Nan! Of course Jason's Nan said yes. Jason was looking forward to this. It was the first time he had any friends over for a birthday party normally it was just family. His birthday came along quick. He had invited his two best friends over, Zach Simpson and Jack Miller. They were interested to see the house, Jason had told his friends about the little girl and the man in the cupboard in his Nan and Granddad house. They were curious to see for themselves these claims.

Susan had decided to do Jason party with her famous double chocolate cake on a Saturday. So they would not have to worry about school in the morning. Jason's friends Zach and Jack were going to be dropped off to his Nan and Granddad's house about 4ish. That gave Ashley and Susan plenty of time to do the food and make the house look cool, with birthday banners and balloons. Plus to make that homemade chocolate birthday cake which was to die for.

Jason came over with his mum in the morning, to give Ashley plenty of time to help with the birthday party's preparation. Jason was really excited. He brought his present over, that his mum had brought for him. Jason wanted to show his sister. It was a game boy, it was really cool! His Nan and Granddad had brought him some games to go with his game boy and a cool outfit to wear. Sarah had brought Jason some sweets out of her pocket money.

Sarah and Jason played in Sarah's room before lunchtime and watched some telly after lunch as Jason had two video's to watch that he had for his birthday, it was Peter pan and robin hood Disney films. By the time the films finished it was about half 3, which gave Jason and Sarah enough time to get ready for the big party.

By 4 all that needed to be done, was done the house was ready. The food and drink had been laid out with the birthday cake as the centre piece on the dinning table.

Jason's friends turned up bang on cue and at the same time, both itching to go upstairs. But first Jason wanted to open his presents from his friends. It was a colouring set from Zach and some funky Colouring stuff from Jack.

"Can we go upstairs and play now please Jason!" Zach asked.

"Please can we" added Jack.

"Ok, come on then I show you my room and I can show you my game boy" Jason said as they ran up the stairs to Jason's room that he stays in sometimes on a weekend. Sarah in the meantime had noticed this urgency to go upstairs, even though to most people they would not think anything of this, Sarah felt as if there was another interest for them to want to go upstairs.

Sarah also remembered her 8th birthday and what had happened to Lucy. So to make sure they were ok. Sarah thought it might be best to keep an eye on Jason and his friends, Sarah went upstairs to join them. Jason friends were only 5 years old like him, if anything happened this could give them nightmares and affect them for life.

To Jack and Zach they thought that seeing a ghost, was a little game. Not how serious it could be, they were so young and it was how a group of five year olds would think.

"Can I join in guys" Sarah asked trying to get involved to see what they were up to and to make sure they stayed clear of Sarah's room, in particular that cupboard in Sarah's room.

"Yes sis" Jason replied glad to see her sister joining in as they played with Lego and did some drawings with the new colouring sets, he had from his friends.

"Do you know about the little girl and the man in the cupboard" Jack asked innocently to Sarah being a curios little boy.

Sarah was shocked, how did they know about that? The only way they could is through Jason and up until now, Sarah had no idea about what had been happening to her little half brother!

Sarah did not want to say too much. She knew it was never a good idea to mention too much, plus she did not want to freak out Jason's friends with the full truth.

"No, there is nothing here, it just a cupboard and my little brother's imagination" Sarah insisted. Then Sarah had another surprise Jason had done a drawing, Sarah knew it was Anna and he had also drawn a man that looked evil and frightening, it was Anna's father Edward, 'this was not good' Sarah thought.

"There is a man in the cupboard and a little girl! This is what they look like!" Jason said in a stern, in matter of fact tone to his sister. Sarah could not think what on earth to say to this, Sarah was still in a state of shock.

How could she convince her brother that this was just in his head? He was little boy, he would not be told any different once his mind was set on something, he knew to be true. This image did not seem to bother Jason, it was an image in his dreams but for Sarah she felt different about this picture, it did bother Sarah.

Sarah tried not to let her fear get the better of her. It was hard, as she felt that she knew this terrible haunting image. Almost like an image from her deep subconscious. That had been hidden from herself. Sarah felt sick to her stomach and this also made her feel very confused!

'Why was she feeling this way about a drawing'? How did she know what he looked like? As she had never seen him just felt him or she may have seen a dark figure but never in detail! She knew those deep piercing green eyes.

Susan called the kids down for food and something to drink. It was time to sing happy birthday and Ashley cut the chocolate cake into nice big slices! Zach and Jack said nothing more at that time about it. They all went downstairs to have food, Jason and his friends were hungry as they eat, the picture that Jason had drawn never bothered Jason friends either, their appetite was fine. Sarah tried to eat but found it difficult, she could not get Jason's picture out of her head.

Sarah wanted to talk to Jason about his drawings but was afraid that if she did maybe this bad entity would harm her little brother! So she said nothing all the rest of the day about it, after all it was just a picture. 'pictures can't hurt you!' she thought to herself, which was images in his dreams and did not seem to be effecting her brother in a bad way at the moment, Sarah thought maybe for now to leave it.

Jason was having a wicked time, after food and cake for the last few hours the kids played upstairs with Sarah monitoring them. It was dark by this time! The nights were drawing in as it was about third week in October. Jason, Zach and Jack were having a nice time playing with Jason and his toys.

Zach could not hold back any longer, his curiosity was getting the better of him. He had to know, especially after those pictures that Jason had drawn! So Zach ran into Sarah's room. He wanted to see the cupboard, to see if he could see this man that Jason had said lived there, but before Sarah could stop him it was too late. Zach had managed to open the cupboard door. Sarah knew this was not good, not good at all.

Jason and Jack ran in behind Sarah who had run in too. The cupboard door in Sarah's room was wide open! Zach went to look inside the cupboard.

"Well I can't see anyone in the cupboard" Zach said grinning, to make fun of Jason's story. But this was not the sort of entity that liked being laughed at. It wanted to teach this little boy a lesson! that he would never forget in a hurry.

The room went cold. The tapes that were on Sarah's dressing table fell to the floor and the cupboard door slammed shut by itself, with Zach trapped inside.

Zach screamed "let me out, this is not funny" thinking that Jack or Jason had shut him in there as a joke to scare him. If it was a joke it was working, it was not funny at all, poor Zach thought.

Sarah managed to open the door after a few minutes, this was enough to shut Zach up and the four of decided that they had enough of Sarah's room, also enough of upstairs. The four of them went downstairs to watch a bit of telly before his friends had to go home.

Zach, Jack and Jason went down the stairs first followed by Sarah. Sarah could feel something right behind her, as she went to go down the stairs and heard a faint sincere laugh behind her with a cold icy breathe on the back of her neck as she went down the stairs.

Sarah was shaken as was the rest of them were. Sarah knew that it could have been worse, a lot worse. It was good that she was there when it happened and it probably prevented anything really bad to happen to Jason's friend Zach.

Zach was a little freaked out by it but at the same time he thought it was brilliant that Jason's Nan and granddad had a haunted house. He wished his house had a ghost too. As all kids that age though it was cool to have a ghost in a house that you lived in! Of course the reality of living in a ghost house was far different.

It was almost time for Jason's friends to go, their parents would soon be picking them up. Susan cut up some more cake for Zach and Jack, then put it in goodie bags for them to take home. The kids mentioned nothing to Michael or Susan about what had happened! Just looked at each other not really knowing actually what had just happened! But Zach and Jack thought it was cool anyway.

Zach's and Jack's parents arrived to pick their children up. Jack and Zach both said thank you for having them and that they had a cool house. On the way home, each of the kids said about the house and the cupboard shutting all by itself with Zach inside it.

It was coolest thing going to a haunted house and explained what had happened. The parents didn't take much notice, they just thought it was their imagination and the fact that it was near Halloween. The parents just thought that the three of them had been trying to scare each other kids did that time of year! No such thing as haunted houses, both sets of parents thought.

Not long after Ashley took Jason home, so he could have a bit of a birthday with his auntie and uncle after they had finished work. Jason never mentioned anything to his mum as they walked home. Jason just said that he had a really good party and that his friends enjoyed themselves too.

For the next year the families Christmases and Birthdays went by. Things started happening it seemed all the time, more so for Sarah, each experience getting more intense! But Sarah was strong, although at the time she did not feel strong. Sarah thought she was weak because she was always scared and she could stick up for herself at school, like other kids would. She would allow the kids to tease her and taunt her. Sarah always put herself down and believed what the kids were saying about her.

But Sarah faced bad things that most other children did not. Feeling different Sarah thought was not good. She really didn't like herself, she felt different but being different was ok, this was something she had to figure out for herself.

Things would move in Sarah's room or randomly fall. The footsteps seemed now sometimes to stop by Sarah's bed in the middle of the night, the feeling of someone trying to grab her ankle, as if to drag her out of bed and the feeling of being watched or followed down the stairs, this was Sarah's constant ghostly terrors. In a bizarre way she became used to this, as if it was normal for her. It always seemed to centre on her! No else seemed to have these experiences! At least that's what she thought no one else mentioned anything about the house, nothing like what was happening to her!

But on the other hand, she did have her best friend, who always helped her, she was kind, caring to her and would never harm her. Anna needed Sarah and Sarah needed Anna. Their friendship had helped each other cope with all that was going on. It gave each other strength for now and Sarah's past that she was unaware of at this time.

Michael was unawares of anything as nothing would happen to him, in this haunted house. Maybe it was because he was a man. He would not scare like his wife and children, so this dark entity would leave Michael alone.

Michael and Susan had a lot of bad times through their marriage but they had come through it all, in some respects stronger and loving marriage but this house was started to bleed into their marriage in a scuttle way, so much so that no one noticed the little cracks, not even Michael and Susan.

The rest of the family had noticing small cracks in Michael and Susan's relationship. It had not been easy with the house. Susan bad break down, which she was starting to be herself but this break had left, lasting scars on Susan in the fact that she was becoming slowly more house bound. Emily and Mark had also noticed her break down and now the fact that, she did not really like leaving the house. This in turn put a strain on things. Michael did not know how to deal with his wife's break down or the fact that she did not like leaving the house so much.

This was Edward doing! He did not want this happy loving couple, to be happy He would have to do something about this. It was working on Sarah his scare tack ticks. Now for the parents but they would have to be handled very differently.

That Christmas Diane came back home to live, this way she could keep an eye on her mum and if Sarah needed to be taken to school, she could do so for her mum. Christmas soon came and went along, a quiet family Christmas, with Michael and Susan's birthday both of which was a quiet affair just them Diane and Sarah. Christmas was nice as it always was but something had changed the things that were going on in the house and the relationship with Susan and Michael plus Sarah knew that Father Christmas was just a fairy tale, Christmas had changed.

Soon after it was Diane's 19th birthday and then it was coming up now for Sarah's 9th birthday! Sarah didn't have any friends and after Sarah's 8th Birthday and in between it was Easter again with Easter it was a quiet one. Sarah would still get flashbacks of Easter memories of when she was a child between 6 and 8 years of age but it memories of a childhood she did not have, at least not in this life but was set in a different time! This would leave Sarah feeling puzzled.

The family had a few days out like to Weston or a day in the park with a picnic, or Ashley would come up with Jason. Sarah and Jason would just play outside in the warm spring sun. Sarah's 8th Birthday being a Birthday would much rather forget, she was hoping that her 9th birthday would be a lot better.

Lucy and Tom were not that keen in coming to the house again for Sarah's party, they made an excuse that they were busy. Michael and Susan decided to do something different, rather than a party. They were going to take them and the kids to the harvester for a meal.

Susan visited her mum with Sarah. She wanted her mum to come to this meal too. Susan would normally visit on the half term weeks or in the week every other week when Sarah was at school. Emily and Mark visited their mum too, again every other week. Hilary was slowly getting over her husbands death but to hard for her as they were together for 55 years; which was a long time to spend with someone! Hilary would still get upset at times. Hilary was 76 years old and she was starting to get forgetful at first nothing was thought about it, probably due to their mum getting older.

Susan and Michael had been invited to a wedding it was Maggie and Keith Barns son, he was getting remarried as his last marriage did not work out. Danny had met a lady called Jennifer Hallow. Karen liked her dad's girlfriend too. They been courting for about a year and decided to tie the knot, Susan, Michael and their kids had been invited to it. This would be something else that would be a pleasure.

Maggie son Danny liked the Jones and knew that they been through some tough times. He thought maybe this would be a nice way to take their mind off their troubles just for a day. At home for a couple of weeks before the wedding the paranormal activity seemed to calm down a little for Sarah around her 9th birthday.

For Sarah 9th it was just the family, Sarah really was not in the mood for a big party. With things calming down this made her feel more concerned as it normally meant something big would happen when things started up again. This made her feel slightly more puzzled but this entity was bidding his time. He had all the time in world to pull this family apart and plan his next move. He done this to many families in the past that lived there.

Sarah thought it was all over but little did she know, as things were happening to her brother, Sarah thought he was just drawing images in his head but he had been talking about it to his teacher unbeknown to his family, things were about to get worse and it was more than pictures in his head . . . .

CHAPTER 15

A friend of Danny's family had offered to do the photos Mr Lee Mills. He was very good with photography and had his own business. He had offered to do the wedding photographs for free as he was a mate. The Jones family meet Danny and his mum and dad down the church, apart from Sarah who was a bridesmaid. She went in the wedding car with the other bridesmaids.

Sarah did not think about the house much that day, too many other things to think of. It was the first time Sarah had been a bridesmaid. It gave a warm happy feeling. Sarah got ready at Maggie and Keith Barns house with the help of her mum, Jennifer was getting ready their too along with the rest of the bridesmaids. Danny was getting ready at his best mans house. 'Jennifer looked beautiful, a long fitted crimson white dress' Sarah thought to herself. They were ready in the nick of time as the wedding car turned up.

Meanwhile at the church all of the guests, family and friends of both the bride and groom were waiting, the groom nervously waiting inside the church with the best man. Jennifer arrived on time, she too was also very nervous but excited too. Hopefully this would be third time lucky for her, her past relationships did not bow too well.

The ceremony was lovely all went off without any problems. It was photo time now with the bride, groom and the family and friends in the church gardens. It was a lovely warm day in mid June, bright sun and blues skies, perfect for a photo shoot.

As Lee was taking different photos Sarah felt uneasy, a sick feeling in the pit of her stomach, from the corner of Sarah's eye in the very far side of the garden of the church an uninvited guest, she noticed a dark figure, it was faint.

Sarah knew that it was Edward Anna's father, what was he doing here? She felt that he was watching her, following her, this almost brought her to tears why would he not leave her alone, just for one day. But she held them back for the sake of the wedding day. She could feel him laughing at her.

Susan noticed her daughter was distant and kept staring over to the far side of the churches gardens. She could see that Sarah looked upset. Susan was concerned by this but knew that this was not the best time to discuss what the matter was.

Susan would have a word with her later on her own. Something was defiantly distressing her. The photo shoot lasted for about an hour. Then it was time for the reception, which Danny's parents had paid for. It was going to be held in a local pub in a private function room. The food was really good and the day went well.

The wedding day was a success but Sarah experience in the church grounds would not leave her mind. She knew that this entity would not leave her alone ever.

Jennifer and Danny really enjoyed their day it was so special for them having their family and their friends to celebrate their big day, the day that Jennifer became Mrs Jennifer Barns.

Their honeymoon was the very next day they were off to sunny Spain sun, sea and Sangria!!! It was a nice day apart from Sarah experience at the photo shoot. Jennifer and Danny were really happy together. It was a lovely day for the most part for Sarah. The rest of the Jones family enjoyed it too.

Harry was getting on well in New Zealand, he called the family every other week, while he was living there to let family know he doing ok and that he was going to be a dad his wife was pregnant with twins and was due to drop in a matter of weeks. The family was growing, with family over New Zealand.

That weekend Jason was going to stay over his Nan and granddad's house. Diane and Ashley had a holiday book for a week in a two bed caravan at Exmouth, the weather was good for them, which was even better as British weather being British weather, not always that good.

Jason enjoyed staying with his granddad, Nan and his half sister, it was nice and they had the swimming pool out, which was even better and lots of simple outdoor games. Like rounder's, space hopper races and playing on the swing. It was going to be fun Jason thought to himself, although he did have school but it got dark after bedtime so it gave him chance to play outside with his sister.

One night in the week that Jason stayed up his Grandparents and Sarah after Jason had been a school, after all the family had gone to bed. Jason was a little restless during the night unknowing to the rest of the family, he was having a visit from Anna's father in his dreams but everyone was fast asleep, so no really noticed that he was not having a brilliant nights sleep.

The house was dark and creepy. Sarah woke up she had that uneasy feeling again 'oh no' she thought here we go again. The heavy footsteps started slowly up the stairs, Anna would not talk either. It lasted for just a few minutes but it felt a lot longer to Sarah, Jason slept through the footsteps.

The next day Sarah decided she was going to tell her mum and dad. She could not keep this secret any longer too much had been going on for too long! Sarah was going to tell them everything. That day after school and tea, when she knew her brother was too busy upstairs playing in his room. Sarah plucked up the courage to tell her mum and dad.

"Mum, dad I have got something to tell you? I know you might think I am making this up but I swear I am not" Sarah continued "Our house is haunted by a little girl and her father who is a really, really bad man". But her parents did not believe her. Sarah wanted her mum and dad's reaction to be different.

"It is just your imagination" Sarah's dad replied, Susan agreed with her husband. They just dismissed her allegations of the house being haunted! She did not know where to turn now 'What am I going to do?' she thought feeling pretty freaked out by everything, she didn't know which way to turn. As for now, it was not just Anna's father that was just one of the problems. There was something else there.

Sarah Knew that there was something outside in the dead of night but she had forgotten that she had seen. It almost as if her mind had stored it away. It was frightening for her to remember, too much for mind to cope with this image. She still knew that there was something there, a shadow in the darkness. Also the figures in her room, she would see the shadows. That was just her mind playing tricks, shadows can look frightening at night' that what she told herself.

Unknowing to Sarah, her mum had seen the little girl herself one night a long time ago in the same room as before Sarah had that room. It was her mum and dad's room at the time, Susan had seen this little girl just before Sarah was born. Susan did feel as if there was something in their house apart this spirit of this little girl.

Anna had floated across the room in front of Susan and just went through one of walls, vanished into thin air. Susan had only seen her once. She knew that in part it might be her fault. What she did with her friends in the house when she was 18, trying to contact spirits through the wee gee board. Something was always there in the background but doing that had invited this entity in. This made Susan feel uncomfortable at times too but thought if they did not speak of it. It would all go away in the end.

Sarah's dad did not want to know and he did not believe in ghosts, Michael was the septic of the family seeing is believing Michael would always say to himself that was his motto, But in life it not always the case, sometimes there are things that can't be seen but they are there!

CHAPTER 16

Jason's week at his Nan's and granddad had gone quickly. His mum Ashley and Auntie Diane, they had returned home from their holiday, also Danny and Jennifer from their honeymoon. They had arranged a get together at Danny's mum and dad's house to look at the wedding photos they had invited Sarah, her mum and dad along. Sarah was a bridesmaid they thought that they, probably want to see the photos of their daughter in her bridesmaids dress.

The evening that the Jones was due, to look at the wedding photos had arrived. Susan, Michael, Diane and Sarah walked over to Maggie and Keith's house. They brought a bottle of wine with them. Maggie had done a little buffet for everyone. The bottle was Susan and Michael's way of saying thank you. It was a nice evening a chance for the Jones to escape their worries. Danny, Jennifer and Karen were already there, Danny and Jennifer looked really tanned and glowing with love for each other. The wedding photos were great. Sarah looked really pretty in her pink checked smocked dress. Danny had done two sets of photos, one of them, one for Susan so she could show her family.

Danny and Jennifer were going to have a house warming party and the Jones had been invited. This was a chance to show their new house off, that they had just moved into before their honeymoon. Susan, Michael, Diane, Ashley with Jason, Antony with Susie and Sarah, had all been invited. They were going to have it roughly in a few months time to give themselves chance to get organised with their house. A new house, with a new life, for Danny and his daughter Karen with Jennifer, who would now be Karen's step mum!

Antony and his wife were getting on well in their home too. Diane was still back living with her mum and dad. She wanted to be there for her parents. Ashley, Antony and Diane were all grown up now with their own lives. Even Diane was always busy with something. Emily with Jessica, Mark with Nicole came round later on in the week to see the photos on an evening. This was also a chance for Susan to catch up with her brother and sister.

Emily still didn't like the house and always had that uncomfortable feeling of being watched, when she went to the bathroom or upstairs but nothing more. So she tolerated the house. Mark and Emily liked the photos but most of all, it was nice to see their sister also their nieces too. Diane was sat in the living room downstairs, joining in the conversation with her Auntie and Uncle while Sarah watch telly and did some homework downstairs.

"You are getting taller each time I see you Diane" Emily commented Diane was a tall and slim girl, tall like her brother Antony. Diane smiled at her Auntie, she liked being tall, Diane was lucky. Sarah finished her homework and herself, Jessica and Nicole chatted about different things, Nicole was 10 years and Jessica was 9 years by this time.

"Sarah keeps looking like her real dad, day by day" Emily said to her sister and brother, Michael came in with coffees and teas for the family, Emily said this. Michael never liked anyone mentioning Sarah real dad, he felt that Sarah was his daughter. But the family had always been open to Sarah about her real dad.

Sarah's dad Michael had poured some lemonade for the girls. Sarah went upstairs with their drinks to listen to some music in her room with Jessica and Nicole as they had brought some tapes over, they played and chatted, Sarah was getting on with her cousins a lot better now, they were actually close now!

"How is Sarah? She seems quieter than normal lately!" Emily enquired. Before Susan had a chance to answer, Michael chipped in.

"Yeah she is fine, just adjusting to her new school" Michael insisting that everything was fine. Susan gave her husband a displeased look and so did his daughter Diane.

"How are you coping with everything?" Emily said than added "BEFORE YOU SAY ANYTHING I did ask my sister that question!"

Michael was quite taken back by what his sister in law had just said. Just gave her a look as if to say 'OK, calm down'

"Well I'm ok I get good and bad days! Sarah is not doing that well she wont say but I think something is bothering her, I have asked but she insists that all is ok" Susan said as Diane looked over to her mum.

"Yes, I know I sense it too with Sarah but have tried to talk to her as well, she says she ok, will just have to let her come to us, your not that good either, you never seem to want to go out and when you do you panic!" Diane said being honest with her Auntie and Uncle as she knew her parents would not be honest and pretend everything was ok.

"Well I will get better but I just need time, Sarah she knows that I am here if she needs to talk, I have always told her that" Susan said in response in a way she felt guilty for feeling like she did. She knew the family was worried about her. This made the feeling of panic, worse by her feeling more stressed.

"Well we are all here for you, Susan and Sarah" Michael said smiling at his wife as if it all just so simple.

"We are here to support you sis" Emily added to give her sister comfort.

Emily and Mark stayed till about half seven as it was a school night so they had to get their kids home. It was nice for the family to catch on things. But it was time for them to go home. They all said their goodbyes and went home.

The next few weeks Sarah would here these footsteps not every night. Diane, Susan and Michael would never hear them. They were always sound a sleep, as they would happen in the middle of the night. One of those nights Anna spoke to Sarah to warn her "Those footsteps you here in the night is my father, he does not like me speaking to you. It makes him angry, when you talk about him!" Anna added "Please don't talk about him"

Sarah replied "Ok, I understand but if I don't talk about him, can we still be friends? I have missed you so much. You're the only person who understands me!"

"Yes, I would like that. You are the only friend that I have, would you like to see me!" Anna asked in a soft kind voice.

"Yes I would, please" Sarah replied smiling, she had talked to this little girl for so long but never seen her. Sarah had seen her once before but it was one of those memories her mind hid from herself.

Then Anna revealed herself this time more stronger image! Anna was same age as Sarah about 9 years old with pale shoulder length blonde hair, blue eyes and was wearing an old Victorian long flowing white nightdress with lace around the high collar and bottom of the long sleeves. Anna had calming and lovely aluminous pale blue light all around her that lit the room around them. Like an angel sent down from above. Sarah felt very special to been able to see Anna. Anna must felt that she could trust Sarah enough to allow Sarah to see her. Sarah had a warm happy feeling inside. There was also something strangely filmier about Anna, in fact Sarah had always felt this way even when she could not see Anna and it was just her voice that Sarah heard. As if she had met Anna before, in another life!

Anna said 'goodnight' then faded away slowly into the darkness of Sarah's room. Anna never left the room, that night. There was a special bond between Anna and Sarah, they both emphasize with each other. They got each other!

There were more footsteps that night for a change! Anna said she would stay with Sarah while she slept so Sarah could feel a bit safer. Sarah slowly drifted off to sleep in the comfort that Anna was there. The night was once again silent and calm for now.

Things were getting more eerie and sincere in the house, Edward's ghost had more intent now than before, this was always worrying for Sarah as she just didn't know what on earth to except next! It felt at times like being on a never ending emotional rollercoaster! He had managed to just scare her up until now. He had still not run this family out of their home. This was still a family, a strong family and always managed to get through all their troubles.

Sarah hated school but she did walk to school with her big sister. Which was nice, gave a little bit confidence just enough to help her through the day, it was someone to talk to on the way to school. Not about school, or the house, other things it was a detraction; for Sarah when her sister was with her. Diane would pick her up too from school. Susan was finding it difficult to leave home.

As per normal the kids were still teasing Sarah. She did try not to take any notice but it was hard. She liked her teacher they were always kind to her, they knew the other kids always gave her a rough time. At least she was doing well in terms of her work and homework. Her school report was always very good. Jason was doing well at school too despite his bad dreams! Jason was a happy child.

It was once again near the weekend a Friday night. Fridays and Saturdays, the Jones favourite nights! Sarah's dad was normally home early on a Friday and did not work weekends, they could all spend quality time as a family. It was joyful and fun times when the family did things together, Sarah loved all her family so very much and Sarah always felt loved too. Antony would sometimes pop over on an evening sometimes with Susie or sometimes without. Susan got on really well with Susie, she the prefect daughter in law.

Sarah family were complicated to explain to others though. Sarah always dreaded doing the family tree, she was adopted and her dad was in foster care. She had no idea about her dad's side and neither did he. But she would not change her family for anything. It was special family, different but very special to her in any case.

The Jones never had loads of money just enough to get by, which to Michael and Susan that was fine, they had all fashioned values. That it time you spend together as a family not the materialistic things you buy for and quality of time. Susan and Michael would try and think of creative ways to give Sarah a nice few days without spending to much and also when Jason came up to stay.

Which Jason and Sarah and the rest of the kids growing up, didn't really mind that their mum and dad could not afford to take them out all the time, the fact that they were together as a family was important to all of them. Often on a weekend the board games would come out to like Monopoly, Connect four and snakes and ladders. None of the kids like losing, so what start of as a good game would normally land up someone being in a mood for not winning, which Susan always tried to drum it in to her kids 'that it not just about the winning but taking part that counts'.

Thank goodness it was the weekend! Ashley came down with Jason they were going to stay over. Antony was going to come down as well but had to work late. Diane was home too she had a day off, Michael came in from work. The five of them sat round to have tea. Susan had cooked chicken and rice with salad, with angel cake and strawberry angel delight for afters, it was yummy as normal.

Then Ashley gave Jason a bath while Susan and Michael sat down to watch telly. Sarah sat by her dad, she had done some of her homework.

After Jason bath they all sat downstairs. It was a nice evening a family get together, Maggie pop over too for a coffee. She wanted to let Susan know that the house warmer that her son and daughter in law was going to be later, than what they had planned as they were still sorting out things in their new house.

Maggie did tell them a bit about the house, as both Danny and Jennifer worked, they had a nice house a four bedroom detached house with a pool and games room, which Sarah and Jason thought that was cool. Maggie just stayed for an hour and went home. She was going out with her husband for something to eat. Maggie said that she would let the family know when the house warming was.

It was movie night Susan had got two videos for them all to watch. Michael on his way home had got some popcorn and snacks, in the news agents just down the road from their house. It was a really good evening and it took Sarah's mind of things. The film was brilliant, it had tired Sarah and Jason, time was getting on by the time the films finished, it was about quarter to eleven but now it was bedtime.

They all went to bed as by this time it was getting really late. Ashley slept in with Jason in the spare room. Diane slept on the sofa, she didn't mind. Sarah went to bed wondering 'what on earth would happen this time' Sarah fell into a deep sleep. In her sleep, she started having a dream like her brother but different, very different!

This was about their house but the house was very old and dated, it felt that it was a long time ago. The rooms of the house were a little different, everything and every room a lot older. It felt it was set in the Victorian times with old furniture and beams across the rooms.

The cupboard was in the dream too but was in fact a secret staircase that went under the house into a dark cold old cellar with had a series of tunnel like an oubliette that seemed to be under the house. Which one of these dark tunnels went outside into some fields by a forest! There were fields, a few little dwellings dotted around the big open fields, also not that far away was a manor house with wide open space. This was definitely a long time ago. Almost like a village, certainly not a town back then.

In this dream that was a nightmare. It would change there was something chasing Sarah that was determined to get her. It chased her through the long grass of the fields near the house. However fast she was, she could not run fast enough. She could feel her heart beating faster and faster, her pulse racing and her chest getting tight, like she was fighting for last breathe!

Then Sarah woke up with sweats and shaking. Sarah could feel her night clothes all sweaty and heart was racing still from the nightmare, the nightmare felt like it was real, she felt frightened for her life. What did this nightmare mean? This really scared her it felt so real! Not like a dream.

The next night, things went from bad to worse. At first it just started as her normal routine after another bad day at school, she had managed to keep one friend at school by this time. Tracy Kindle was still talking to Sarah but she was not a close friend, well not as close with Anna. Even with a friend, school was never wonderful, Sarah would still get teased, so it was always a bad day at school.

Sarah had her tea did her homework and went to bed early. She had not had a good the night before due to her nightmare. Susan had noticed a change in her daughter, she was now started to get concerned for her. Sarah was becoming withdrawn and losing confidence, low self esteem. Susan had decided to have a word with her husband the next day after he had finished work, see what he thought about Sarah becoming withdrawn and less talkative!

That night Sarah woke up in the middle of the night. As she would always want to go a toilet in the night, she hated this happening. She always felt something was there and now after her nightmare, this made her feel more afraid but she had to go. The feeling of fear came over her, her palms sweaty and heart was pounding hard and fast, she felt like crying.

Sarah got up ran downstairs as fast as her legs could go, to the toilet then ran upstairs after straight into bed. Trying not to think of what had followed her all the way down the stairs and all the way up the stairs! Even though she could feel his cold breathe on her back ever step she took, 'that was horrible' she thought.

Sarah was drifting off to sleep, it was late about half one in the morning, she was so tired by not having a lot of sleep the night before! Sarah was awoken by the footsteps once again coming up the stairs. 'OH NO' Sarah thought. These footsteps would normally stop at the top of the stairs but this time they didn't, this time her bedroom door that she had close to, opened wide. She knew something was there! She heard something getting closer and closer to her. This spirit had malicious intention on its mind! Sarah hide under the duvet, hoping it would go away and leave her alone. If she hide and keep really still, pretending to sleep but no not this time!

All of a sudden she felt cold icy hands on her around her ankles that happened to be sticking out at the end of the bed. Sarah felt her angles being pulled and tugged. Something was trying to drag her out of bed. Sarah was terrified and tried to hang on to the bed as tight as she could, she tried to kick out hard with her feet, hoping to kick what had her ankle tight off of her but this force was too strong for her. Sarah's duvet flew off the bed; she still hung on to the bed tight, Sarah was not letting go for anything. "Let me go, please" Sarah screamed. "Why are you doing this to me?"

Then she heard a deep voice whisper "You will die this time Sara, but slowly" the voice said in a menacing tone.

Sarah mum and dad came rushing in, when they heard their daughter shouting. Diane was oblivious to what had happened to her sister, she was in a real deep sleep. When they came in the bad presence had gone, it did not want any witnesses to what just happened to Sarah. They saw that her duvet was on the floor and she was half way off the bed.

"WHAT ON EARTH is wrong" Susan asked she could see her daughter was in a state, she could see in her daughter's eyes that something had scared the living daylights out of her. Something terrorised her daughter!

"It was a bad nightmare" Sarah said she was too afraid to say anything. But she did ask, if she could sleep in with her mum and dad. As they could see that Sarah had some sort of a scare they agreed. They both were worried about their daughter. They never see her shaken as this.

Michael said that he would sleep in Sarah's bed so his wife and Sarah could have their big bed. That night Sarah could not settle, she cuddled into her mum this had really scared her, like the time when she was push under the water in the bath. Susan was really worried. She could tell that her daughter was really freaked out by something.

Sarah had to talk to someone she could not cope with this all alone anymore! Even though she had Anna, she knew that Anna was very nervous to speak of certain things. So Sarah decided she would speak to her mother finally and tell her everything, well nearly everything! Even though she was unsure of her mother reaction surely, after telling her all that she knew and her nightmare; Sarah's mum would have to believe her. Sarah though to herself 'Right I am telling my mum everything on Monday, I have an inset day, my dad and sister will be at work, it just be me and mum. I can have a proper talk with her'

The next day Susan was due to have a chat with Michael, she would do this after tea later, when Sarah was upstairs playing or doing something. She wanted a quiet word alone with Michael. Then she would try and get to the bottom of what was the real problem from her daughter, she knew this was not just a nightmare.

Michael went to work as normal and Diane took Sarah to school, after she went straight to work. Susan had her sister Emily and her friend Maggie coming round that morning for coffee. Susan told them about Sarah to get their take on things.

She told them that Sarah screamed in the night. When she and her husband went into Sarah's room the covers were on the floor, she was halfway out of her bed clinging to the bedposts. Also that Sarah was shaking like a leaf. But Michael had said it was just a bad nightmare that she had.

Emily was not really shocked in one way. She had her own ghostly experience in the house. For Maggie she never herself had much experience, apart from the footsteps she had heard sometimes, when she had stayed over and that the feeling of being watched from the top of the stairs. Everyone felt that also, Maggie had never forgotten what they did with a few friends in that house when they were 18, 19 years old with the Wee gee board. Emily and Maggie knew there was something there.

They both agreed that it was a good idea to have a chat with her husband and with Sarah but separately. They also knew that Michael did not believe about this sort of thing but whether or not he did, that was besides the point something was affecting their daughter and needed to be talked about.

This was about Sarah and what she needed right now, the strength of the family behind her. Sarah did not feel strong enough to take it alone anymore. She was only an 9 year's old little girl and had these experiences as long as she could remember. It was getting worse week by week, month after month.

Emily and Maggie went back home lunchtime, it would be a few hours then Sarah would be coming home with Diane. Susan would have to have this chat to Michael about Sarah. In the mean time Susan just pottered around doing some cleaning and tidying until that time, to keep herself busy.

Diane picked up Sarah and came home. Susan by the time she had done what she needed to do in the house. It was Friday by this time which helped in one way. It would give Michael chance to think things over, after Susan talk through the weekend.

Sarah and Diane came back to their home. Diane and Sarah could tell that their mum. She had something on her mind, when they got home! Susan was a little quiet as she sorted out tea. Sarah sorted her bag out and got out of her school clothes.

"After tea Diane and Sarah, I need a word with your dad on my own, so if you both can go in your room for an hour after tea, then I get your bath sorted, Sarah" Susan said to her daughters being very vague of what was on her mind. Diane and Sarah looked at each other, wondering what this chat was about!

"OK mum" Sarah replied curious about what the chat was going to be about? Half an hour later Sarah's dad came home and all had tea. Sarah went upstairs after and put her music on, she played with her dolls a little worried by what her mum and dad were going to talk about. Susan had tided up and went to the living where Michael was watching telly.

"Ok no worries mum" Diane said looking over to her dad and went upstairs, just listened to some music.

"I need to talk to you about Sarah" Susan said in a straight talking manor.

"Oh this is not about the other night!" Michael responded as if to say oh what now, kind of way.

"I know she said it was a nightmare but I know Sarah, that's not it! Something is going on with Sarah. She seemed to be too scared to say what!" Susan said in a slightly raised tone.

"Well if there's something, we have already said that we are there for her. If she doesn't want to talk, we can't force her. Its just school, kids can be cruel" Michael said trying to take the emphasis off the house.

Michael was just not having any of it about the house which Susan half expected with him. The next was to talk to Sarah. Susan was not happy leaving things as they were. Even if Michael did want to push it aside and pretend all was fine. Susan felt as sometimes, she could not talk to her husband.

"Well you might be happy leaving it I'm not. I know it not just about school. You know it too!" Susan said in response, Susan was frustrated with Michael.

"Well talk to her then, if it's about this house there is nothing wrong with it" Michael answered back. He knew it would be the house. He just did not want to know.

Susan just sat in the arm chair in a mood. She would have a talk with Sarah at some point. She was a bit annoyed with her husband at that time with his lack of understanding, with their daughter.

Susan had decided that she was going to talk to Sarah over the weekend, not knowing that Sarah was actually going to talk to her mum about things on the Monday, when her dad was at work. Sarah knew that her dad, as much as she loved him and knew that he loved her. Her dad simply did not in anyway believe in that sort of thing and nothing would persuade him otherwise.

For the whole evening Sarah's mum and dad, did not talk to one another. Susan sorted out Sarah bath, Sarah heard the slightly raised voices from upstairs; Diane didn't hear anything as she had her music fairly loud. Sarah could not tell what they were saying though. Sarah had her bath then put her pyjamas on, then went and sat downstairs to watch the soaps with her mum and dad. Diane came downstairs too to watch the soaps as well. Diane could tell that her mum and dad had been having words. She looked over to her little sister and smiled, to give a bit of reassurance that it would all be ok.

Sarah could feel that her mum and dad were not happy with each other. Even when they had a disagreement which was not that often they did not take long to make up than an hour. It all be forgotten about, yes in the end they speak that night but it was a bit longer than an hour!

Susan could tell that Sarah and Diane were picking up on the vibe that their mum and dad were not speaking. Susan looked over to her husband and smiled, she did love him. He was annoying sometimes were he was a little narrow minded in that sense.

Michael felt his wife looking over at him turned and smiled back, he could never stay angry with his wife for that long, Michael tapped the sofa as if to invite his wife over to sit by him and she did, they cuddled and smiled over to Sarah and Diane, who were really happy to see that their mum and dad seemed to be ok at last.

Sarah came over and sat on the other side by her dad, the three of them sat and watched the rest of the soaps together, before time for Sarah to go to bed. Diane stayed downstairs too. It was nice to see their mum and speaking again.

The next day Susan went into Sarah in the morning, Michael was still a sleep as was Diane but Sarah and Susan were a wake. Susan wanted to have a chat to Sarah before she sorted out every ones breakfast. After they had their talk Susan had planned a full English breakfast.

"Morning sleepy head" Susan said as she went into her daughter's room to give her a kiss and a cuddle good morning. Susan left the curtains pulled too.

"Morning mum" Sarah said rubbing her eyes. She was still a little tired.

"Is everything really ok? I know you and lately you are not yourself!" Susan queried her daughter in soft and kind tone. Underneath very worried about her.

"Yes I'm ok mum, just don't like school that much, it's hard" Sarah said she did not want to anything yet. She wanted to talk to her mum when dad and sister were at work as her dad would not understand. She did not want to worry her big sister.

"ARE YOU SURE it's just school? There's nothing you want to say? It is just the other night it looked more than just a nightmare! You were half way off the bed and clinging on to the bed post, your duvet was on the floor!" Susan said trying hard to understand what was going on.

"Mum it was just a really bad nightmare, I'm really sorry if I made you worry about me" Sarah replied, Sarah really wanted to tell her the truth but just felt it was not the right time plus her brother was due over later with Ashley. She wanted to hopefully enjoy her weekend, not have to think about that at least not until Monday.

"OK but you know that I 'am here for you if you need to talk" Susan said trying to be supportive to her daughter with another hug.

Susan left Sarah's room and went downstairs, while Sarah got dressed. Michael got up shortly after to the smell of sizzling bacon, ten minutes after Diane came down. They all got up and had breakfast. Sarah's mum and dad were on speaking terms once more and they looked happy.

Lunchtime Jason and Ashley came over for lunch and tea, it was a nice day. Sarah and Jason played outside most of the day. They played with Felix and Tabby! They both came back in when it was teatime. Sarah and Jason had a snack too in the garden of runner beans. Sarah's dad runner beans, they had a little buffet for tea. Sarah and Jason watched telly, Jason and Ashley stayed a little bit after tea, so Jason could watch Dr Who on telly with his big sister then they went home.

Sarah had enjoyed her day, she knew that her talk with her mum was looming. The next day was Sunday it was normally a relaxing day. For Sarah it was not, she tried to hide that fact that she was a little nervous and she hid it well.

That day went rather quickly and over the course of that weekend, nothing that bad happened in the house. Just the feeling of being watched and the footsteps but they did not come to her bedside this time.

Although Anna was quiet that weekend, she had warned Sarah not to speak of her father. Not in a nasty way, just being a friend and trying to keep Sarah safe from the clutches of her father. Anna loved her father but knew what he capable of also!

Monday came Diane didn't have to walk Sarah to school, she normally would. Sarah had no school that day, Michael and Diane had to go to work. Sarah prepared herself to speak to her mum. She let her mum do the normal set of cleaning that her mum did which took about three quarters of an hour. This would give Sarah time to think of how she would word, most of what had been happening!

Sarah also knew that by telling her mum Anna's father would make Sarah pay, in one way or another. She could not deal with it anymore on her own, it was intense by now.

Sarah was really unnerved! She could not wait to get this off her chest. She had been keeping everything a secret for so long and now she was about to tell her mum absolutely all that had been going on, well most of it! Sarah heard her mum come down stairs from tidying. Susan had put the kettle on in the kitchen. Sarah waited till her mum had got herself a hot drink and had come in to sit down to watch her telly.

Sarah had made a point before her mum did the cleaning, that she wanted to tell her mum something important after her mum done what she needed to do.

"I am ready for you now Sarah. Did you say you wanted to have a talk" Susan asked her daughter. As she could tell that something had been playing on her daughter's mind for a while.

"Yes, I do mum" Sarah replied. Sarah and her mum sat downstairs on the sofa. Susan could tell that something was really troubling her daughter. Susan held Sarah hands for reassurance.

"What's the matter?" Susan asked for concern for her child, trying to comfort her "You can tell me anything, I am there for you, like I have always said"

Sarah took a deep breathe and told her mum most of what had been going on in the house. Sarah was excepting her mum to turn round and say 'it is just your mind playing tricks on you' like she did around Sarah 8th birthday party but to Sarah surprise she didn't instead she understood.

"The house is haunted by a little girl and her father, the little girl is my friend but her father scares me, I swear to you I am not making this up!" Sarah started of saying, to see what her mum's reaction was.

"Why didn't you say anything when I ask you last" Susan said first then added, Sarah looking a bit shocked by her mum's next line.

"I know about the little girl, I seen her a few years ago just before you were born" Susan said and gave her daughter a big supportive hug. Sarah was shocked by this statement. She thought her mum and dad did not believe her. After all this time she had said nothing to her. Sarah felt slightly hurt by this.

"Why! Did you not say anything to me, mum? As that why I didn't tell you when you spoke to me last on the weekend. I thought you not believe me! When I told you and dad that time before, you and dad dismissed it" Sarah asked feeling very confused and a little hurt, she though that her mum always told her everything.

"I could not say anything with your dad and your sister a round. You know what your dad's is like with that sort of thing! It is best to leave things like this alone. It can only lead to trouble". Susan said sternly to her daughter. She was concerned for all her children and Grandson. So she had kept her encounter with the girl a secret for all those years. Susan hoped it would go away, she also unbeknown to Sarah had been hearing the footsteps too.

"I CAN'T it gone too far for that now! He is there all the time" Sarah said feeling tears welling up but holding them back.

"You have to try" Susan said "I know it's hard and I will help you and support you. You have to push it out of your mind" Susan was so concerned about her daughter welfare. She knew that this entity was very bad news!

Susan gave her daughter a cuddle. Sarah went to her room for a bit. She told her mum, that she was going to be ok and said that was going listen to some music to take her mind off things.

Sarah went to her room she felt confused, hurt and upset by her mum, she did understand that her mum did not say anything because her mum just wanted to protect her from getting hurt. It still hurt to think mum kept this from her. Sarah could not hold back the tears. Sarah turned her music to drown out the sound of her sobbing. She felt alone now. Sarah just didn't know what to do!

Susan was not happy either she was very fearful for her daughter by now, she knew that there was a lot more to Sarah story and knew that her daughter was not ok. This entity had been taunting her daughter. She too did not know what to do for the best!

This house had always been haunted everyone in the family knew it, even if they not told each other about each others experiences, before now. It had not harmed or threatened anyone up until now.

In fact Jones family had got use to living in a haunted house and did not really think anything of it! It never bothered them. Yes at times they felt uncomfortable but not much more than that. It seemed to change when Sarah came along! This was their family home! Susan did not ever want to leave. In one way why should she leave this house it was their house! It was their children's home too that they had grown up in that house.

CHAPTER 17

The next day everyone in the morning did their normal things. Michael got ready for work and went to work, while Sarah got ready for school. Diane walked her little sister to school as she normally did. Diane could see that her sister was distracted by something that was bothering her. When Diane asked her sister if all was ok, Sarah did not say anything just that she was ok. Sarah found it hard to concentrate getting ready for school.

That day Sarah could not stop thinking about the conversation she had with her mum and the nightmare she had, Sarah was quite all through her lessons that day. Sarah was stressed and depressed to, 'what could happen next?' these dreams still puzzled her 'What did these nightmares mean? This entity would not leave her alone why? Why was she such a threat to him? She was just a 9 year old little girl?

Why would she have a dream about the house but the house was different and old? Sarah really did not like her school. Sarah could not do her work either properly. She did try her best to keep her mind focused. Even the teacher told her off for daydreaming.

The normal things that would upset her, like other kids calling her names. Sarah did not take any notice of this name calling, which would normally upset her so very much so that it would make her cry! Sarah was num, felt nothing, complete emptiness. Sarah could not take her mind of everything that was going on at home, it was started to feel like too much on her own!

Sarah was in a daze, a dream world all day not quite with it. She could not just forget about it all, do as her mum did and pretend it was not happening to her. This would not just go away for her.

This entity would never ever leave her alone, the things that were happening to her and the dreams meant something. She would have to figure it out for herself it was obvious no one was going to help her!

Then Sarah thought back to the first day she heard Anna voice 'Anna called Sarah, Sara. And so did Anna's father too just the once Why!' Sarah thought to herself. At the time Sarah thought nothing of it, when Anna had got her name wrong. After all that had gone on her mind was going into overdrive and 'also Anna never mentioned about her father what was so bad about him, when he was alive!'

Anna never said what had happened to her mother Helena only that she died when Anna was very young. What happened to Anna's mother? How did she die? These were just a hand full of questions that were buzzing around in her head. There were still more questions that she had! More questions than answers that was the problem.

All this questions in Sarah head, she needed to know. Maybe these dreams would give her the answers why! Why was Sarah having these nightmares? Sarah felt as if there was a link between these nightmares and what was happening in the house with Anna and her mother Helena. Were their deaths natural, or was there something more sincere at hand here!

A few days later after Sarah came from school with Diane, that day something was not right! Sarah felt that something had happened in the house as soon as she walked through the front door, the house felt different! The atmosphere had change, unnerving. Sarah knew her mum could not say much as Jason was there. He had come over for tea, straight from school with Ashley who had dropped him off as Ashley was going out with a few friends. Diane even felt a change in the house that made her feel tensed too.

Sarah felt very unwelcome in her own home. The house had an eerie and suspicious feel to it. Sarah's mum was quite not her usual self. Susan gave Sarah a kiss on the cheek and a hug like she normally would. Sarah felt as if her mum was very tense and nervous "go and put your school things away before we have tea" Susan asked as she gazed up the stairs! Jason would not go upstairs either, like he felt something very wrong too.

"Are you ok mum? You seem a little on edge! And so does Jason" Diane enquired she could tell that her mum was edgy about something.

"No not really but don't tell Sarah let me speak to her if I need to! I heard a little girl crying coming from Sarah's room when I was up stairs tidying" then she added "when I came downstairs I heard noises in her room bangs, like things were being moved, make sure Sarah safe up there, just go up to the room now" Susan said to her daughter. Susan didn't want Diane to go up there either but Diane was a grown up now, maybe she would be ok.

Ashley was not happy too, she could see that her son was feeling uncomfortable to go upstairs, she wanted to upstairs with her sister but she could not leave her son on his own in the living room. Jason watched telly, while his mum, listened out for any trouble.

Diane could see her mum was shaking "Ok mum, you sit down in living room and go upstairs to Sarah" Diane said trying to pretend to be brave but she was frightened too.

Sarah had gone upstairs to put her things away in her bedroom. It felt very cold in her room like ice the rest of the house was warm; something or someone had been in her room. She knew it was not Anna.

Diane came upstairs into Sarah's room "Are you ok? Shall I stay with you?" Diane asked her little sister, she was worried about Sarah.

"No it's ok I be fine!" Sarah said to keep her sister calm and it make out she was fine being the brave one.

"Well I will just be down stairs with mum if you need me?" Diane said she had to check on her mum as she seemed to be in a state of shock. Diane had noticed that things had moved in Sarah's room.

"Ok sis I will be fine! I will be down in a minute, just putting my school stuff away" Sarah said smiling at her overly concerned big sister, before Diane went down the stairs.

Things had moved in her room too and the cupboard was wide open 'Oh no' she thought in horror, she knew now something had happened. Sarah went to close the cupboard door but it would not close like something trying to stop her from closing it. She felt like something on the other side of the cupboard door was trying to push it open while she was trying to close it. So much so when she let go because the pressure was hurting her hand, it swung open with force.

Sarah felt like she had angered something. She had a real horrible feeling, she felt fiscally sick to her stomach and faint. Sarah felt like something was trying to drain her energy. Something did not want her there in that room. Sarah was not welcome there.

Then Sarah's Barbie house that she had for Christmas by her bed fell on the floor by it's self. This was not natural, the Barbie house falling down. This was not a small doll house; it was about 4 feet high with Barbie furniture in it and dolls.

Sarah then felt very strange it was a very bad feeling, as if she was not alone in the room and it was not her friend Anna. Sarah hairs stood on end. A cold icy stare behind her! The side of her hair move as if something was heavy breathing on her hair. Sarah felt a cold hand on her back, something was trying to tell her in no uncertain terms to get out or else.

All of a sudden she felt the ground from beneath her go. This spirit had pushed her to the floor! She felt intensive force, which caused her to lose her balance, causing her to fall. She felt immediately threatened, it was time to get out of her bedroom her instinct was telling her to run. Plus she really did not want to stick around to find out what would happen next! This was her queue to leave!

Diane, Ashley, Jason and Susan heard the bang from downstairs, when the Barbie house fell and when Sarah fell to the ground too. Susan, Ashley and Diane wanted to go up stairs to see what was going on.

Sarah ran down the stairs, all the while feeling this cold stare following all the way down. A cold chill that went though her bones, a cold hand that felt as it was after her very soul. Susan said nothing to her daughter, just a vague expression on her face. Her mum looked as white as a sheet.

"What were those two bangs we heard? Are you ok Sarah?" Diane asked getting really scared now. Then Sarah turned to her mum and sisters.

"Those bangs I just knocked my stereo on the floor, when I was trying to put things back" she did not want to tell them the whole truth at this time. She could see how freaked out her sister, her real mum and her mum were. Then Sarah added.

"Mum there's something very wrong with this house, it is not good and for some strange reason it does not like me" Sarah in a desperate attempt to get a response from her mother and wondering at the some time 'why her? Why does the father of Anna not like her! Why does she feel so threatened by him and no one else! Sarah could not take it anymore.

"I don't know but your right something did happen to me today" Susan explained, she could see her daughter face it was near to tears.

"What happened mum? Tell me" Sarah asked wondering what was wrong.

"I was cleaning upstairs and I heard a little girl crying in your bedroom" Susan continued "When I went into your room the crying stopped, then I heard the girls voice she said 'tell Sara to stop making my father angry, I don't want anyone to get hurt' that's when I seen the cupboard in your room was wide open. I came downstairs after. Then I heard noises like things being moved around in your room" Susan added.

Ashley and Diane were in shock they didn't want their mum and sister to stay in that house a minute longer. Susan did not want to tell her daughter about what had happened to her that day but as she was nine years old, she knew her daughter was going though similar experiences and that she had seemed to of made friends with this little girl Anna.

Susan felt her daughter was old enough to deal with it better, than she first thought. Susan was quite shaken by this experience but she tried not to show it for her Sarah's sake.

"Oh no" Said Sarah in concern for her mother and feeling slightly confused "But I don't understand that the second time, Anna has called me Sara" Sarah replied rubbing her forehead.

"You know the girls name" Sarah mum asked even though. She had heard to distinct voices coming from her room sometimes, one was Sarah and other sounded like another little girl. Susan knew that there was no else in Sarah's room at the time, just Sarah but it different voices. Ashley and Diane were surprised.

"Yes it is Anna. I talk to Anna most nights unless I hear the heavy footsteps. I am not afraid of her she means me no harm. Anna my age, she listens to me when I need to talk and I listen to her. Her voice is kind and soft" Sarah tried to explain as best she could, about Anna so hopefully, it would ease her mum mind in one way, that the house was not all bad!

"OH right" Susan did not know what to say in response to her daughter's admission that. There was something there in their house, their family home. Susan was slightly disturbed by this!

"I don't like the thought of you Sarah being here" Ashley added with Diane nodding in agreement. Ashley didn't want to leave mum with Jason but did not want to stay there with her son. She knew her dad would be home soon, that would be a good thing.

"We will be ok, your dad is back soon" Susan said giving a false smile.

Diane was due to go to work on a night shift. She didn't want to leave her mum and sister either, Susan reassured her daughters that she and Sarah would be fine and in any case their dad would be home soon. So there would be a man in the house. So reluctantly Diane went to work and Ashley left to go home.

Susan left it after that she had to figure out what the next move was, for her family. Susan knew that Michael would not agree to move, in way he would be right. They were not the ones in the wrong but it was starting to get a little worrying.

CHAPTER 18

By this time it was Christmas again, Jason had his 6th birthday. It was just a quiet family get together for Jason's birthday, as a lot had gone on that year. The family just wanted Jason's birthday to be about the family. Jason didn't mind that it was not some big party as long as he was with his family. Michael and Susan had a quiet anniversary too. Things in the house, was starting to put a stain on this marriage.

Sarah was not in the festive spirit to celebrate Christmas! She had too much going on with school and the house. Jason was still into Christmas being the age he was. For that year they all went over Danny and Jennifer for a belated house warming. It was a week before Christmas and then over her sisters for Christmas day. It would be nice to have things to look forward to for the Joneses. The family was determined to get Susan, Diane and Sarah away from that house as much as possible.

For Christmas it would be no cooking for Susan this time, which was nice for her to have someone else to cook the Christmas dinner and tea! Emily could see that there was something going on with her sister and her family. Emily wanted to get them away from the house for just one night. There was something not right with her sister's house!

It soon came round to Danny and Jennifer's house party. The house was done out lovely with all mod cons, it was very fresh and chic feel to the house; Wooden flooring through out and light and airy rooms with plenty of space. Spot lights all around. In the living room the trimmings were up and big Christmas tree in the bay window of the living/dinning room. The trimming looked again very chic and nice but Sarah thought 'not as nice as when they trimmed up'

Susan was pleased too that for one night, she would not have to worry about her daughter or her Grandson, also the rest of the family. The things that were happening in the house was starting to effect her older and grown up kids. They could see by how Sarah was that things were getting worse and the paranormal activity was increasing. Susan knew deep down there was something seriously unbalanced with the house that once they called home. Something really had to be done.

House warming party went by quickly and a long day that had started from about 6 in the morning till about 1Am the next morning. It was nice for Susan to be able to relax for once! The kids were having a great time too.

At the end of the day the adults settle down in the living room. Having drinks and listening to music and chatting, while the kids played in the games room with toys that they had and playing in the swimming pool. Sarah thought it would be nice to go for a swim after all the food they had that day, while Jason carried on playing with the toys.

Sarah got changed into her costume and went into the swimming pool area. It was indoors and heated which was nice with patio furniture in cream, it looked really smart. It was not huge, just right for a little swim. Jason had a little swim earlier in the day. Jason wanted to carry on playing and did not what to have a swim.

Sarah got in the pool it was nice, warm and peaceful. It was relaxing with just some dim lighting on. It was around about half 5 so it was dark outside. Sarah did a few laps around the pool then relaxed in the pool by the side. Sarah closed her eyes.

Sarah had a real uncomfortable feeling. The feeling she only got when something was about to happen to do with Anna's father, which did not make any sense as she was somewhere else not at home. 'Surely not here' Sarah thought. It should be safe here. Sarah tried to ignore her gut feeling, closed her eyes again, just relaxing at the side of the pool.

Sarah opened her eyes she felt the temperature drop around the pool side, it was difficult to tell as the lights were dim. She was positive she saw a shadow figure at the other side of the pool that moved from left to right.

It could not be any of her family. She would hear them come into the swimming pool. Plus this was a dark mass but in shape of a person. Sarah was frozen again afraid to move.

Sarah was terrified she dare not move! She could feel butterflies in her tummy. A sense of dread, she knew it was him. How could this be! This dark figure started to come closer and closer. Sarah prayed for it to go away.

Sarah tried to call for help but nothing came out, she was in trouble. Then the shadow disappeared with Sarah thinking thank god for that, hoping that it was all over at for now.

Sarah got out of the pool, she had bad feeling that it was dangerous for her health to stay any longer. Sarah listened to her instincts, Sarah was bewildered by this 'it can't be Anna father, surely' Sarah felt uncomfortable all that evening. Nothing else happened but it was something she could not just forget. Another one of Edward's mind games!

Sarah changed back into her clothes and went into the games room with Jason and Karen was there too playing with Jason on the football table! The rest of the evening was fun for everyone. Sarah played for a while then went to find her mum and dad who were mingling in the living room with Danny, Jennifer and other guests.

"Having a good time?" Susan asked her daughter smiling, Sarah's mum looked happy for once and her dad.

Sarah was in shock at what had happened, she didn't tell the truth she was too scared if he could do that to her. What could he do to her family! She could ruin her family's evening as they were enjoying themselves, so Sarah told a white lie.

"Yeah the party is good" Sarah answered hiding her true emotions for her family's sake.

Ashley, Antony, Susie and Diane were enjoying the party too, Antony had arrange a taxi to take them home, all home that night, they got the bus up. But they all had a few drinks so a taxi was the best thing. Diane was a bit tipsy she did however notice that her little sister seemed to be drifting around the adults, not playing like Jason and Karen. Diane could tell that things were still playing on her little sister mind. She had no idea that there was more to it than that! She went over to her sister who was just sat on the sofa watching every one else enjoying themselves . . . .

"Hi how is it going, you don't seem to be enjoying yourself" Diane said out of curiosity smiling at her little sis.

"Yeah I'm ok, just tried" Sarah could not tell her big sister the truth.

"Well we will be going soon, just think soon it be Christmas!" Diane replied trying her best to put a smile on her sister face.

The rest of the family noticed Sarah talking to Diane and wondered if everything was ok with Sarah, as could tell that she looked a little bit unhappy. Susan and Michael went over to Ashley, Antony and Susie as Diane came back over to where they were standing.

"Is Sarah ok?" Susan asked Diane noticing that, she was sat on her own. Just staring out into space!

"Not sure, when I asked if she was ok! She said she was fine" Diane answered back she could tell the family were a little worried.

"Sarah is fine just it has been a long day for her!" Michael being his logical self, he went over to Sarah to give her a cuddle and sit with her.

Diane had told her brother what had happened in the house a few weeks ago with Sarah, what her mum had heard, also the bangs that both heard when they were downstairs and Sarah was upstairs?

The rest of the family kept their eye on Sarah for the rest of their time there. The evening flew round and it nearly time for the taxi to arrive for the Jones. Ashley went and got Jason from the games room, which he was not happy about. He looked very tired as it was about 11ish for a little boy was late.

The taxi arrived five minutes later. They all said their goodbyes and thanked Danny and Jennifer for inviting them. Ashley and Jason were dropped home first, then Susan, Michael, Diane and Sarah, Antony and Susie were dropped off last.

It was a nice evening after that scare. Michael and Susan cuddled up on the sofa. That day Susan was not happy, Susan did have the house on her mind, the stories that her daughter had said also feeling things herself. The feeling of uncertainty was not far from her mind. She knew her daughter well and felt that she was hiding something. Susan also was thinking about what had happened a few weeks ago with herself and then what happened to Sarah when she came home from school that day on her mind too.

'This house was indeed looked like it was haunted! There could be no other explanation' Susan thought to herself, she was very concerned for daughter now. Susan was nearly in tears to think 'what is going to happen next!' Susan thought she knew that her daughter was being affected by that house.

That night Sarah did not sleep well. It was playing on her mind what could of happened next, if she would stayed in that pool, Things were getting more serious now, she also thought to herself 'what next?' Diane did sleep but she was a little uncertain about her sister too.

Christmas time came round once again and for this year it would be different as Susan, Michael and Sarah were going up Emily for Christmas dinner and staying over. After they had opened presents at their house Diane was going over to her sister for Christmas dinner that year. It would be nice a chance to get out of that house.

Christmas morning had arrived Diane and Sarah were up early, followed shortly by their mum and dad. Michael did his usual and lit the fire, Susan put the kettle on.

That day they did not bother much for breakfast, just some toast as they all were going to have a big Christmas dinner. Diane got some smelly sets and make up also some money. Sarah got a new outfit to wear; some dolls and bit of money too, with some colouring books and felt tips pens. They both were very pleased.

Susan and Michael were pleased with what they got too, then after that it was a mad rush to get ready as Emily was coming to pick them up in an hour, she had offered to pop Diane over to Ashley's house too. It was Christmas day there would be no buses.

Leading up to Christmas it was a little calm in the house, these events happened like waves. It would build up and up to a point then calm, then all of sudden intense, the calm before a storm. The footsteps still happened and things would still move. This entity like playing games with peoples emotions and now for the Jones family the mind games were working.

Susan, Michael, Diane and Sarah were ready they all looked really festive and Christmassy, the snow was upon the ground, Sarah looked out of the living room window. Ten minutes later Emily pulled up outside the house, beeped her horn to let them know that she was there and waiting. They went outside as they already had their shoes and coats on raring to go. Diane was dropped off, then it on to Auntie Emily's house. Meanwhile at the Jacksons, Jessica was looking out of the window for her cousin. Peter poured the adults a glass of sherry and a put a mince pie out for everyone, for when they came in of course for kids it would something fizzy or squash to drink.

Five minutes later they had arrived, it would be a nice Christmas day and for Susan a chance to relax, it normally a very hectic day for her. She was not cooking this time. She had offered to help with the buffet for later. Susan was not sort of person to sit down and relax for to long, she felt she had to do her bit to help.

Jessica and Sarah went upstairs to play as Jessica wanted to show Sarah her Christmas presents. While Michael, Susan, Emily and Peter sat downstairs and had their glass of sherry, Emily could relax a little herself as the turkey was in and the potatoes, the veggies were prepared. Emily had her sherry then brought the presents down for her sister, brother in law and Sarah. Susan gave Emily, Peter and Jessica presents. Sarah and Jessica had come down stairs at this time as Jessica saw her mum with the presents.

They opened up their presents and Emily got on with the Christmas dinner. There was a lovely smell coming from the kitchen as the roast turkey was cooking. The day went brilliantly, a good day all in all. Susan enjoyed spending the day and evening with her sister, Peter and Michael were getting on great and Sarah was enjoying her time with her cousin too.

The next day was boxing day their was no need to rush to get up, Emily was going to drop Susan, Michael and Sarah home later on that morning. Susan was going to do a roast but that was for tea. They all would be full up from the amount that they ate Christmas day, so it a snack for lunch and not much for breakfast a slice of toast most probably.

Later on that morning when everyone had got up and adults had a tea or coffee and the kids a squash and Emily felt almost human as it morning after the night before, She dropped Susan, Michael and Sarah home.

Diane was home too, she had walked back. It was a half an hour walk but she needed the fresh air as she slightly hung over. She was drinking the night before with her sister, brother and sister in law. Diane looked how Susan and Michael felt.

The next night when Sarah had gone to bed the nightmares started once again. This time she would feel like it would be more, than just a simple dream but horrible nightmare. Things were increasing a lot now. No one said much that day, it was a nice day but things were not right in the Jones household that Boxing Day.

This nightmare started out as if something or someone was chasing Sarah running through the woods. These woods in her dream were not far from their house. She could never run as fast as she wanted. Sarah did not like this dream! She felt something was going to happen, if her nightmare continued. She woke herself up. Sarah was quite shaken up for the rest of the night and could not settle back to sleep properly in fear of the return of the nightmare and it consequences.

The next day Sarah never mentioned her nightmare just tried to ignore it. Hopefully it would not happen again. She knew that was just wishful thinking. Sarah felt this would not be the end. Christmas was gone for another and under the circumstances it was not a bad Christmas, better than what the Jones family thought it would be.

CHAPTER 19

It was coming up for Michael and Susan birthdays also Diane 20th birthday once again and this time. They spent their birthday at home, a family meal. Diane went out with her sister's for her birthday. With all that was going on Susan and even Michael felt unhappy leaving Sarah. Susan decided on a big family meal, at home with all the family would be better. Michael agreed with Susan and thought a family at home would be a better option, even though Michael had never actually said he was worried, being a proud man.

Soon it would be Easter, the kids always enjoyed Easter they were not religious but it was a happy time plus two weeks off school, even better! Easter egg hunt and lots of chocolate! This year nothing seemed that exciting for Sarah or even Susan and also for Ashley and Diane who were becoming concerned for their family. Things that could not explained in the house, their mum's panic attacks and things that seemed to be going on with Sarah and Jason.

The months seemed to go quickly and with each passing month the nightmares and experiences seem to grow, like it all was building up to something for Sarah. Anna did talk to Sarah as always would not talk certain issues. She was still reluctant to talk about her father. Sarah did not push it. She knew Anna would not talk about her father. This was Anna way of protecting her and Sarah understood this.

It would be a hard and testing time for the Jones family for the next year and beyond. By this time Sarah was coming up for her 10th birthday. This year she did not feel like a party. Sarah just wanted her mum dad and brother with her on her birthday.

Susan was letting all the stresses and worries of the house and general life get on top of her. The nervous brake down that manifest itself happened, after her friends lost their baby boy. Bringing the memory forward, of the loss of Susan and Michael's child had really tolled on Susan. She was getting nervous of going out any where by this time, Susan was not coping.

The rest of the family had been aware of their mum's problem and had tried to support her as much as they could. This was with everything was being to effect Susan and Michael marriage. The cracks were getting deeper and harder to hide from the rest of the family.

Sarah 10th birthday was nice just the six of them, Sarah, her mum and dad, also Diane, Ashley and Jason. The rest of the family just popped their presents into her through the week as her birthday was in the week.

The sun was shinning for her, on her 10th birthday. The warm rays of the sun warmed the house through. There was still a cold feeling about her bedroom and a sense of sadness that Sarah tried desperately to hide from her parents. Almost like a mist of negative feeling had fell upon the house, Sarah felt this although that year. Really from the age between 8 and 9 years old, as time went on she felt as if it was getting worse, leading up to her birthday.

Sarah felt wrong as if she was not meant to be there or anywhere for that matter the wrong time, misplaced. She did not understand at all the reasons for these strong senses that she had. Sarah had never felt right all her life, like she did not belong. It was puzzling and confusing for her. 'Why did she feel this way? Why more strongly after her 9th birthday!' Sarah thought to herself. Things seemed to happen more to her from her 9th birthday, more intense! This strong feeling would not go away!

Sarah had a really nice 10th birthday Susan had tried her best to make her 10th birthday, a really nice birthday but for Sarah too much was going on in the house, too many confusing thoughts. She could see things were affecting her mum too. Sarah was worried about her mum. She knew as did the rest of the family their mum was becoming agoraphobic, her mum could not go out like that. She got panic attacks, if she had to go out for long.

After her birthday about two nights later, Sarah fell asleep after her normal routine of the day. Sarah had decided on an early night, that night, the night before she had not had a good night sleep, once again with things playing on her mind. It would Saturday the next day. Sarah would be able stay in bed a little. Hopefully that night the ghost of Edward would leave her alone, just for one night!

As she was in her deep sleep, she had one of her nightmares again, this time it was a dream were she was running from something or someone. The faster she ran the harder it was to run as if something was trying to stop her from getting away. Something was really wrong, she knew that she had to get away something terrible would happen to her if she did not!

Sarah held her chest it felt so tight, she could hardly breath as if something was taking her very breathe away, reaching out to her very heart and her soul. Again before whatever was trying to get her, it had managed to get her. Then she woke up with shock, she felt a cold hand try to grab her leg and when she did awake something felt different. When something had her leg at first she was not to sure if she dreaming it or if it was real!

Sarah was shaking she was about to call out to her mum, when she realised the top of her nightdress was wet. She touched what appeared to feel like it was sweat on her nightdress, her heart was still pounding and chest still tight, it was hurting too for some reason.

As she put her hand up to see what it was, she was horrified! It looked like blood. It was dark in colour, it was hard to see. It was night time and for some other reason, when she tried to get up to see what this was properly by turning on a light. She could not move her legs, like she was pinned to the bed! Something did not want her to move, she could feel pressure from something holding her down. This was no dream! This was happening to her! Her whole body was pinned to the bed, she had felt herself being pinned to the bed on more than one occasion but this different; Sarah was terrified what was going to happen next.

Her chest got tighter she realised. This that appeared to be blood was indeed blood! She looked down to her chest and saw strangely, what looked like three claws or scratch marks going down her chest by her heart, this really frightened her. Sarah did not know what to do! She was too afraid to do anything!

Sarah wanted to call for her mum or dad, she knew that it was not safe and she feared they might get hurt. She felt her cold tears roll down her face, she was more scared then she ever had been. Sarah's room was ice cold. She could see her breath as she felt her heart slowing down. Something had hold of her and was not going to let her go. This thing wanted to harm her!

Her eyes felt heavy she barely keep them awake, as she her heart slowed down even more. She managed to whisper "Help me, please" as she passed out, the temperature return to normal. Sarah laid still, eyes closed. The bad presence had gone.

Anna that night came to her, while she slept she had her heard her friend's plea for help. Anna stayed with Sarah until the morning light to keep her safe and so Sarah would not be alone. Sarah was indeed now not safe. Her subconscious thoughts had awakened; her thoughts were trying to tell her things about Anna and Anna's father.

When Sarah awoke she noticed that the claw marks had mysteriously vanished and blood stained nightdress was gone too. Not one mark of blood anywhere to be seen. She felt almost fine just a little bit sore where the marks had been, like nothing had happened!

Sarah also noticed a daisy chain by the side of her bed side cabinet that she had made the day before! Sarah Knew that Anna had been with her through the night. This was Anna's way of letting Sarah know that she been there. It did make Sarah feel a little easier knowing that Anna had been there, that her friend had heard her call for help but she was still in a little bit of shock, this was a frightening experience.

Sarah knew and felt Anna had been with her after her experiences, she was still upset. She was afraid, scared and confused more than ever now. There were so many questions, no one to answer them. Sarah just didn't know who to turn to! Sarah felt so alone yet again as Sarah could not ask Anna or she could not tell family either! What could she do!

CHAPTER 20

Jason was starting to worry his teachers at school by this time. Totally unknown to the rest of his family as he for the most part have always seemed not to have a problem with the house nothing really happened to him only that nightmare that time and that drawing of Anna and her father that Sarah had seen, at least that's what his family had thought!

Sarah too was drawing pictures of things to do with Anna, her father and the house with her dreams. It was Sarah's way of trying to make sense of everything. Things in the house were definitely starting to get more intense for the whole family, different for each member of the Jones family, as for the rest of family it was other things that were worrying like how Susan was!

This house was affecting all of them. The negative feelings was spreading, it was not over yet! This bad entity had a lot more. This entity was pleased to see this family slowly being pulled apart.

The teachers knew that there was nothing wrong with Jason's family. Jason on the surface seemed to be happy at home always saying how great their house was. That he was happy with his mum and he loved his sister and grandparents and the rest of his family. Also that he knew he was well loved by them. They would never harm him but they could not explain what the pictures that he had drawn were about? 'What did these pictures mean?' they were not the usual pictures that children would draw. The school did find it very odd indeed.

Jason was starting to draw more strange pictures at school of this menacing figure and the pale blonde little girl in white. This menacing figure was of a tall dark haired man and in black Victorian suit with green eyes that could stare right through you, into your soul, the man just had a look of plain evil. It was a disturbing picture!

The teacher became more concerned about Jason all though on the face of it Jason seemed a normal confident little boy 7 year old, these pictures were very disturbing and strange. This was just the beginning for Jason, the stuff of nightmares and things that go bump in the night for all of the Jones family . . . .

The house was also starting to have a negative effect on Mr & Mrs Jones marriage with things that were going on Michael feeling the strain as he could not and didn't know how to help his family. Seeing his wife suffering with a break down and now due everything, she could not bring herself to go out of the house that much, the agoraphobia was getting worse.

Michael just wanting to put his head in the sand, hoping it would all go away, Susan wanting to protect her kids and run away from the house and everything else. This house and everything that was happening were starting to tare this family into pieces.

Susan and Michael were starting to really row for the first time, about the house and other things too. In fact it didn't seem to take much for the sparks to fly. They had strong words before but never like this. They had started to fall out of love with each other. Even so much so that they started to sleep in separate rooms most of the time, Susan still in their room but Michael sleeping in the spare room.

Michael and Susan had started to drift apart, floors were starting to show. This upset Sarah she could see her mum and dad's marriage falling apart and powerless to do anything about it. Ashley, Diane and Antony could all see that their parent's marriage was braking apart and there was nothing they could do about it.

The negative presence of Anna's father was also witnessing this. This was most empowering for him, a family in turmoil. This would make the family vulnerable, easy target now, easy pray.

Susan and Michael tried not to row in front of the children. The rows would be mainly at night thinking that Sarah was asleep. She would be awake listening to them row and fight, with tears of unhappiness. Sometimes she would hear the front or back door slam; her dad would walk out in the night after a big row. Those nights felt so cold and empty, wondering if her dad would return, maybe he would walk out forever. Michael always returned an hour later, her dad would sleep on the sofa, those nights.

Sarah felt very uneasy about the house and this presence. She also wanted to be there for her friend Anna. 'Was these dreams Anna in a way of trying to tell Sarah what had happened to Anna and her mother? Was Anna's father involved in their deaths?' for the sake of family, she needed some answers but how that was the 60 million dollar question!

Some how this feeling would not go away, she knew the more she tried to find out about this presence of Anna's father, it became more angry, so how could she handle this! She was in a catch 22 situation. What ever she did would not be a good outcome regardless!

Sarah wanted to help Anna find peace in herself, to help her anyway she could. At the same time this was a dark and evil force that she knew if she tried to fight against, people could get hurt. Her mum was already in a fragile state and her dad was close to breaking point. Sarah was already incredibility fearful about her own family. This spirit had a dark and evil past, intent in harming for whom ever dared to get in his way or if Sarah were to cross his path or past! Anna needed someone to listen to her story, or she would suffer in silence for all eternity. How as telling Anna story would cause Anna's father to enrage! Maybe for Anna the only way was through Sarah's dreams! Maybe this was Anna ways of giving Sarah some of the answers that she needed to find!

That night for the first time that Jason had stayed at that house, he wanted to be in with his sister that night. Jason who had always slept through the heavy footsteps that would accrue and the voice of Anna would speak to his sister . . . Suddenly he woke up in a daze "The man coming to get me" Jason cried, "Don't let him get me!" Jason screamed, at the time he was asleep, he was shouting. Jason woke up his grandparents and Sarah. Diane was out that night with Ashley, she as well as Ashley was unawares of everything.

Sarah went over to Jason who was sleeping on the spare mattress in Sarah's room, when Michael came in from the spare room and Susan ran from her room into Sarah's bedroom to find him sat up in bed. Just staring into space, wide eyed open, but non responsive to anyone!

Jason's granddad Michael just thought "He is having a nightmare as kids often do at his age all the time" Michael said trying to play down the situation "Probably something he had seen on telly"

Susan was not happy with the situation at all, she knew this was not just a case of child's nightmare. Susan knew her grandson and yes children do get nightmares but not like this. Jason had never acted like this with any nightmares! It was strange and erratic behaviour. "I'm going to stay with Jas, just in case he wakes up with another bad dream again" Susan was very concerned for her grandson, this was not normal. She had never seen him react like this and she knew it was to do with the house.

"Ok, I understand" Michael replied trying to give his wife a bit of support as he could tell she was worried about their grandson. "Goodnight" he said while giving Susan and Sarah a cuddle and a kiss goodnight. Michael went on to bed.

Jason's Nan cuddled him and put her arm out for Sarah. Sarah lay down with her mum and Jason on the bed with her blanket and cuddled into her mum tight. She was worried too, about her mum and her brother, which Susan could see in her daughter eyes, Susan looking down at Sarah and said to her in a whisper "It will be alright, it's just a bad dream, nothing will harm either of you! I will not let it". Susan said trying to reassure her daughter. Susan Stroked Sarah's hair to give her a sense of comfort but deep down Susan knew there was something terrible wrong in this house! It had eating away at this family for years.

This was a lovely family home at one time for the most part, problems along the way. Susan never gave up on the family and held them together, always tried to make her children feel safe and comforted. Now it was a terrifying house that her children did not feel safe in. This nasty presence wanting to harm Susan's children and play with their minds! No longer was this a loving family home, Susan thought to herself. This also had become a trap for Susan, with her issues that had manifested after a long period of time.

No one spoke that night of what had happened. Susan or Sarah could not sleep either. They just stared across the darkness of the room listening for the slightest noise or sound. Feeling on edge as Jason slept though the night, totally unawares of his nightmare or his reaction to his dream, just in a deep sleep. Nothing else happened that evening.

In the morning there were stern looks exchanged across the breakfast table from Mr & Mrs Jones. The atmosphere you could cut with a knife, it was not good at all. The household had an uncomfortable feeling.

Ashley came round in the morning to pick up Jason, Michael mentioned that Jason had a nightmare, just added it probably something he seen on telly, as Susan got Jason ready for school. Ashley could tell that things were not well with her parents.

Sarah knew her mum was worried about things even though her mum was good at trying to hide it. Sarah could tell that her mum was not happy at all, she could see it in her mother's eyes. Sarah knew her mum completely.

Sarah knew there would be strong words said later between her mum and dad. This was awful; they had never really rowed, so much as late. Well not that Sarah was aware as when she came along the marriage was better. Before this they have a turbulent marriage. They were always a loving couple to Sarah's mind. Yes they had their problems, what couple did not have problems! This was different now.

Ashley offered to drop off Sarah and Jason into school on her way home. She too could see that there was tension between her mum and dad. All that day at school Sarah did her school work, but her mind was on what was going on at home with her parents . . .

Meanwhile at home! It was Michael's day off, as Sarah had thought her mum and dad were not getting on very well at all. This year was the first time in the last ten years of marriage they had rowed and mostly about the house. What was happening, in what they thought was their family home? That they had nearly 30 years of good memories and it's fair share of bad. The last few years had bared its toll on this once happy and joyful family.

"Our Sarah and Jason are not happy here or our grown up children and neither I'm I, there is something very unsettled in this house. There's always has been something wrong!" Susan said in a very firm tone "You are not taking any notice on how our daughter and grandson are feeling, you are so wrapped up in work these days and everything else but what's going on in our own home, I cannot take much more!"

"There's nothing wrong with this house, nothing happens when I'm here! It's just in their heads, your too sensitive since your break down, trying to find a problem that does not exist?" he said raising his tone of voice.

This continued for a few hours harsh words were spoken until Michael had enough and he stormed out of the house! Michael was infuriated by his wife comments and Susan was annoyed by her husband lack of understanding, rather than being supportive.

"I need some air, I've have had enough of this house and you, your just bloody stupid woman falling for our kids stories. They got you wrapped round their little fingers" Michael said as he shut the door behind him with a big bang. This rattled the whole house.

Susan started to cry, she felt so alone for the first time in their marriage, although she knew their marriage was in trouble! it was not just the house, she felt the last year the closeness they once had was fading, they were drifting further and further away, as a couple. She could not take this house much longer. Susan was really worried about her children and grandchild. She wanted to protect them. Since her break down things had started to go wrong! But more so in the last year!

Susan didn't know how! She felt threatened and feared for her children safety. That day while her husband was out and Sarah was at school, Susan tried to keep herself busy in the house, she found it extremely difficult. Susan was still very upset about her husband lack of support. 'After all it was about their children'. Things going around and around in her head 'Why would Michael try not to understand for their children sake, she needed him to be the man of the house and help protect his family' Susan thought to herself. She could not cope with this on her own, it was too much. She did not feel strong enough, she felt weak after all that gone on! She needed her husband to be by her side.

It was the afternoon by now, Susan did not bother much for lunch, as she not that hungry. Still too upset by the harsh words of her husband. There was a gloomy and dark cloud that was hanging over her family.

Susan kept her mind occupied by tidying up around the house. She knew Sarah would be home from school soon. Sarah was 10 years old now, Sarah wanted to walk back from school by herself, before Diane would take her in and drop her off but Diane was working now, could not do it all the time. Sarah didn't mind walking home by herself, hoping by the time she got back her parents would had a chance to talk things over, if they were left alone for a bit.

Susan went upstairs into Sarah's room to put some washing away. Susan had an idea, it might not work but she had to try for the sake of their family. Susan thought maybe if she could talk to the little girl Anna, then it might help in some way. Susan was desperate and didn't know what else to do! So she sat on her daughter's bed and called to the little girl "Anna; are you there?" she said quietly feeling slightly unnerved, she didn't know what to expect, if in fact it was a good idea in the first place but she had nothing to lose! "It's Sarah's mum, I don't know what to do! So I have come to talk to you, can you help me, please?"

At first there was nothing, just a deadly silence that fell all over the house, the calm before the storm, just the sounds of an old house. The creaking of old floor boards and the rustling of the wind blowing through the leaves on the trees and through the house;

Susan had a bad feeling that something was about to happen. The temperature dropped drastically. So much so that Susan could see her own breath, her fingers felt num with the cold air. Her whole body shivered with the cold, the room felt like ice, as if winter had fallen upon Sarah's bedroom like blanket of frost!

Susan noticed from the corner of her eye the door coming into Sarah's bedroom was going back and forth by itself. This was very strange there was no draft none of the windows upstairs were open! Or was this something else more sinister going on? She never had this happen before in all the time she had been alone in this house, many times.

Maybe the feeling of being watched from time to time, if she came down the stairs from upstairs or having a bad feeling about Sarah's cupboard and seeing the little girl float across her bedroom, one time at night but that was about it. This was a really bad intensive feeling.

Susan felt the hairs on the back of her neck raise up. All of a sudden she heard the heavy footsteps the ones that Sarah had described to her mum. At first Susan did think it was her husband back home, at least she was hoping it was him . . .

Then the footsteps stopped at the top of the stairs, Susan called out very sheepish "Is that you Michael" but knowing deep down, it was not Michael. Susan knew she was not alone in this house and a very uneasy feeling of discomfort.

But there was no answer to Susan's call, she sat frozen on Sarah's bed unable to move, she was afraid to move or to call again for help. Susan felt a cold hand stroke the back of her hair and a cold eerie breathe on the side of her head. Cold fingers running through the side of her hair, along with cold breathe on the back of her neck, she could not move frozen with fear. Then she heard a man's voice whisper in her ear "Helena".

Then Susan was glad when she heard the downstairs front door open and she heard her daughter and her husband voices. Susan ran down the stairs, trying not to let it show that she was shaken up a bit from her experience that she just had.

"I'm back! I picked up Sarah from school on my way back home. I am so sorry we had words honey. I should have been there for you and the kids." Michael said feeling he had let his family down. He could see that his wife was scared and freak out. Michael thought it was about Jason and his bad dreams or Sarah. He had no idea of what had just happened to his wife.

Susan said nothing to her husband or daughter, she was just so happy to see her husband and daughter after what had happened. Susan didn't mention any of it all that day. She gave her husband a huge kiss and big cuddle, Sarah jointed in the family hug too and looked up to say to her mum and dad "Is everything ok now between you two" she asked in a concerned voice, knowing that her mum and dad were having marriage problems and they had not been sleeping in the same room for a few weeks.

"Yes everything will be fine now" Michael said smiling to reassure his daughter. "Well we don't have a treat very often now, how about a take away, followed by double chocolate ice cream" replied Michael, at the same time knowing that his marriage was falling apart before his eyes.

Susan glazed upstairs briefly "I get the take away menus" Said Susan still unhappy with everything. This made her uneasy for the rest of the night and she was feeling discontented in her marriage too.

Sarah noticed that her mum had looked up the stairs and gave a strange bewildered look. Something had gone on, but Sarah didn't know what!

They had all decided on a couple of pizzas. Michael ordered the food, while Susan and Sarah sat down to watch telly. "It's ordered" Michael said as he too sat down to watch telly.

The phone went, just as Michael put the phone down and went to sit down "I'll get that;" Susan insisted. "Hello, Mrs Jones speaking"

"Hello this Mrs Price speaking from Combs Hill Primary School. I'm head of year. I have been speaking to your grandson's teacher Mrs Woods. We did try and contact Jason's mum on her number but no answer, so we thought we would have a word with you."

"Yes go on" Susan was very worried about Jason. He had never been in trouble in school, so this sudden phone call was not welcome news.

"Your grandson has been drawing in his art lessons, he has always have had a board imagination. We always thought he was very expressive in his art. The drawing of the little girl in white and the man that so say lives in your cupboard but now more recently his drawing are very horrifying for a little boy of seven years" Mrs Price continued.

"A little girl in white and a man in the cupboard, oh right!" Susan didn't know quite what to say to the teacher, she no idea about these drawing that her grandson had been doing at school. She wondered what the drawings were about! In fact none of the family knew apart from Sarah.

"Well as I was saying, your grandson drawn a picture in his lesson this afternoon it's was a dark figure a Victorian man, very menacing with what appears to be blood dripping from his fingers! When I asked your grandson about this, he said that this man comes to him in his nightmares" Mrs Price was very concerned about this, it was clear in the tone of her voice.

Susan was horrified "Oh no, I shall have a talk with him tonight and his mother too" Susan was speechless. Now Susan REALLY was worried.

"Ok, please do, if you or his mum would like to come and see his teacher or me about anything please do feel free to do so" Mrs Price replied offering her assistance.

"Thank you for your help" Susan said and put down the phone, trying not to show her concern.

Susan looked at Sarah wondering, what she could say to her daughter and her husband. She could see they both looked very puzzled, to what the phone call was about! She didn't know weather it would better at this point to lie. Susan felt uncomfortable lying, she told her children always to tell the truth. Shall Susan tell them what the call was about? This needed to be handled carefully and her husband was not a believer of things beyond the grave, this was what it seemed to be! A message beyond the grave . . . .

"What's wrong" Michael asked looking very puzzled "What was that about?"

"Oh just about a picture Jason did well in his art work" Susan replied. She didn't like being dishonest to her husband but he would not of taken it seriously. She felt, she needed to have a private talk with her grandson, before she said anything.

"Oh right; we have got a budding artist in the family" Michael said jokingly smiling feeling proud of his grandson.

Shortly after the phone call their take away arrived, two large meat feast pizzas, Susan set the table and they all sat round. The pizzas were nice, Susan and Sarah were not that hungry both of them with things on their mind.

No one spoke, each in their own thoughts of the day that each one of them had. Michael was thinking of work, Sarah about the house and her dreams. Susan was worried about everything. She had thoughts about the house and what was going on with her grandson and daughter. Little did she know but all her children had their own experiences over the years growing up in the house. Not as bad as Sarah! She seemed to be this bad spirit main target.

In fact anyone that stayed in that house, they had something happen meaning, the footsteps at night. In fact anyone who had lived in that house! But it was an old house. It was at least 80 years old. It had a lot of families that had lived there in all those years.

After tea Michael sat down in the living room to read the paper, while Susan did the dishes and tidy up, all while deep in thought on how to approach things that was going on with Jason. After Susan had tidy up, she came into the living room. Michael always knew when his wife was worried about something or she had things on her mind but he didn't say anything as it would only been over the house, so say that it is haunted.

Susan had to speak to Ashley first to let her know about the phone call from his school and take it from there. Ashley might want to talk to

Jason being his mum or Ashley might prefer it coming from her mum, sometimes grandparents can speak better to a child.

Susan managed to get hold of Ashley and Diane. They had been out with Jason for something to eat as a treat at the local harvester, had just got back.

"Hello. How are you?" Susan started off

"Yes were all fine just been out for something to eat at the harvester, got in about 5 minutes ago. Diane will be back a bit later, it was nice. Jason enjoyed himself, stuffed his face" Ashley said unaware of the bomb shell her mum was about to drop about her son.

"I'm glad you had a nice time, tell Diane I see her later then. I have got something to tell you not sure, how to tell you as it a little worrying" Susan didn't really know what to say or how to say it?

"Right what is it? Your tone is a little worrying mum" Ashley was now concerned to what this news was!

"Jason's school called me as they could not get hold of you! I spoke to Jason head, Mrs Price she said that Jason has been drawing strange and disturbing pictures, of a man that Jason says lives in the cupboard in our house and a little girl" Susan added Susan did not know how bad Ashley would take this.

"Oh my god" she was in shock. She had no idea about any of this.

"There is more! The last picture he did the man had what appeared to be blood on his finger tips!" Susan could tell that her daughter was upset by this but knew that she had to be told, both Susan and Ashley unsure how to handle this news.

"Poor Jason, how do I handle this?" Ashley just didn't know what to do for the best. How to speak to Jason about this? She had no idea how to approach it.

"Shall I talk to him for you?" Susan asked trying to offer a bit of support to her eldest daughter.

"No it ok mum, I speak to him" Ashley replied upset and confused. Ashley knew that the house was haunted. She had heard the footsteps growing up in that house. Even heard a little girl's voice from time to time or feel like something would touch her leg when she was in bed but that was about it. The house never worried her till now. At this time Ashley had no idea about what was happening to Sarah.

"Ok as long as you are sure? Let me know how you get on with him!" Susan asked anxiously wanting to know how her grandson was doing!

"Yes I'm sure, wish me luck? Bye mum" Ashley said as she put the phone down. Michael and Sarah heard the phone call. Michael did not say anything about the contexts of the conversation she had with their daughter, but could see that his wife was upset and worried.

Michael looked up at his wife "Come here love" he said putting his arm out for her. Susan sat by Michael as he put his arm around her. "Things will be ok" he smiled. Trying to ease her stress, he did not show it, he too was worried but wanted to stay strong for his family. Sarah didn't show it but she too was concerned for her brother, she had no idea that it was getting that serious with him.

Ashley meanwhile had the task of talking to her son about these pictures that he had drawn at school. She would have word it right, in such a way as not to frighten him even more or to make feel like he cannot come to his mum.

Before she had a word with Jason, Ashley spoke to her sister Diane and told her about the phone call, Ashley needed a little bit of extra support. Jason was up in his room playing at the time.

"OH NO poor Jason, I had no idea" Diane said after she was told by her sister.

"I know it's that house! It has always been that house" Ashley replied she was nervous about having this chat. Diane stayed a little longer before she went home to her mum and dad's house.

Ashley went up stairs to have this chat to her son "Jason can I have a word with you alone" Jason's mum asked, smiling at Jason.

"Yeah ok mum, what is wrong?" Jason said as he could tell that there was something on his mum's mind.

"Your Nan had a call from the school today when we were out. Don't worry your not in trouble" Ashley said holding her son's hand. Jason could tell her mum was upset about something.

"What is it mum? Tell me?" he asked innocently, not knowing what to except.

"You drew a picture at school, a not very nice picture! We and your teachers are concerned by this" Ashley said leaving it open for Jason to have his say and what the pictures meant.

"Oh right that picture, don't worry mum he doesn't want to hurt me, he just comes to me in my dreams and so does Anna, Anna is really nice" Jason said in a matter of fact voice.

"Well, I don't like you drawing these pictures anymore, I want you to ignore that man" Ashley said she was hoping if he left well alone, this man would leave her son alone, she hoped!

"Ok mum, I will try" Jason said cuddling his mum and then went downstairs. Ashley did not know how to take her son's reaction. He did not seem phased by this at all. Ashley seemed more worried than him.

Ashley went downstairs and later when Jason had gone asleep, Ashley told her sister Diane everything about the phone call from the school and what Jason had said also how he reacted.

Diane offered to stay but Ashley just wanted it to be her and her son that night, just the two of them. Diane left and went home to her mum and dad. She felt her family needed her. She went home and stayed in to be with her mum, dad and sister.

The next day Ashley called up her mum and told her, how she had got on with Jason. That day Jason was due to come up to his Nan and granddad's house for tea. Ashley was not sure being in that house was a good idea for Jason under the circumstances but Jason really wanted to see his sister, grandparents and Auntie so she agreed to let him come over.

That day after school Ashley brought Jason over, Susan was so pleased to see her grandson. She gave him a huge cuddle, a big kiss on the cheek along with his granddad and sister also Auntie. Jason did not say anything about the picture, his family thought it maybe best not push, let him speak about it in his own way just be there for him, when he needed them.

After tea Sarah took Jason upstairs to play, she could tell the grown ups needed to talk. Sarah took Jason into her room. She had an idea that might help him. At least she hoped it would help him

Jason looked up at his sister "I don't like this house anymore. It scares me". Jason said holding his big sister's Sarah hand tight.

"I know Jas me too but we are not alone, there is someone here that is good and kind, not scary at all. Would you like to meet her? Her name is Anna and she is my friend, my special secret friend. I'm sure she will be your friend too" Sarah asked trying to help him. Sarah knew that Anna would never hurt or scare Jason, she was kind and caring.

"YES! I would love to speak to her. Please" Jason replied, he had always wanted to meet this little girl that been his sister's friend. He felt a little nervous and afraid to see her but in a way too, excited. 'He had never met a real ghost before,' even though he was nervous and afraid, his instinct told him not to be afraid of this spirit, it meant him no harm.

"Ok come and sit on my bed, I will see if she would like to talk to us! Don't be afraid she will not harm you, not ever" Sarah said to Jas trying to calm him. Sarah continued.

"Anna, it is Sarah. This is my brother Jason he would like to talk to you. He is afraid and has had bad dreams like me" Sarah asked in a quiet voice.

Sarah closed her bedroom door to and put the night light on. It was starting to get dark outside. Then they sat back on her bed with her brother Jason, she put her arms around him to give him support and comfort.

Then Anna spoke softly. "I'm here, please don't be scared Jason. I am not here to hurt you in anyway, I promise." Anna voice was gentle and soft. Jason was not scared that night. He had a new special friend, someone he could talk to and not to be scared of, that no one else knew of.

Susan, Ashley, Diane and Michael heard Sarah and Jason from downstairs. It seemed a long time ago, since Susan heard the children's laughter. Susan wanted to have this talk with her grandson but as he seemed happy at the time, she felt it would be better to leave it to another time 'I will let the kids have a bit of fun for tonight as they seem happy' Susan thought to herself. Maybe everything was going to be alright after all. At least she was hoping it was . . . .

"See I told you, it will be ok" Michael said to his wife not knowing the full story of what had happened that day. He looked up and continued "Looks like their having a grand old time upstairs, told you it would be ok. It's just a ghost story they probably be telling each other to try and scare each other, it's what kids do, nothing more, nothing less. Ghost stories are not really real."

If only he know the truth. Susan was still unsure about things and about the conversation with her grandson's head of year. Later that night they all went to bed and for one night it was all peaceful and still. Maybe it had all ended! Or maybe not . . . .

CHAPTER 21

It was coming up to Ashley's birthday at the end of June by this time she was 24 years old, the family treated her to the harvester. It would be her son, mum, dad, Sarah, Antony and Diane. Susan thought it be nice for the family to have a day off from the stresses of life. She did find it hard to go out. She made the effort for the sake of her family. The family had a nice time on Ashley's birthday but the thoughts and feeling of the house would not go away from Sarah's mind.

All the while Jason was having his nightmares, so was Sarah but hers was slightly different. By now her nightmares were becoming more frequent and more detailed than before, like they were memories of a forgotten life. These dreams would not happen every night but about twice a week. Sarah would dread her nightmares! She never knew what nightmare it would be and how it would end, while she was asleep or awake. It was a frightening time.

The other dreams would start off the same, in their house but as before the house was different in its layout. The house looked more like a large country cottage or maybe servant's quarters to a country house. She was not sure about that side of it. The house was old that she was sure of that, with old wooden beams going across the individual rooms, They did in cottages a long time ago and the cupboard in Sarah's room, was as before indeed a secret staircase, this cupboard door was open every time in her dream, a dark and sinister looking stone staircase.

Sarah felt as if this was a secret doorway for someone to hide, for good or bad intentions. But in her dream she felt as for this particular time, it was for hiding some ones dark secret, the secrets to another man life. Sarah felt it had something to do with Anna's father Edward, a dark side of his past that no one knew about!

This time the cupboard door was closed in her dream, which was soon to be a nightmare. Sarah would be in the secret cupboard looking out to a room that looked a little like her room but old and with the old wooden beams going across. Sarah would look through the key hole and then she would see Anna.

Anna was crying and looked frightened, as if she had found out something terrible; Anna was scared of someone or something. Sarah could feel her friend's pain and wanted help, as her best friend was really upset. Anna found something about her father, Sarah felt and scared of what he would do, when he realised his daughter knew about of whatever this bad, terrible secret.

Sarah would try to call out to her but Anna would never hear her, as though someone was stopping her voice from being heard. A second later Anna's father walked in the room shouting at her and shaking her violently with rage. Sarah saw Anna's father put his hands tightly around his daughter's neck.

Then Anna's father turned his face to the cupboard as if he knew that Sarah was there, seeing everything! This scared her to death. He was not a nice man! 'How did he know that she was there? She was as quiet as a mouse?' Sarah thought to herself 'this is just a dream he can't see me in a dream and Anna's father doesn't know what Sarah dreams are about!' it still scared her though, it was puzzling too.

Then Sarah would wake up in a cold sweat, almost as if her natural defences kick in, stopping her from seeing the whole truth. She knew now why Anna was so afraid of her father. Sarah could not believe what she had just dreamt! It was indeed a nightmare, a nightmare she didn't want to have. 'What happened next? Was Anna alright in her dream or did father really strangle his own daughter. Surely not and if so what happen to Anna's mother Helena!' Sarah thought to herself. Sarah felt too that Anna's father was actually in her dream. That was the bit she didn't understand, Sarah was very confused. It felt as if he was looking straight at Sarah through the dream.

This was not good news, how could she keep this to herself but she knew that she did not have a choice in the matter, now she knew just how dangerous he was. Even though he was a ghost, he was an evil ghost. Which made all the difference but how could she fight something like this. If he ever knew that Sarah now knew about this dream. What would happen to her or her family? If he did indeed kill his own child and maybe even his wife!

Sarah did not sleep at all that night and for quite a few nights, this really freaked her out! Sarah did not sleep as well as every time she drifted off the dreams would start or the footsteps. Sarah also found when she would try to talk about Anna's father she would feel hands around her neck! It was as if Anna's father was warning Sarah not to speak of what she knew, to keep quiet or else.

Sarah would also have things throw at her too in the bedroom at random, dolls or books would fly across the room or things would fall to the ground from her dressing table or bed and this would happen when she was on her own. Anna's father made sure that there was no witnesses, that he only targeted her, so that she would fear him and would keep her silence.

Sarah had to know the truth for sure. Maybe if she did all the nightmares and the footsteps would stop! Anna would be free too. At first these things that would happen felt more like a warning to scare her. But as the days and weeks went by she became more aware that it felt more of threat and intense. This presence wanted to harm her, Sarah knew too much already.

It would be the summer holidays soon which would give Sarah a brake from the house. They always had a week holiday in Devon at the end of July. The weather was getting warmer now, lighter mornings and dark later at night. Sarah played outside a lot when the weather was good, she felt more uncomfortable in the house now. She still spoke to Anna when she could.

Sarah would also feel the creature at night laying in wait in the garden or she would feel it in the room with her again a warning to make keep her silence, to keep her mouth firmly shut but with the darkness coming later, she would not see the creature so much. It needed the dark to hide itself to slip into shadows of the night.

Susan could sense her Sarah still was not happy in the house at all, however much Sarah tried to hide it. Susan knew her daughter and all her children, she could sense when there was something terribly wrong as a mother instincts would. Susan was blissfully unaware of the latest nightmares that her daughter was having and the things that were going on with this presence. That this entity was trying to hurt her daughter or throwing things around her daughter's bedroom, Susan knew something was up but not at the extent of how much!

Michael unbeknown to the rest of the family was putting a brave face on, he was lost. He needed to protect his family too but just didn't know how! How do you fight something you cannot see! He never believed in ghost up till now, however he knew something was going on but did not know how to explain it!

Michael also unknowing to his family did have one experience himself quite a few years ago. He had woken up in the night as he felt something had hold of his leg and trying to pull him out of his bed. He was half asleep at the time and it only happened the once, just for a minute, so he dismissed it. This happened when Sarah's mum and dad were in her room.

Jason was still getting his dreams but it was more images of the girl in white and the dark sinister Victorian man by now. But if he got scared in the night he would think of Anna and feel comfort by this thought or if he was at his grandparents he would go in with his sister. He would feel Anna presence which would calm him enough to go a sleep cuddling up to Sarah, which in one way made them closer as brother and sister.

One night after the usual night of scares, Sarah decided she was going to talk to Anna the following night! She had to know what really happened to Anna and her mother . . . .

The next day Michael went to work as normal, while Sarah walked to school on her own, normally her sister would take her to school. Sarah wanted to walk by herself. It was only about a 15 minute walk away, Susan said that was ok. Sarah wanted to think of what and how she was going to speak to Anna.

The day was wet and windy, grey clouds and cold. This wind was harsh as if it had intent and purpose as it swirled all around Sarah and through the trees. The wind seemed to whisper her name, as if something else was with her in the wind that day. Something dark and an evil force, an unseen force; this made Sarah feel uneasy.

That day nothing seemed as it should be. Sarah was on edge for the rest of that day in her lessons. It felt as if something was watching through the window from outside her classroom, from the playground, from the window by where she was sat.

The figure in her dreams was there, she could not see him but she knew he was there, watching her every move. Sarah's her heart was pounding with fear, she felt sick to her stomach. He was taunting her. Those dark green eyes staring though the glass pains of the window right into her eyes. It felt like he was threaten her not to ask or speak of anything, she knew or she would be very sorry indeed.

Sarah knew now things were going to get worse this ghostly figure knew that she knew. In the playground when it was her break time, as usual she kept herself to herself and did not speak to anyone. Her one friend Tracy did say hello but that was it. Tracy could see that Sarah had things on her mind, so Tracy left Sarah alone.

The children once again tease her, she not only heard the laughter of the other children teasing her but she could also hear a man's laughter! An evil laugh; "Go away and leave me alone" Sarah cried, she was near to tears. She could not take it. Sarah wished that she could run away or disappear.

"ALRIGHT, come on lets leave the freak alone" the other kids laughed egging each other on.

Sarah sobbed 'I'm really a freak, I must be or WHY would this be happening to me and my family!' she thought to herself. Sarah hated herself, she wished she was like the other kids, well liked, confident and popular, instead of the source of amusement for the other kids and different.

The end of the school day was finally there and when it was time to go home again, as she walked back the wind started to blow again. It was harsh, bitter with a cold edge; blow hard around and through to her bones. She could hear her name being whispered through the breeze. Then she heard a voice 'I'm coming for you; but not just yet, I want you to fear me more.' Sarah was freaked out by this and ran home the rest of the way, which by that time she was already half way home.

Susan knew something was up when Sarah came in the door! She was as white as a sheet. Sarah clinched her chest tight as she found it hard to breathe! Her heart was bruised, pounding fast; she felt pains to her chest.

"What on earth is wrong? You look as pale as anything!" Susan said in a concerned manor, noticing Sarah clutching her at chest, as if she was in pain.

Sarah was too scared to tell the truth. She did want anyone to get hurt "I'm ok, it just started raining and I didn't want to get wet, so I ran in from the heavy rain" Sarah said trying to give a smile to hide her fear.

Susan didn't know if she believed her daughter. Yes it was starting to rain heavy but she knew the way her daughter looked as she came in. It was as if someone had scared her to death, Susan was still anxious for her daughter.

Sarah went upstairs as her mum sorted out the tea! Sarah's dad came in ten minutes later. Susan just smiled at her husband as he gave her a kiss on the cheek "Everything ok HONEY" Michael asked his wife as he felt something was up.

"Yep everything is fine dear" Susan could not say that she was worried for their daughter. She was not too sure what had actually happened.

CHAPTER 22

It was the summer holidays coming up soon, Susan and Michael had planned a summer holiday in the end of July to Sandy Bay in Exmouth, Devon for a break. Ashley was going as well. She felt that Jason also needed some time out too. It would be good for all the family, in a way of giving Sarah something else to think of, rather than that house.

That year flew round quick with that was going on in the house. It would be Antony's 22nd birthday in August in the summer holidays. After their holiday, the rest of the summer holidays went by quickly, gone in a blink of an eye. The summer holidays were nice. Susan and Michael tried as much as they could to give Sarah a nice time. They deserved it with day trips and a holiday down to Devon, along with Antony's Birthday.

Sarah and Jason in the summer played in the garden a lot as the sun always shinned in the summer holidays. Michael and Susan were still not on getting on but try as much as they could to keep this fact from their kids! They seemed to row now at least once a week about something, hiding this fact was not easy, a lot of times they both were sleeping in different bedrooms.

It was the Sunday before they were back to school but back to a start of a new secondary school. Which Sarah was really not looking forward too, she had worried about it all day. It was bath time they had had their tea just sandwiches and cake Susan could tell that her daughter was worried about school. The family had tried to reassure Sarah all day that school would be fine and offer support, if there are any problems which was nice to know but did not stop her from worrying.

Susan ran her daughter's bath as Sarah was ten now she wanted to sort her own bath out herself. Sarah got in bath and washed her hair and then body. Sarah laid down in the bath to try and get the stresses of starting a new school out of her head. Easier said than done! Plus the incidents in the house and her nightmares! She was not scared of the bath as it felt a long time ago since her incident in the bath, over a year ago. She had never forgotten it, it only happened the once.

Sarah just relaxed and empty her mind. The temperature suddenly dropped by the bath, she was not alone. Sarah felt the temperature change along with the atmosphere. This time was different. Sarah knew she could be in danger as she knew something about this entity that should not know.

Sarah decided it time for her to get out of the bath before anything occurred. It was too late as she went to get up, she felt a force on her chest push her back down and her head into the water, it was happening again but it was not just to scare her, this time it had nasty intensions.

Sarah tried to struggle but the more she struggled the tighter the grip, the more she kicked, the more she was pushed down into the water in the bath by this time, she started to swallow water and breathing became erratic. Sarah was chocking and coughing, she could feel herself loosing consciousness.

Meanwhile in the living room Susan was sat down and Michael was in the garden, Diane was out with her friends. Susan could hear splashes coming from the bathroom at first she did think anything of it. She thought it was Sarah playing in the bath but some motherly instinct came over Susan as she felt something was terribly wrong.

Susan went rushing into the bathroom and saw Sarah head under the bath water. She was not moving, by this Sarah had completely blackout. The evil entity had gone! Susan was shocked but quick too as she got Sarah out of the bath and wrapped her in a towel! Sarah came to and started to cough sputtering out water. Susan had got there in the nick of time.

Susan could tell this was not time for questions, Sarah looked pale in colour and weak, she was not well enough at the moment to answer anything! Susan just gave her daughter a huge cuddle. She was just so glad that she had got there in time. Susan knew what could happen to her daughter, if she had got there any later!

Susan got her daughter dressed than picked her up and took her to the living room, laid her on the sofa. Susan quickly went upstairs and grabbed a few blankets to put round Sarah then put the kettle on for a hot chocolate.

Michael came in from the garden into the kitchen. Susan was in the middle of doing Sarah her hot drink. Michael could see straight away from Susan's face that he had missed something very bad. She looked frustrated and annoyed in turmoil almost to the point of tears.

"Has something just happened?" Michael asked looking slightly puzzled and noticing Sarah on the sofa.

"Our daughter nearly drowned!" Susan replied frowning, feeling all sorts of emotions going round and round in her mind.

"What is she ok?" Michael added "how did it happen? That is something that would happen to a 5 year old but Sarah is ten!" Michael said really feeling confused how's to how could this happen.

"I don't really know what happened to be honest but I got an idea! We will talk about this later just go and see, she is on the sofa" Susan said making Sarah a hot chocolate. Susan did want to talk about, what had happened but for now she wanted to concentrated on her daughter and making her feel well again.

"Hi how are you feeling?" Michael asked his daughter this was upsetting to see his daughter paled faced and weak, Michael wanted to know what could have happened too. He also felt now was not the time to ask and his daughter had to get some rest as she had a big day ahead of her. Susan brought in a hot chocolate.

"Mum, dad I be ok, I just mucking around in the bath and I slipped that is all, really sorry if I scared you" Sarah could not bring herself to tell the truth, she could see her mum and dad face was near to tears already.

That evening Susan and Michael did not quiz Sarah on what had happened! They both agreed as it was a big day the next day, they would leave it for now. Michael and Susan did not say much to each other that evening too. Sarah had an early night, that night. Sarah was upset this really scared her so much.

The next day it was school for Sarah and Jason. Sarah first day in her new school, it felt very strange but it was nice for her big sister to take her for a bit of support. Diane could tell that apart from starting a new school, her little sister had things on her mind. It was hard for Sarah to concentrate on her classes. She felt that she was being stared at and laughed at once again. This would be like the other two schools. Sarah was given dirty looks and made to feel uncomfortable once again.

It was an upsetting time for Diane. Diane and her boyfriend Sean had broken up. They had been braking up and getting back together for a few years now. Diane had decided to give him the flick, as he not the one for her. He always put her down like she was never good enough. Diane had enough and they were no longer to be an engagement. Which meant Diane was at home more, she was single once again like her sister Ashley.

Susan and Michael's kids were not stupid. They could pick up on this fact especially their older kids, Ashley, Antony and Diane that things were not ok at home, with their mum and dad, that something was going on to do with the house, something was effecting Sarah!

It was now back to school and back to normal routine of work and school. Jason birthday was not far off once again, his 7th birthday. It was slowly approaching. But with all that was going on, it was hard to think of birthdays or any sort of celebrations. The Jones family was finding it hard to put a brave face on.

Jason was having his 7th birthday at home as by now Susan's family had noticed changes in Michael, Susan, Ashley, Antony, Diane, Sarah even Jason. The whole family was being affected also that Michael and Susan marriage was heading for stormy weather. Ashley wanted her mum, dad and Sarah away from that house for one day. Ashley could tell something was up and she had an idea, as did the rest of the family it was to do with the house. She knew by her own feeling in their house, that something was never right in that house, it was poison.

No one realised though that each of the outside family had also had their own personnel experience with the house. Only that Jason and Sarah was being affected by it. The feeling of being watched, at night the footsteps, even the sounds of a child's laughter or seeing from the corner of their eye something move. But neither of the family had told each other about it, they all kept the experiences to themselves.

Michael and Susan's anniversary was coming up! Ashley had offered to have Sarah for the night, so Michael and Susan could spend a bit of time together. Maybe even sort things out with each other, they didn't really feel like celebrating but time alone would do their marriage good. The evening of their anniversary came it was nice to have some time together alone. For one night they kept their thoughts about the house out of their conversations.

Michael gave his wife a nice bouquet of flowers. They had a big box of chocolates from their kids. It was a nice evening but they knew that they would need to have a serious chat at some point. But it was easy to pretend for now all was prefect.

The following week it was Jason's 7th birthday party at his house with his family. It would be a full house Michael, Susan, Sarah, Ashley, Antony and Susie, Diane, Hilary, Emily, Peter and Jessica, Mark, Vivian, Nicole and Natasha. Ashley had sorted out plenty of food and drink for everyone. No one would starve or be thirsty that night.

It was really cool the kids thought and the adults thought it was very good too. A chance to catch up on everyone, have a laugh forget about things for just one day. A chance to forget their troubles, have a nice time.

Smoothies for the kids and Asti for the adults! It was really nice everyone was really enjoying themselves. Even Nicole and Natasha enjoyed and said it was a great party, that was high prays coming from 2 typical teenagers.

It was fun, fun, fun all round. The evening had passed quickly and it was time for everyone to go home. Michael, Susan and Sarah got a taxi home along with Emily, Peter and their daughter Jessica. The Jones family did returned home that night.

Jason, Jessica and Sarah went into Jason's room and played games. Sarah was enjoying it but she could not get her mind of all that had happened to her and what terrifying ordeals were to happen next!

Sarah played with Jason and Jessica in his Jason's room, after of course Jason had opened his birthday presents. The kids had stuffed their faces, this year Jason had Lego, transformers, a train set and a garage, lots of sweets and chocolates, also some colouring. Jason had a lovely birthday, it was fun for him.

Michael and Susan went home with Diane and Sarah. It was nice to be home in one way. Mind you after the party as it was a long day, all of them were very tired. Sarah did enjoy herself. It had been a fun day.

Susan and Michael got ready for bed, while Diane and Sarah got themselves ready for bed. Sarah and Diane said goodnight to their dad and mum then went to bed. Michael and Susan also went straight to bed as they felt a little tipsy.

Diane went straight to sleep as she was really tired, Sarah was tired but was a little afraid of going to sleep as she was afraid of what might happened! That night nothing happened as sometimes nothing would. The house was still, silent and dark. Not a ghost in sight. But the worse was still to come . . . .

Sarah still had her nightmares, each time with a bit more detail than the last, like pieces of a jigsaw coming together. Sarah felt like a bit of a detective, trying to analyse the evidence and trying fit the pieces in place.

Anna was always there for Sarah, however as much, Sarah tried to get the truth out of her best friend. Anna would not speak of what happened to herself and her mother Helena. Sarah knew the more she had these dreams, the more it seemed that something terrible had happened in that house. All those years ago, somehow this house had retained the imprint of the terrible events of past in its very walls; Which in turn gave this bad entity power to scare and harm by the house's negative energy of the past.

What had happened to Anna's mother Helena? Sarah did feel that with everything that was going on in the house. That these horrible sequences of events stemmed from Helena death! It where it all began so Sarah would have to go back to the beginning starting with Helena!

Somehow Sarah was connected to this, the past and present but she did not yet know how! Maybe it was because she felt and sensed things about people and places that not many other people could not. Like a beckon she attached these things.

However she was connected with this, Sarah knew that Anna knew why and so did her father but Anna would not say how! The pieces of the puzzle were not all there yet. Sarah would have to find the answers herself but trend with corrosion.

The rest of the time went quick in the lead up to Christmas, by the time Jason birthday was over it was the end of October. Susan and Michael would have to start buying the odd Christmas present although this year no one seemed, to be that enthusiastic about it.

CHAPTER 23

The run up to Christmas was eventful in many ways, getting ready for Christmas with the buying of presents and thinking about trimming up, for Michael and Susan, trying to get along for the sake of the kids. For Jason he was looking forward to the unwrapping of the Christmas presents and seeing what Santa had brought. For Sarah it felt different. She knew now it was her mum and dad that sorted out the presents not Father Christmas, which made Christmas feel different and all the things that had happened to her through the years! It had been too much to handle for Sarah and had put a damper on things for her.

Anna's father Edward had started haunting Sarah once again, for some reason the experience always seemed to increase near Christmas as if Anna's father did not like Christmas, and no he did not like Christmas! November flew by very fast in a blink of an eye. As it normally did with the rush to get the families Christmas presents.

It was the 1ST of December now! The countdown to Christmas had begun and the build up to Christmas. Sarah was hoping for a better Christmas this year, in terms of hoping that Anna's father and the creature of the night would leave her alone, deep down she knew this was wishful thinking.

That night on the 1st of December, Sarah had another horrible experience to add to her many horrible experiences, she often did at night, when she was a sleep and her parents and sister were fast asleep too.

It was one of those nights were she was desperate to go to the toilet but as normal she did not want to go, she feared of what might happen. As most of the time it did but she could not hold it in, she got up, ran down the stairs and ran into the toilet all the time feeling the ghost of Edward behind her. She could feel that he was waiting for her at the other side of the toilet door, the door handle turned as if someone was trying to open the door! Lucky for Sarah she had locked the door.

Sarah finished opened the door quickly and went to run up the stairs, but this time halfway up the stairs, Sarah felt a cold hand grab her ankle with force. Then she felt herself being pulled down, Sarah fell. Edward's ghost was too strong for her. She felt her legs give way as she fell onto the stairs.

Sarah held on to the banister tight, she tried to get up and kick her leg out to try and get him of her ankles, she managed to brake free. Sarah ran upstairs to her bed and wrapped her covers right round her. But it was not over.

Five minutes later she heard the footsteps coming up the stairs. He was determined to give her hell and make her suffer, to keep Sarah from knowing the whole truth! He enjoyed it too, making Sarah fear him.

The footsteps stopped by her bed! Then she felt as if something was trying to take her covers from her. She could feel a strong force pulling and tucking at them. Sarah felt her whole body starting to rise up, she grabbed the bed post as tight as she could. Sarah was terrified! She knew that this spirit was capable of killing her if he wanted to. Her covers were thrown to the ground. Her neck felt tight and her heart felt heavy; Sarah was so terrified by this!

She tried to scream but nothing was coming out of her mouth, the harder she tried to scream the tighter her neck felt. This lasted for what seemed forever was about 5 minutes and stopped. That night yet again she could not sleep, he just wanted to traumatise her and could kill her any time that he wanted to but never did. It was a terrifying little game that he wanted to play with her emotions.

The next day once again Sarah said nothing to her mum, dad or sister. Just kept her feelings bottled inside, Sarah did know at the time but this nasty ghostly presence had plans to make their Christmas one they would not forget in a hurry.

It was getting near Christmas now! The snow had started to fall. It started to really look like Christmas once again, even with the pretty snow glistening all around. Sarah still could not feel that festival, she did hide it well though.

Susan could tell her daughter was feeling down. To take Sarah's mind off things, Susan thought it would be nice if they trimmed up together with Sarah's dad and her sister Diane. Also get Jason to help as well. Susan invited Jason to stay the night. Ashley dropped him of mid afternoon after school. Ashley was not very pleased about Jason staying over but he was excited about it, she could not let her son down. It was a Friday night so no school in the morning which was a nice time to trim up. They all trimmed the house it looked amazing when they finished. The Christmas tree was pretty with the fairy lights, as always.

Michael came in from work and saw the decorations "WOW! You guys have been busy! The house looks great" Michael was full of the festive season! He had brought some mulled wine for Susan, Diane and himself and some limeade for the kids and was wearing a Santa's hat. The kids thought he looked silly but it nice to see someone being festive. It did put a smile on every ones face.

Sarah and Jason really loved Christmas as all kids do, even Diane loved Christmas and she was 20 years. It was nice sitting downstairs watching telly with just the Christmas lights on. Christmas had started, with the trimmings and the snow outside, which made it feel like Christmas. Michael lit the fire, so it was warm and cosy. There was a warm glow that they all felt, it was lovely.

Michael had planned a night out with a few of his work colleagues for the following weekend, it was for Christmas. He was looking forward to it he had not been out for a while. Michael went out for an odd drink in the local pub up the road with his work mates but it was not very often.

Michael was a little concerned about going with everything that was going on at home and the problems that Michael and his wife were facing in their marriage. After work Michael come home his normal time about four. "This night out I have with the lads on the weekend, I don't have to go if you want me home love" Michael said to Susan trying to support his wife.

"No you go me and the kids will be fine" Susan replied she knew her husband had been looking forward to it for ages, plus a night out was not going to make any difference to their problems.

That week at home nothing that much happened to Sarah with this menacing figure! Just the feeling of him watching her and the footsteps a couple of nights that was about it, much to Sarah happiness. Diane did her normal school run taking Sarah to school for her mum.

But this was not the end! It was just calming down till the next wave of terror for the Jones family. Anna spoke to Sarah that week too, she told Sarah do not be foaled that just because it was a quieter, Anna's father was not going to stop haunting the house. He was not the sort of person to give up on anything.

The weekend came round fast. It was Michael big night out! Michael was looking forward to it! 'It will be nice to catch up with the lads outside of work' Michael thought to himself. He was coming back in the morning. He knew he would be having probably quite a few drinks, he thought he would be a bit drunk that night.

Michael said goodbye to his wife and children then went out. Susan, Sarah and Diane were alone in the house. WHAT kind of night lay ahead for them? Sarah stayed downstairs with her mum. Diane went upstairs to listen to some music as she often did, when she was at home.

Sarah could see that her mum was not that happy that her dad had gone out because of being left alone in the house with just herself and her two daughters. Sarah knew that something bad was more likely to happen with their dad not being there, then if he was.

Sarah could see that her mum was nervous and her mum was quiet. Not her usual self. "Are you ok mum?" Sarah asked a little worried. Her mum looked really scared for the first time!

"Yes, I'm fine." Susan replied trying to pretend she was ok. Sarah could see right through her mum and knew she was not. She was just putting a brave face on for the sake of her children.

"Come on MUM, I know you are not ok! You did not want dad to go out tonight! Your not alone Diane and I are here" Sarah said trying to give her mum a bit of morel support.

"OK you are right but your dad has planned this Christmas night out with his work friends for ages" Susan said with a stern look.

"I know mum. But we need him here, what if something happens!" Sarah knew when her dad was out or fast asleep in bed things were more likely to happen.

"I just worry about you and Diane. But it will be ok I'm here, I won't let anything bad happen to either of you" Susan said trying hard to reassure her daughter and gave her a big hug.

That night Susan slept in with Sarah in her room. Diane came into Sarah's room too, she knew that weird stuff had been happening to her little sister and didn't want to leave her mum and sister alone. The three of them slept in Sarah's room. They brought the spare mattress in from the Diane's room. Sarah and their mum slept in Sarah's bed and Diane had the spare mattress. At least that way she could keep them close if anything were to happen. Diane fell fast asleep. Sarah cuddled into her mum and drifted of to sleep, in the end, so did her mum, her mum was trying hard to stay awake.

It was about three weeks to Christmas by this time. The house was still and silent. Not a sound, peaceful.

Sarah was cuddled up with her mum, feeling safe and comforted, WHEN all of a sudden the room went cold. Susan opened her eyes she felt a cold breath on her face and felt a dark eerie presence over her, Sarah and Diane. "GO AWAY" she shouted "LEAVE MY CHILDREN ALONE" she could not see anything but knew something demonic apparition was there.

Then Sarah woke up with Diane still funny enough still sound asleep. Then they heard a familiar voice, it was Anna come to warn them. "You are in danger! My father is angry" Sarah and Susan did not move.

Downstairs there was a huge crashing noise! It sounded like the Christmas tree had fallen down. They could hear other banging sounds coming from downstairs but they kept still. It went silent for a moment to Sarah and Susan sighed with relief. Then the sound of footsteps started up coming up the stairs getting closer and closer.

The bedroom door was open Susan wanted to close it but she would not leave the children even to close the door. She felt lost; Sarah held her mum. Diane started to stir. The bedroom door opened wide. Then the door closed shut, this woke up Diane.

The next ten minutes the bedroom door rattled and shook as if someone was trying to stop whatever was trying to come in. Diane screamed she had never experienced anything like this in this house. Sarah and Susan were frightened too.

The door would not open, it was Anna trying to protect her friend Sarah and her family from the evil clutches of her father. Anna used all her strength to keep her father away and door shut tight. Sarah felt Anna was in the room she knew that Anna was trying to help. Then all of a sudden it stopped and if by magic. In a whisper Sarah said "Thank you" to Anna. That night Sarah, Diane and their mum could not sleep!

That was it for Susan she could not stay in the house any longer. She knew whom ever those footsteps belong to was intent on harming her, her daughter's and grandson. Susan could not bare the house any longer.

That morning they all got up. Sarah, Diane and their mum was not very happy at all. In fact they were very nervous and shaken up on what to expect when they went downstairs. Diane got dressed as did Sarah and Susan, while Diane was finishing getting herself dressed Susan and Sarah plucked up the courage to go down the stairs.

They had a huge shock when they went in the living room. They gazed at the room in complete horror it was an utter mess. The trimmings and Christmas tree were spend all over the floor; Susan burst out in tears as Diane came into the living to see why her mum was crying. 'What a mess?' Diane thought to herself. Diane could not believe it. Their Christmas was ruined. Diane was upset to the trimmings all over the floor! The Christmas tree was in bits. 'What did this?' Diane thought

Diane knew that the house was haunted but could not believe that a ghost could do that! Even an evil ghost! Diane was upset too, just like her mum and sister. She loved her Christmases at home with all her family. This made the house feel different. Not warm, not a safe home anymore. The three of them felt like they had been violated.

"What are we going to do, mum" Diane said feeling very confused.

Susan did not know what to say. That morning they all tidy up before Michael was due to come home. Sarah did not go to school that day. Diane did not go to work either. She ran in sick, so she could help her mum and sister.

Susan did not like Sarah taking time off school, she felt their education was very important but she knew that Sarah was too upset. So she ran in and said she was ill with flu. Susan contacted Ashley to let her know what had happened, she had no idea how to explain this to her husband. With no trimmings or Christmas tree there was no Christmas for the Jones family. They could not afford to replace, the trimmings, the trimmings that they made growing up were ruined too. They were irreplaceable.

Ashley with Jason and Antony came round to help tidy the mess up. Too give massive support to their mum that she really needed. Ashley gave her mum and sister Diane a huge cuddle. She could tell that her mum and sister needed it. Ashley gave Sarah then gave Jason cuddle too, he was upset and confused too to see the trimming, torn and smashed all over the floor, although a few trimmings had managed to stay in tact.

They had all managed to clear up the mess before their dad got back. Ashley, Antony and Diane offered to help their mum sort out Christmas, getting more trimmings, lights and Christmas tree. Susan at the time was still in shock. Ashley thought it would best to give her mum a bit of time to think things through and left with Jason. Who was still upset and confused about what happened to the Christmas stuff.

Ashley contacted the rest of the family like her Nan, Auntie Emily and Uncle Mark. At the time she just said that her mum and dad had been burgled in the night. Ashley left it to her mum if she wanted to tell them the truth. The rest of the family were in shocked too, this was not the sort of thing you would hear around were the Jones lived. It was a quiet and peaceful neighbourhood.

Auntie Emily was not convinced by Ashley's story. She knew that there was something evil in that house, the rest of the family were not really convinced either. They also too knew about the house and its eerie atmosphere, at times.

The family all wanted to do their bit to help. This was a time for the family to come together. Put what ever differences they had aside. Susan was devastated about the house. Susan and her kids had worked so hard, to make the house look so nice for Christmas, then to be ruined like that. The mess felt like her and her husbands marriage a mess, it had all been too much. Susan had enough of the house and in part her marriage too. Susan knew now this was not going to go away, that it would just keep getting worse, she had to do something about it.

Susie had looked into council flats, just in case the worse scenario happened between her husband's mum and dad. If they did spilt up at least Susan and Sarah would have somewhere to live! She also knew that they would not move just like that.

Antony did not really like Susie doing this. It was not nice to think that his mum and dad were to separate but Susan would have to think about her options. It was no longer safe for Susan and Sarah to stay. Antony's mum and dad had not been getting on well in while, so it was a possibility.

This time these problems could not be fixed, too much pain and suffering had happened between Michael and Susan but what ever happened it would not be happy news.

CHAPTER 24

Susan had enough and she was determined that she was going to tell her husband Michael. Susan felt as if her family was falling apart round her by what was going on in the house. The children were terrified of the house. They had Anna to help them. All her husband wanted to do was to bury his head in the sand and hope it would all go away. Susan knew that it would never just go away. Susan had to protect her children, she knew her husband would not want to move but maybe after what had happened that night. Maybe just maybe he would feel different. She was going to move whatever with or without him. Susan had made up her mind!

Michael and Susan loved each other as they had children together and had been a married couple for 30 years. They were not in love with each other anymore. The problems of the house just highlighted that. Before Sarah had come along they were a happy family at times but their marriage was not perfect. Michael was not the best dad or indeed the best husband but in his own strange way he did love his wife. When Sarah came along Michael had mellowed a lot, he tried to make up for not being a brilliant dad or husband.

Michael had tried to be a loving husband in the past but living in a foster home was not the same as living in a real home with a mum and dad. His foster family were not the most loving of people, he did not have a good role model that children depend on to mould them into a good person or how to show love in the right way.

Susan back then would not give up on their marriage, to be seen as a failure in her eyes and her family's eyes. After Sarah, Michael and Susan wanted their home to be a warm family home. Somewhere

where the memories could be full of fun and laughter! After all that gone through there was no more fun and laughter just terror, feeling unsafe and scared;

Sarah was miserable too! She knew that this would affect her mum and dad's marriage. That day she spent her day in her room, just played music on her new stereo she had for her birthday, Diane played her music in her room upstairs waiting for their dad to get back, both Sarah and Diane did not feel very festive. Everything was a mess including their mum and dad's marriage, they both knew there would be a full out because of this.

Sarah had her best tape on, while she just sat on her bed when the sound seemed to slow down almost, something was distorting the sound. Then the air turned cold she heard a wicked laugh by her ear.

Sarah knew that it was Anna's father, mocking her. She felt he was laughing at her family taunting her as if to say 'NOW! You fear me and I am destroying your family ha, ha' she heard him say as a whisper.

Then her tape just went back to normal. Sarah tried to be strong. She could feel that he wanted her to brake, to crush her spirit and cry but Sarah wanted to be brave. It was so very hard. She had never felt so desperate and low, in her whole life.

Ashley had managed to rally around with the family and had brought them a new tree, fairy lights and trimmings but as the last ones were destroyed they would leave it up to Susan, if she wanted to put them up!

Ashley popped them over before her dad got back. Susan was still an emotional wreck about it but she was not going to put them up to be ruined again! So she put them up in the attic until she had decided what she was going to do with them!

When Michael got in lunchtime he notice there was no trimmings up or Christmas tree, which he knew that they all had work so hard to make the house look really nice. At this time Sarah and Diane heard their dad come in, they both went downstairs to see their dad's reaction to what had happened!

"What happened to the trimmings and the Christmas tree? Where are they?" Michael said looking very puzzled, thinking what on earth had happened! At first Michael thought they had broken into. But most buglers don't go round stealing Christmas trimming or trees, normally its televisions or video recorders.

"They had to be thrown away there all broken. I will chat to you later about it!" Susan replied trying not to give too much away. She could not say too much in front of Sarah and Diane, Sarah was already having nightmares. She had to bind her time. Wait till Sarah had gone a bed, then she knew THE talk that she dreaded would have to happen, this would no longer keep.

"OK if that's what you want? BUT we do need to talk about this!" Michael knew by his wife tone that something serious had happened that night, while he was away. He could tell by her tone this was not a case of them being broken into. Susan did not say much for the rest of the day to her husband. Michael noticed that Sarah was very quiet too.

Later that day Susan had a number of phone calls from the family asking if they were ok! Maggie popped round too, she had heard the news that her best friend had been broken into. Michael was in the garden, he needed space.

"Hello, are you all ok?" Maggie said to her friend giving her a much needed hug, worrying about Susan.

"Not good really, were pretty shaken by it" Susan said looking very upset, worn out and depressed by all that was going on.

"Did they take much?" Maggie asked not knowing at the time it was not a brake in. Susan could talk about it a little Diane had taken Sarah out with her to see Ashley and Jason.

"It was not a brake in! Nothing was taken! Just the trimmings and the tree ruined" Susan replied she had to tell somebody the truth. She was not looking forward to, when it was time to have a chat with her husband, he would not believe.

"I don't understand!" Maggie said in a slightly bewildered manor.

"It something in this house, it always been here but since Sarah came into our lives it has got worse, more intense" Susan replied back, it felt strange to tell someone that was not family but she knew that Maggie always felt that there was something in the house too.

"You mean the house is haunted! I did already know that! We did that Ouija board here when we were about 19 years old! But I didn't take it that seriously I must admit, it a bit of a joke although I have felt something here at times" Maggie said trying to make sense of it in her head.

"Yes up until now, it not threatened us like that and I did not know how bad things were with Sarah" Susan said feeling like she had the weight of the world on her shoulders.

"Well if that is the case, Sarah is not safe here! She seems to be a target! Mind you she has always been a sensitive little girl and quiet" Maggie said worrying even more now about her friend, she realised how serious things had become.

"Yes I know I am going to chat with Michael tonight. I except that you noticed it yourself, me and Michael just have not been getting on very well! You know I have put up with a lot through the years. He has not always been the best of husbands or best of dad's but you work through it and keep going. I don't think I can anymore" Susan said consulting her friend.

"Well you do what right for you and Sarah now, the rest of the family will understand. Marriages sometimes do not last forever! It sad but if all your doing is arguing then that not good for any of you. Plus in this sort of house it's not good either" Maggie said giving her friend the support she needed.

"Yes I know but it's a hard decision I have to make" Susan replied not looking forward to the conversation that was going to have later. Maggie stayed for a little bit till just before tea time when Sarah and Diane were due to come home.

Michael was out in the garden most of the day as he taking the day off work. He had told his company that they had been broken into, his boss were very understanding about it and he understood that Michael could not come in, that Michael needed to be with his family. Michael really was not happy! He knew already what the conversation would be about.

Meanwhile that day at Ashley's house Sarah and Diane were glad to get out of the house, it did not feel like home to either of them now. What once was a family home was just a house. A house that did not want them in it!

Sarah and Diane were still pretty shaken by the events of the night before. They both were going to stay over Ashley's for the night, before that Diane and Sarah were going to go back home for tea, after come back to Ashley's. Antony had got a car by this time so he was going to drop them up home. Antony wanted to see his mum and dad too.

Sarah played with Jason that day, in one sense did not feel like playing. Ashley had a chat with Diane. Antony had come over for the day too. He wanted to see how his sister's, niece and nephew were doing!

"It's not good, that house is haunted" Diane said worrying about her mum, dad and sister.

"Yes I know. It was not like that for us growing up in that house. Yeah we all knew that there was something there but it's never been that bad" Ashley replied thinking to herself about the years that she had been growing up in that house.

"Well I think we got to be more worried about our mum and dad's marriage. I don't believe, In that sort of thing, ok I cant explain it but mum and dad have really not been getting on especially since mum's breakdown two years ago!" Antony said trying to be the voice of reason.

"That's not that bad, they row all the time lately about different things. It would not be that bad if they split up" Ashley said as she could see this coming for a while even if her mum and dad lived in a normal house "They have had problems all through their marriage, it's never been that good, they rowed when we were kids and our dad had a nasty temper back then, he only calmed down when Sarah was born" Ashley added.

Diane and Antony both sighed and agreed with their big sister, they carried on their chatting, while Sarah and Jason just played with Lego upstairs in Jason's room. Sarah tried to be the big brave sister to her little brother, she could tell that even though he was not showing it, her little brother was upset seeing his Nan and granddads house in a mess like that, seeing the trimmings torn up and Christmas tree in bits.

Later that day Antony came over to his mum and dad's house with Diane and Sarah for tea. Susan did not fuss like that, it was obvious that no one would be that hungry, so she just made a load of sandwiches and make some fairy cakes.

Maggie had gone home by then. Maggie told Susan that she would ring her in morning, to see how Susan got on with her chat with Michael. It was just five of them Michael, Susan, Antony, Diane and Sarah for tea.

When it came to teatime everyone sat round the table in silence barely a word spoken between them all. "OK, what is it with you all? No one has spoken to each other, so what's going on?" Michael demanded

Antony and Diane could see the raw tension between their mum and dad! It was building up and up like a coyly on a spring! After tea

Antony was going to take Diane and Sarah back to Ashley's house. Sarah did not want to leave her mum and dad. She could also feel the raw emotion.

Sarah could not hold it in any longer "Anna's father did it. I'm scared just like mum and Diane" Sarah said as she ran upstairs sobbing with her sister Diane following her upstairs. Diane was afraid too, she wanted to keep an eye on her sister.

Diane didn't want to stay in the house she knew her sister was upset but Sarah wanted to stay home and told Diane that she would be fine. It was just a bit upsetting with the house, so Diane went back to Ashley with Antony but did say that if Sarah needed her she was there for her.

Diane and Antony wanted to give their mum and dad space to talk. Sarah just stayed in her room and listed to music, in an attempt to take her mind off everything. It was not really working that well, downstairs Michael wanted to know 'what the hell was going on?'

"WHAT does Sarah mean Anna's father! Who is that? No one tells me anything any more." Michael said banging down his knife and fork "Yes we will talk later" Michael said angry that no was letting him know what on earth was going on. He stormed off to the living room. Turned on the telly, not in the mood to talk, just angry;

Susan was upset with the harsh words of her husband, who she needed more than ever. The reaction of her daughter, how upset Sarah was! Susan just cleaned up the kitchen. She could feel the tears coming, she had to be strong for them all and held them back . . . .

Her heart was torn in two between her husband and her children. She didn't want to give up on their marriage either. 'What was she going to do?' she thought to herself. She had never felt so lonely. Susan needed the warmth of her husband loving arms around her, telling her that it was going to be ok but instead she felt the cold arms of aloneness around her. She knew that her marriage could possibly be over.

The talk that Michael and Susan were going to have was huge thing. This was their future! Everything had to come out. Susan could not hold anything back for the sake of the children. This house was not a home any more just a place of nightmares.

Michael could no longer ignore his wife and the children, what they were going through on a daily bases now. Something had to be done! Or it was the end of their family.

Sarah was nervous about the conversation. This talk her mum and dad were going to have. She heard her dad raise his voice to her mum when she was upstairs. She could feel the tension between them even from upstairs. Sarah thought to herself 'oh no, Mum and dad are getting a divorce, I know it!' Sarah could here the raised temper between her parents. Sarah just didn't know what to do! She felt helpless.

Sarah did not want to leave the family home because of Anna what would happen to her if Sarah left! She would feel really guilty. Sarah really wanted to help Anna. She felt that she would be letting her best friend down, Sarah one and only real friend that understood her; even though Anna was a ghost.

That night Sarah stayed upstairs, she knew her mum and dad had a lot of talking to do. Sarah did her homework and listened to her music. It was a way of keeping her mind of what her parents were talking about!

Susan had finishing her cleaning in the kitchen and had sat near her husband while Michael was just looking at the telly not really taking it in by now he had calmed down a little. Susan took a deep breathe and turned to Michael. "Michael we need to talk" she said in a determined tone

"OH right! What is the problem? Don't tell me the house is haunted!" he said with a stern attitude; then added "apart from us"

"This house is not right for us any more; there is something very wrong with it!" Susan said in a concerned tone, Michael might not want to hear it. He would have to listen at some point.

"There is nothing wrong with this house." Michael replied. In a way he knew something was up but he hoped that if he said nothing it would all go away. Michael felt lost he wanted to protect his family, he did not know how! But at the same time he was not in love with his wife anymore. He loved her because of years they had together and their children. He had realised by now he just was not in love with her.

"We can't stay here anymore. There is something that wants to harm our children, last night there no burglar, it was an evil ghost" she continued "Our children DO NOT feel safe in this house; we have to protect our kids. We have to move" Susan was very animate about how she felt.

"We can't just move. If we ignore what ever it is, it will go away. This is our family home" Michael responded trying to calm his wife, trying to play it down.

"This is not something that will just go away. It's gone to far now" Susan said getting angry with her husband that would not understand, closed his mind off.

"The problem is us, I don't want this anymore" Michael said trying to push the blame on what was going on in the house, to their marriage.

"Well I can't stay here and neither can Sarah, I am going to move out with Sarah. I won't see our child suffer anymore. It's not just us but the house, its ripping our family apart" Susan went upstairs in a mood. She went into her bedroom and slammed her bedroom door shut. Sarah heard everything.

Michael was so angry he went out slamming the front door behind him. Susan stayed in her bedroom, apart to say goodnight to Sarah, then she went back to her bedroom and stayed in there all night.

Sarah wanted to know what had happen she did not hear properly, what been said by her mum and dad only raised voices. Although she knew it was not good! She knew that maybe at the moment, may not be the best time. Sarah was worried that her dad would not return, he sounded so angry and even if he did return, what would he be like as he was angry when he left?

The house was calm and quite all night. Sarah felt that Anna's father would be pleased with the fact Sarah's mother and father had fallen out. Angry words were said. She felt his presence a little that night, almost if she could feel him grinning and laughing at her. Sarah could not sleep properly everything weighing down on her; she was upset and stressed that night, tears fell yet again.

Michael return home later that night but he slept downstairs. This was the first time in over 30 years of their marriage he had done this! Sarah knew that her family was in trouble they were falling into disarray. This house and all that had gone on had cut their family apart. Sarah tried to fight back the tears. There were no footsteps or the sound of Anna kind voice once again Sarah felt alone! She was lost in the mists of own personal hell . . . .

CHAPTER 25

The next day it was a weekend no school for Sarah and no work for their dad.

There was silence around the breakfast table that morning. None of them spoke a word to each other. Then Susan turned to Sarah and said. "We are leaving this house!"

Michael and Susan had drifted far away from each other, they had tried to hide it from their children but this time they could not counsel it, how they felt from their children any longer. Susan was determined to leave the house, she could not cope with it any more.

"What about dad" Sarah asked in a tearful tone of voice.

"Your dad is not coming and I cannot stay here a moment more. It is not safe here anymore for us" Susan replied trying to be honest with her daughter.

"Well I am not leaving our home. I am not going through all that again in finding a new home. I have not got the money to move either. I am really sorry Sarah" Michael said in a very stern voice.

"Well, I and Sarah are staying with my sister Emily for now. You do whatever!" Susan said as she got up from the table. "I am going to arrange it with my sister now" Susan was annoyed with Michael again with his lack of support.

"OK you stay with your sister Emily but I'm staying right here" Michael shouting also leaving the table, leaving Sarah on her own around the breakfast table.

This family was finished, there was no way back! Michael was determined that he was not going to leave the house. Michael could not see that the house was effecting the children; this was the first time him and his wife had really argued loudly like this in front of their children, to the point that they family was on the brink of separation. He had saved a lot of money and time into their home, there was no money to move. They were comfortable with money but not rich. There was a huge amount of tension in the air. Sarah was upset to see her family broken in two. She could not stand the thought of her mum and dad not together this was something she never thought in a million years this would happen to them!

Sarah could see both sides of the argument, even at just 10 years old. Her dad had spent a lot of money at the time getting their home. Her mum was just trying to protect her kids. Sarah could tell her dad was feeling lost and see a weaker side to her dad. Who had always been in her eyes soft but strong for his family!

Michael had calmed down a little after breakfast he had chance to think it though. Sarah sat in the living room on the sofa just looking at her mum and dad, who were just sat down watching telly not speaking! Sarah heard her mum on the phone to Auntie Emily just before she had sat down. Michael could see that his wife, even though she was in a mood. His wife was holding back the tears! As despite everything they still loved and cared for each other.

Michael looked over to his wife, he got up and sat by his daughter he gave her a cuddle, he could see that his daughter had been affected by him and his wife's row's. This was not good environment for her. Susan though her marriage was going to end. Michael looked over to wife at the same time, said what himself and his wife had been thinking for a while, none of them strong enough to say as it would still hurt. Michael said something that surprised his wife.

"I and your mother have not been getting on. I think deep down you know that too! I will never divorce your mum. I still love her but sometimes, mums and dads fall out of being in love, like us. I am staying here" Michael looked at Susan with tears but as hard as it was to say, it was the truth.

"No dad, please tell me that you are making this up because of the house" Sarah pleaded with her dad, Sarah was devastated.

"Your dad is right, we need to live apart but your dad will always be there for you and me" Susan said also with tears, this was a big moment but it was right thing to do, not necessary the easiest thing to do!

"Ok, your mum is right you. Your brothers and sisters happiness and safety comes first I love all very much". Michael looked over to his wife and smiled. Michael was putting a brave face too. He knew that his wife and children for whatever reason were not safe in the house. Regardless how he felt about the house, he had to put them first. Seeing his wife and daughter move away was the hardest thing he would to face, he thought it was for the best right now.

"I will help you sort out what needs to be packed and get some boxes to put stuff in. I will stay here for a bit until I can sort something out for a new home for us" Michael said he felt like a husband and a father again the rock of the family. He knew he could not be with them straight away. He felt his family were back on track. He could not give up on his family, neither could his wife. They were going to get through this together as one.

The phone went. It was Diane she wanted to see how her mum and dad were, also Ashley and Antony were anxious to know too. Susan answered the phone.

"Hello" Susan said in a quiet voice, you could hear in voice that she was not happy.

"Hi mum, how are you and dad?" Diane asked "how is Sarah?" she added feeling slightly nerved of what her mum was going to say especially, she could tell that mum was upset.

"Not good to be honest, Sarah and I are leaving the house but your dad is staying it is up to you if you come or you can stay at your sister's for now. Till we have a proper place to live, at the moment were staying at your Auntie Emily's house" Susan replied being as honest as she could, her children needed to know what was going on? Regardless of how upsetting it was to hear!

"Oh no, you and dad are separating? How is Sarah taken that news?" Diane said concern for her little sister, although she was glad that her mum and her sister were leaving that house, in a way it was not a huge shock that her mum and dad were separating.

"Sarah is upset about me and your dad separating but she does understand why, it has to be done!" Susan said with big sigh.

"I know, doesn't make it any easier though. I give you another call later over Auntie Ems" Diane said she knew once she put the phone down her brother and sister and her little nephew will want to know what was going to happen? She would have to break the bad news somehow!

"Ok love, speak to you later, got to sort out our things now" Susan replied not looking forward to the task ahead as it was a huge one, even though Susan and Sarah was staying over her sister's. This was only a temporary measure and would have to pack, some things away in readiness when they would eventually move to a new place.

"Love you mum, bye" Diane said as her mum said bye too, Diane put the phone down and sat down in the living room of her sister's house.

Ashley and Antony stared at their sister nervously waiting to hear the news. Lucky enough Jason was upstairs playing, this would have to be broken gently to him being only 7 years old, this would be very upsetting so telling him would have be done in a way that 7 year old would understand!

Ashley and Antony was not surprised to hear about their mum and dad's separation, upsetting in one sense to know that their mum and dad's would not be together. They were glad as well that their mum and Sarah were going to move out.

After Ashley and Antony had found out the news, Ashley went upstairs to her son's room, so that she could tell Jason the bad news about the move away also that his Nan and granddad would no longer be living together.

Jason was a little upset about his Nan and Granddad would not be living together anymore, that Sarah and his Nan would be moving away but was a little young to understand what that really meant. Ashley reassured Jason that Sarah and his Nan would not be moving far, at first they would be staying with his Auntie Emily then they move into a new home, it would be still be in Bristol.

Meanwhile at Susan and Michael's house, Susan got up and sat by her husband gave a huge hug and kiss "Thank you for understanding" Susan said with a sigh of relief but she was not happy, in one way she could not stand the thought of leaving her husband behind, they had never been apart but this was the only way.

To live apart but Michael would still always be there for his wife and daughter. They were not giving up on each other, just separate to give each other a little bit of space that their marriage needed. They could not give up on each other but they could not live together any longer.

"We are still a family, even if we are not living together! We can be strong and get through this!" Michael said being supportive to them. This was Michael way of protecting the most important thing in the world to him, who he loved more than anything, his family! It was his way also for making up for letting his wife and children down in the past, he could not change that but he could do the best thing by them now.

Susan went upstairs to make a start on packing things up, while Michael got some boxes sorted from the attic. Then Michael gave his wife a cuddle and kiss, "I will always love you, I will be there anytime you need me or if Sarah needs me" Michael said embracing his wife to give her a much needed hug of comfort, the comfort that she needed for a long time.

Michael realised now that his wife and daughter was moving, just how important they were to him. He loved his wife he knew that but they could not live together anymore, loving someone sometimes is not enough. Michael was grown up enough now to understand this.

"I know, I love you too, we can't argue in front of our kids anymore. We have to do this for them and for us" Susan replied given a little smile even though her heart was braking. They had been together for so long and through so much. Although they were not in love, they still had all those cherished memories, some were bad but there were good and fond memories and these were the ones they would cherish. Still cared deeply for one another, this was still heart wrenching, they also had three children together which would bind them for life.

Sarah went into her bedroom. She had one last look around before she started to pack. She felt sad; "Anna, its Sarah" She whispered. "I am so sorry but my mum wants us to leave, it's not safe for me and my family anymore! But my dad is staying behind for now" Sarah really felt bad for leaving her friend Anna.

Sarah was upset that she had to leave her friend. Anna did not reply. Sarah started to pack her suitcase with her clothes toys and music. Then Anna came "I understand it is ok. I don't want you or your family to get hurt because of me" Anna said with tears in her eyes.

"I am really sorry" Sarah replied holding back the tears of sadness. Sarah would visit as her dad was still going to be there, it would not be the same.

Anna faded away. Sarah got her things and went downstairs. She could feel her eyes swelling up with tears; but she held them back really well.

That day they packed most of their personal things apart from Michael's stuff. It was put into boxes. Susan's sister Emily was looking forward to spending time with her sister. She did not have a big house, so it was going to be a squeeze. Emily had a small three bed house about ten minutes away from their house. Emily Jackson had her husband peter with their daughter Jessica.

"We will still be together as a family but not living together again and I will visit all the time. I have to stay here for now till I will find somewhere for you to live and a place for myself" Michael explained to them. "Auntie Emily is here now, I get the ball rolling" Michael said. Emily pulled up outside their house, to collect Sarah and Susan.

Michael could see that his family were upset. He hated not being able to be there with them either, even though he would not be living with his wife and daughter, he knew this had to happen. "Come here you guys. How about a Jones super hug" Michael asked with his arms open wide to embrace his wife and Sarah. They all hugged with tears of sadness.

Antony was in the car too he had offered to help with his mum and sister's things. Antony waved to his dad from the back seat of Emily's car.

"Ok let's go. We will miss you." Susan replied even though it was only temporary. She still hated it. Michael put the boxes of things in Emily's car, Susan and Sarah got in.

"I will pop round later and see you all" Michael said as his wife got in the front of the car and Sarah went in the back seat of the car, next to her big brother, all very tearful. This was an emotional time for them all. The sadness brought out all the past, in their emotions. Things that had gone on to do with the house and just memories in general, the good, the bad and the ugly brought to ahead with the emotion of the move.

As Sarah sat down in the car, she looked up to what now was her old bedroom window. She noticed the ghostly figure of Anna was standing by the in the window in her room. Sarah could tell that Anna was upset, Anna looked afraid too. Then she saw another ghostly figure but a dark ghostly figure behind Anna, cold icy hands on Anna's shoulders. She knew that this was Anna's father and this was not the end even though she was moving away. The dark figure looked straight at her with an eerie grin. He put his thin finger up to his mouth as if to say don't tell anyone about me or else as they drove away. Sarah felt really upset now she knew she had let her friend down.

Susan was glad that they were leaving, she had feared for her children's life. Now she was relieved she knew or at least she hoped that her children would be safe. It was all over. She didn't want to leave her husband, knew in her heart there was no other way.

Emily pulled up outside her house. Emily's family were waiting outside to greet them. Sarah got out of the car, she looked up at her cousin and uncle then smiled, they were both quiet each in their own thoughts; Then Susan got out and helped her son Antony get the boxes of their things out from the car.

Antony looked at his mum and could tell she was beside herself, he could see that even though she was out of the house, she was upset. "It will be ok! But this needs to happen, mum, you could not of stayed there anymore, I'm here for you and so is Ashley and Diane" Antony said to his mum holding his mum's hand. He wanted to give his mum comfort, be supportive and strong for them. He knew right now that was what his family needed.

Sarah went over and gave her big brother a hug too. She was glad that he was there to support their mum and there for her too. They all went inside with a box of things each. Antony stayed for a cup of tea, after he had to return home to his wife Susie, whom would want an update on how his family was doing.

"Thank you for helping out Antony" Susan said as they all sat down to a hot drink after sorted out the boxes.

"That's ok mum, anytime" Antony said giving half a smile, wondering how his dad was getting on, all alone in that house. Antony stayed for his cup of tea, said his goodbyes and left to go home.

CHAPTER 26

Susan liked being with her sister. They were never really that close as kids so maybe this was a way of building some bridges. When they were growing up Emily was always busy, she never really had time for Susan but they were adults now, things change!

Susan missed her husband he had always been there for her, even when they were just friends. But their marriage in the early years was not perfect! Michael was a bit hot headed and didn't know how to show affection properly being brought up in a foster home. It still was not the same there without him! They had been together for over 30 years. That's a long time to be with someone, Susan and Michael would no longer be living together. Their marriage was not over.

Sarah played upstairs with Jessica. Emily's husband Peter went on his computer to do some work, while Susan and Emily had a coffee and a frank chat about what had been going on with the old house!

"So are you going to tell what has REALLY been going on?" Emily said she knew her sister had not told her the whole story about things.

"It's the house! Just could not stay there any longer also myself and Michael are just not in love anymore, we can't be together anymore. We would end up hating each other. Plus it was not good for Sarah hearing us argue all the time after all she went through in that house" Susan was nearly in tears, she had been keeping her feelings hidden to put a brave face on things.

"Go on, we all could see about you and Michael but please tell me about the house" Emily replied she could see that her sister had been bottling a lot of raw emotions.

"It's just not safe, Sarah and Jason were having nightmares and the house had something terrible inside a bad spirit. There were footsteps that would freak the kids out, there was also a little girl that would visit Sarah" Susan had finely said what had been going on. It felt good to talk to someone about it, she was surprise that her sister did not try and dismiss it.

"I know about the footsteps, that's why I never really visited you that much while you were in that house. That night I stayed over when Sarah was younger. I heard them and I always felt as if something was watching. Whenever I went down the stairs! I did not say anything. I thought you might think, I going completely mad." Emily explained also pleased to get her horrible experience in that house of her chest.

Susan was shocked she had no idea that her sister had felt that way. She never once said anything about it!

"OH right, I never knew!" Susan replied raising her eyebrows in surprise.

Sarah and Jessica were getting on very well. Sarah tried to have fun but she had her mind on other things. She was missing her dad but that not her main concern. Sarah was worried about Anna 'What would happen to her without them?' she thought. She knew her dad would be ok in the house on his own, as nothing ever happened to him!

At the old house in the meantime Michael was packing up some boxes before he was going to meet his son Antony and daughter in law Susie for a drink. They had wanted to meet him. Antony and Susie wanted to do their bit to help. He had packed up some things from Diane's room, some of Jason old toys and some of Sarah's things. The door to Diane's bedroom happened to be open so he could see into the landing and onto Sarah's old room. All of a sudden from the corner of his eye he seen Sarah's bedroom door open by itself. Being Michael he did not think anything of it, thought it was a draft coming in from somewhere that caused the door to open.

Michael just went downstairs to take the box down ready to take with him. After he had seen his son, he was going up to Emily's house to see Susan and Sarah. He went down the stairs he suddenly felt something stare at him from behind; so much so that it made him turn to look up the stairs! This had never happened to him before so again he ignored the feeling. Michael left to meet his son.

Susie had managed to find some council flats that were close and had vacancies, it was just an idea and because it was council run Susie wanted to pass it by Michael first.

Michael met his son and daughter in law in the local pub for food and a pint. It was good to see his son, he was always working hard. By now Antony was working with a taxi company and it was going well. Susie did work for the council but had been made redundant a year ago, now just doing some shop work to tie her over till she got a better job.

"Hi dad good to see you, how is mum and Sarah?" Antony asked feeling a little concerned for them and his dad.

"Hi how is Diane too? What is really going on?" Susie added also worried for the family too. She had become very close to Susan, Sarah and Diane.

"Well our house so she says is haunted by an evil presence. Sarah and Jason were having nightmares! You know me I don't believe in that sort of thing son but I had to take it seriously, it was destroying our marriage. I didn't want your mum to leave but I just not in love with her anymore, we have been drifting apart for a while" Michael explained to his son, just been good at hiding it, he felt his son how ever upsetting it was, he deserved his dad's honesty.

"I never really liked that house dad to be honest, it always felt unwelcoming a cold feel! as for you and mum you cant stay with someone your not in love with anymore, it sad but I suppose its life and you cant stay together just for us kids sake it not fair on you or us kids" Antony replied talking sense.

"Will be there for you and Susan, you have to do what's right for you now!" Susie added trying to give her support too.

"I just don't know what to do about the house. I don't want to leave it, at the moment. I'm quite happy staying their on my own at the moment, nothing happens to me but I do need to find something for your mum and sister" Michael said rubbing his forehead.

"WELL I think I might have a solution not prefect but it's something for now anyway. Before I said anything to Susan, I wanted to run it by you. You know Susan better than me" Susie said she had already told her husband the idea. Antony thought was a really good idea. Michael was intrigued by this.

"Ok what idea is this?" Michael asked in curious manor, giving Susie a puzzled look.

"Well you know I use to work for the local council, I still have contacts and it just so happens there some flats not too far from here. They have got some flats free! I know it's a step down from a house but they are really nice flats. You do have the option to buy after three years" Susie said trying to give some sort of practical help.

"No thank you, it's not a house but it is somewhere, I will have a word with Susan and get back to you on that!" Michael said he had a feeling he knew the flats she was taking about and yes is was in a nice area, nice flats. Only six flats in each block.

Michael had a nice time catching up on things. After they finished Antony, Susie and Michael gave each other a hug and said goodbye.

"Speak to you soon dad! Let me know what mum thinks?" Antony said as they left. Antony dropped off Michael at Emily's house on route to his house.

Diane was going to stay with her sister Ashley, till her mum and sister got settled in a more permit place.

Michael got out of the car, waved goodbye to Antony and Susie, he knocked on the door. Susan opened the door with excitement. Michael and Susan embraced and kissed each other on the cheek. Like they had not seen each other for days, it all was due to the emotions of what had happened or nearly happened to their family. They had nearly lost it all. This would be a new chapter in all their lives . . . .

Sarah came rushing down the stairs. She saw her mum and dad kissing. "Mum dad, do you have to do that in front of me!" Sarah said she was glad that they were. It meant that her mum and dad were still together. Not getting a divorce, even if it meant they were moving to a different house.

Jason had come over for tea to see his Nan and Sister, Antony had dropped him over and Emily was going to drop Jason home later, that evening.

Sarah knew that her dad would be close, he promised faithfully. She did think at one point her mum and dad marriage was over, now just separated. But in fact her mum moving out of the house, making that hard decision was probably what had saved their marriage and family, Sarah's dad decided that they moved apart is what saved them.

"Here is some more of Jason toys and some of your things too Sarah, why don't you go up stairs to your room and sort them out with your cousin and brother. Leave us adults to have a chat" Michael said to his daughter, while coming in and handing Sarah the box of varies things. Sarah was worried as soon as she heard her dad say about a chat, her dad could see it in her eyes; so could her mum. "Don't worry Sarah it's going to be alright. Me and mum are staying together, just not living together, there will be no arguments I promise" Michael said giving his daughter a cuddle.

This made Sarah feel a lot happier, she went upstairs with her cousin and her little brother. "We do need to talk!" Susan said smiling at Michael holding Michael's hand.

Susan, Michael and Emily sat in the living room, on a weekend, it was sometimes a take away night for the Jacksons so Peter went out and got fish and chips for them all, while they rest of them had their chat. "I am really sorry I did not support you, like I should of. I will always be there if you need me" Michael said to his wife she could tell he meant every word, which meant a lot to her.

"I know you are sorry, I hate fighting! I am sorry too for not thinking how hard it must been for you not knowing what to do!" Susan replied. Then she asked how their son was" how is Antony? How the taxi business going? How is Susie?"

"Yes ok, Susie said something at the end. When we were about to leave that can help us! Well more for you but it would mean that your not far away, she didn't say Where, just that they would let me know" Michael replied feeling a little excited by what his daughter in law had said.

"Oh right" Susan said feeling a bit puzzled.

Peter came back and they all sat down stairs with the kids, they had their tea. It felt good that they were all together again, even though they knew for now that Michael had to go back to that house but for now they were happy. Just before bedtime Emily dropped Jason off home to Ashley's house.

Later on that night before the kids went to bed it was time for Michael to go, back to the house. Michael's family did not like the thought of him going back to the house. They knew for now he did not have a choice, so he got up said thank for his tea, said his goodbyes and returned to the house on his own!

It was bedtime for the kids and for the first time in a long time Sarah had a really good night sleep, like she had not had a good night sleep in years. There were no footsteps and no nightmares for them that night. When Sarah went to sleep she could not help but think 'is it really all over?' she had been so use to the footsteps, Anna's voice and those nightmares for so long, it felt kind of strange.

Susan also had an ok night sleep. She could relax in the knowledge that her daughter was safe, no reason to be afraid anymore. As she fell asleep, she thought about her husband.

Susan missed him giving her those kisses and cuddles! Their chats they had. Even though they were not in love, they still cared deeply for each other and had never been away from each other. Plus as well as being husband and wife, they were soul mates, best friends and that still remained. Even through they had tabulate marriage in the beginning.

When Michael was a teenager the only family he really had was his foster parents, who were not brilliant and Susan. Susan became his one and only friend, her family took him under their wing, they did feel a little bit sorry for him.

Meanwhile at the house Michael was getting ready for bed. It did not feel right in the house without his wife and daughters, or the sound of his other kids or Jason. He was not use to not hearing his children play upstairs on an evening, while his wife and he would cuddle up on the sofa talk about their day.

The house was cold, dark, empty and lonely. He missed his wife and him when the kids were in bed their long embraces and kisses, the feel of his wife body next to his at night in bed together. Michael went to bed alone. He noticed that Sarah door was open again, he was sure that he had closed it earlier. Michael closed it again along with the spare bedroom door. Thought nothing of it and went to bed.

The next morning Michael had a little lay in. It was a Sunday but knew he had more sorting out to do. On Monday he had an appointment with the asset agents to get a valuation on the house for when he would eventually sale it, so he had to dig up the paperwork for the house in readiness for Monday morning.

Michael got dressed and went to go downstairs. He noticed that both Sarah's bedroom door and the spare door were wide open again! Yet he could remember that night, he had closed both doors before he went to bed. This made Michael uneasy he did not like it, when things happened that he could not explain with a logical explanation. Michael just ignored it again and went on doing the things he knew he needed to do. Still at back of his mind trying to work out what had happened!

In the Jackson's household the kids were up with Susan, who was not the one for lay in, plus it was not the same waking up without her husband by her side! The kids were watching morning telly, While Susan got some breakfast on the go. Susan was missing Michael like crazy but tried to hide it. Sarah knew her mum too well and came out to the kitchen to give her mum a cuddle.

"I will be alright; just not use to your dad not being here" Susan said a little sad but glad to be away from the house. Also she hoped that her husband would be ok alone in that house, even though nothing ever happened to him! He was on his own it might be different. This bad spirit only had Michael to scare or threaten now as Sarah, Diane and Susan were gone.

"I know mum, I miss dad too" Sarah said giving her much needed support.

Michael came over that day to spend time with his wife and Sarah but did not mention what strange thing had happened at the house! Susan and their daughter were glad to see her dad. He was staying for Sunday Dinner, they were having a lovely roast dinner with all the trimmings. It was nice. That day the Jacksons trimmed up for Christmas with every ones help it looked wonderful. But Sarah could not help it although it was nice, this was not their home. She remembered when they trimmed up at their house last and for it all to be ruined. It was a painful memory!

Michael could see his daughter was not happy and his wife. Michael said to his wife "I might have a bit of good news for you and Sarah but I am waiting on a phone call before I can tell you what it was!"

"Oh right! That sounds interesting!" Susan enquired she was a little puzzled, this gave her a bit of hope "A phone call from whom?" Susan added.

"You'll see" Michael said smiling and grinning as if he was up to something!

Later on that lunchtime they all sat round the table in the living room to have their Sunday roast, it was delicious although, Sarah thought her mum's roasts were better but did not tell Auntie Emily this, after lunchtime Emily put the kettle on.

They all sat down to watch telly with a hot cup of tea or coffee, Emily's phone went it was Antony. He wanted to speak to his dad. Michael went into the hallway to take the call Susan could not help wondering 'what the call was about after Michael had said that he had some good news but he was waiting on a call and how this to do with their son' this was very odd.

Michael came back into the living room as Emily brought out cups off coffee for them all. Michael had a huge grin on his face, he looked over to Susan.

"What is it? What did our son say?" Susan was curious to hear what he had said!

"Well I have found you and Sarah a new home! It's not far and we can afford it." Michael was beaming with joy.

"Where;" Susan asked.

"Susie has found you a three bed flat for you and Sarah. Well you know she use to work for the council, she still has contacts in the council. She phoned around on your behalf, she has found some flats available that are not far away about 5 minutes from Sarah's school. Its council flats but they are nice flats clean and quite new, you have the right to buy after three years. We just got to let them know if you are interested!" Michael said he knew Susan and the fact that they were council flats would not bother his wife, as long as they were nice flats, in a nice area.

"WELL OK. That's brilliant! That was nice for Susie to do that for us, I give Antony a call later. I will let him know that it would be prefect and thank Susie for us" Susan replied and started to feel excited too. It might be a flat but it didn't matter. "Is that ok to use your phone in a bit to call Antony" Susan asked her sister full of joy.

"Well I was hoping you were going to yes. That means that I would not be too far away either just about 25 minutes walk away, or ten minutes on a bus" Michael said. He was happy his wife had got somewhere to live, also that it was not too far from him so he could visit Sarah on a regular basis, which Susan did not mind him visiting a lot but it would be strange, they were not moving in together. They were on the move once again, this time it would be for the very last time.

"Hope you don't mind us leaving you soon" Susan asked her sister.

"No that's fine understand totally plus this house is not big enough for you lot" Emily was pleased for her sister, she knew she had a rough time at that house and just wanted her sister to be happy.

"This going to be good for us mum, I do understand about you and dad but that's ok as dad is not going to be far from us" Sarah smiled at her mother. She gave her mum a huge hug.

Susan called her son up to let him know that it was a yes, that it would be really good, to thank Susie for going to all that effort to finding her and Sarah a new home. Antony and Susie was just glad to help and that where Susan and Sarah would be. It meant also Susan was close to them about 20 minutes away in fact and Antony's dad. Susan was getting a little better with going out but the family still felt they wanted to able to still be there for their mum.

Later on Antony phoned his sister Ashley and told her the good news that he and Susie had found their mum a place to live, in a nice area not too far from the family.

This would be good for Sarah too, she would be close to school and she could walk to school by herself, which meant also Diane would not need to take her or Susan. Ashley let her Nan know that Susan and Sarah were moving. By this time Hilary was getting really forgetful, this was also a concern for the family. The family had been keeping a close eye on Hilary too.

"Ok can we hang on here a bit longer if that is ok with you Emily" Susan said. Susan knew that it would not be straight away that they would move.

"Yes that will be fine" Emily replied, Emily had no problems with that.

Michael not long after went back to the house said goodbye to Susan and Sarah. He had to sort out things for Susan. Michael had packed Susan and Sarah's stuff into boxes. Susan would also need to decide between her and her husband, what big items they wanted. Things like furniture, bedding, towels and kitchen utensils, the weeks did go by quick. Michael visited Susan and Sarah everyday as he promised. Then Susan and Sarah were off to start their new life in their new home. It was only a ten minute drive away. Susan could still see her sister anytime.

Sarah did go back to old house quite a few times, while her dad was still living there. He still had to find a home for himself. Sarah friend Anna would not speak to Sarah, when she returned to the old house to visit her dad. She would still feel her presence. This would be upsetting, she had let Anna down. This would not be the end for the house and its menacing ghost! Sarah moving away meant she would no longer be a threat to this entity's dark secret.

Lucky for Susan it only took two weeks to sort the flat out with Susie's help and her contacts that she had through the council. As Susan did not work for health reasons, with the break down and being acrophobic, plus before when her and her husband was together, she was a housewife. She had always been a housewife looking after the kids and the house, which Michael was quite happy to be the bread winner!

Now Susan would have to rely on benefits which Susie helped Susan fill out the forms, that she had fill out to get the money that she was entailed to. Susan did have a little bit of money put aside, which would cover getting the big things she needed for the house like furniture for the flat.

CHAPTER 27

It was the day of the big move, the weeks leading up to this had gone past very quick. Mark and Michael helped Sarah and Susan take their stuff over to their new flat. Sarah and Susan were tearful to see Michael go home without them. He had a brief look around the flat. Then he left to go back to the big old house but he was only a walk away! Michael promised he would go up later that day, to see them as soon as they were settled. Michael thanked his son and brother in law for their help.

"Thank you SO much Antony" Susan said as she got out of the car with a few bag of clothes.

"No worries mum, just glad I can help. You all have had a few rough years. Come on in to yours and Sarah's new home. I will get the boxes in you just relax" Antony was glad to help his mum, it was nice to know at least his mum and little sister was going to be ok. Antony was not that worried about his mum and sister anymore. He felt sure his dad would be fine in the house on his own.

Michael told his son that he was going to move a bit later, as the house market was not a good time to sale a house. Also at least him staying at the house, he would not be too far from Antony's mum and sister. Michael and Susan separating was a way of saving their marriage, a chance to reflect. Realise what they had!

Hilary called up later on that day. Emily had given her mum, Susan's new phone number "How is the move going?" Susan's mum asked knowing, what a huge deal this was for her daughter.

"Yes mum it all going well. I have plenty of hands to help Mark and Antony have been brilliant. Michael has been sorting stuff out mine and Sarah's from the old house. Just need to pop back to the old house at some point to sort out the other things in the house!"

Later that day Antony popped down to the Susan's old house with his mum to go through other stuff. To who wanted what and bring back the stuff that his mum had chosen. Sarah stayed at the flat with Susie, who help put things away and to help Sarah sort out her stuff.

Someone needed to be at flat. Susan had a delivery of a 3 piece suite and 2 single beds, a telly, 2 cupboards for the bedrooms and 2 cabinets for each of the rooms. Susan was not at the old house for long just an hour and a half, in that time the items she had ordered had come all at the same time more or less. So very busy day lucky for Susan this move had fallen on a weekend.

They had moved in around about Michael and Susan's birthday mid January and just a week before their daughter Diane's 21st birthday. Michael and Susan did not celebrate their birthday like that. It was too busy with the move and they were not together anymore.

Michael thanked his son for helping his mum out with the move, this had meant a lot. It was going to take time for the adjustment but at least his wife and daughter were not far away. This would make things a little easier for all concerned.

Michael came back with Susan and Antony. He could help put things away that Susan had picked from the house to the new flat. It was nice for Susan to come back to flat to see all the new furniture there.

With the help of Michael, Antony, Susie, Diane, Ashley and Mark, It didn't take to long to sort the flat out and to fill in the paperwork for the flat, what she was entailed to. Susan was keeping herself busy by sorting out boxes and boxes of things for the individual rooms. Sarah sorted out her room it was about the same size as her old room maybe slightly smaller, still plenty enough room to put her stuff in.

Sarah was also keeping herself busy too! She was missing her dad lots; it was going to take time to adjust to her mum and dad not living in the same place. Sarah knew that how ever upsetting it was she would have to get use to it. At least she didn't have to listen to them arguing all the time! Hopefully they should get on better living apart.

Susan and Sarah were also concerned as he was still in that house, nothing ever really happened to him, when they were all together there. Now he was on his own, this could change things for him.

In the flat there was a living room about medium size with sliding doors leading out to a medium sized garden that looked onto a big field. They kitchen lead of from the living room was not huge but not a bad size. There was medium square hallway with a big storage cupboard, a toilet room, a bathroom and two medium sized bedrooms and a small box room. Susan had one medium bedroom and Sarah had the other medium room. The small box room would be a spare bedroom.

Lucky for Sarah which was a good thing, Sarah's school was only about 5 minutes walk away from their new home. Susan went into Sarah's room to see if she needed a hand with anything, "Well what do you think of our new home! I know it probably feels a little strange without your dad" Susan asked her daughter.

"Yes it's nice, I do like my room but it is odd without dad. I can't help it mum I miss dad but I know it will get easier as time goes on" Sarah said then added being very grown up "Don't worry mum, I will be fine"

Later that day Michael came around with some fish and chips for tea. He knew that his wife would be really busy and probably had not eaten. He thought he would check to see if, she needed a hand with anything and of course he did miss Susan and Sarah too.

Susan answered the door and Michael gave Susan a hug. He seen that she needed it more than ever, then Sarah came running to the door. Michael came in and Susan closed the door.

"I've missed you dad" Sarah said so happy to see her dad.

"It's good to see you too, both of you and I have missed you too" Michael said

"Well you going to let me come in properly or these fish and chips are going to get cold" Michael added jokingly.

"Thank you" Susan said smiling, Michael knew by her smile that it more about the support than the food.

"No problem" Michael said smiling back. It was a nice rest of the day almost like it was; what seemed a long time ago! when they would have a laugh together as a family. There had been no laughs for a while just tears and anger.

"Is there anything you need for here or anything you need me to do?" Michael asked showing his support, as promised that he would be there for them both and he meant it, Susan could tell he meant it too.

"No but thank you" Susan replied "As you can see all the big things are here now. It just the little things to sort out but I got tomorrow to do that! How are you being in that house on your own?" Susan asked, she still cared she needed to know that her husband was going to be ok!

"I am fine, just feels really strange without you and the kids, too quiet" Michael replied. It was nice to talk not to row. There seemed to be less tension between them.

Later that day on evening Ashley popped round with Jason. He was dying to see their new home. He was upset about his Nan and granddad not being together. This meant however he had two places he could have a sleepover, and two lots of presents on his birthday or Christmas rather than just one lot from the both of them.

Ashley was upset but she knew that her mum and dad have not been getting on for a while, so she was half expecting it to happen. It came as no surprise.

"It's not a bad size flat" Ashley said "I THINK Jason likes it too" Ashley added as Jason went out to play in the field with her sister with his new football.

"Well it will do for us" Susan said smiling watching her daughter and Grandson play outside, happy and joyful as children should be.

Ashley had brought a bottle of champagne to celebrate the new move. Michael didn't really feel like celebrating at the time, he separating from his wife but in another, he understood why Ashley had thought it was cause for celebrate. If Susan had not of made that tough discussion the marriage would have been over. It would of ripped them apart staying in that house; or someone might of got seriously hurt like his daughter Sarah! Physically hurt by whatever was in that house. Michael understood these things now.

It was a nice evening. Later that week the rest of the family came down to see Susan and Sarah to give their royal approval. Emily and her mum Hilary with peter and Jessica popped over. Later Mark, Vivian, Nicole and Natasha also popped over too see the flat. They all were impressed even though it was a flat, it was a lovely flat. Most of all Susan and Sarah were smiling once again with sound of laughter. Something that this family had not done in a long time!

Susan and Michael's kids were happy for their mum, dad and Sarah. Even though their parents were apart, they seemed better for it. So in turn this would be better for Sarah too, not seeing her parent's row. Michael visited Susan and Sarah most night for an hour. Sarah would visit her dad sometimes in the old house.

The evil menace seemed to leave Sarah alone, for the coming weeks when she would visit her dad. Just the footsteps and feeling of being watched that was it, well at least for now anyway. Sarah still felt Anna's father about in the background, keeping an eye on her. But he left her alone at this point. She was not scared as before.

The future looked promising for them all. Sarah never stopped thinking about Anna. To Susan and even Sarah it was nice, NO bad ghosts, NO feeling unsafe, nothing to harm them, in this flat. It was over!!!!

This was a chance for their family to mend, to heal and nothing would stand in their way. They felt stronger than ever. Even Sarah felt confident now. She was away from that house. It gave Susan the strength and courage back again, that she had once lost. This was the happy ending they wanted. Susan and Michael lived apart, they were still happy. They were a family once again. Sarah and Susan bright future had started! Right here, right now!

THE END

(OR IS IT?)

Lightning Source UK Ltd.
Milton Keynes UK
UKOW05n0807271114

242252UK00002B/23/P